ISLAND DREAMS

Barbara Angermeier Malcolm

Barbara Writes

Barbara Writes
Barbara Angermeier Malcolm

eBook: ISBN 978-1-970552-19-5
Paperback: ISBN 978-1-970552-20-1

Published by Barbara Writes
Printed in the United States of America

This book is dedicated to Pat, Eileen, John, Dave, Scotty, David, and all the other "dive guys" who taught us and befriended us. You were like our family.

CONTENTS

CHAPTER 1

Ella looked down at the swirling water. Had she run out here to fling herself into it? No, she had just run away from Dan and his hurt blue eyes. She hadn't meant to hurt his feelings when she said that she thought they had made a mistake moving here. He was doing what he wanted to do, teach SCUBA diving and lead dives, but she didn't have anything she wanted to do. She was bored. There were no dive shop jobs for her on Bonaire, not that she had some impressive career that she left behind.

She had worked in the dive shop in Green Bay, Wisconsin where Dan was an instructor and that's how they met. She fell in love with him almost as soon as he walked in the door. Dan had an easy manner and was especially good with nervous students, mostly women. He flirted and cajoled them into trying skills that they were afraid of and talked them out of quitting altogether. Ella thought at first that he was flirting with her like he did with all the women but then he asked her out for a drink. He talked the whole time about his dream of opening a dive shop on a Caribbean island and living where saltwater met sand.

Ella had never imagined anything so exotic. She was happy to dive in cold Lake Michigan which was accessible to home and save up for a warm water vacation every few years. Dan changed all that. He rhapsodized about the joys of living where you wore sandals and shorts all year round. Where all you had to do was drive a bit with your SCUBA gear in the back of your pickup truck and you'd be at the seashore where you could walk across the sand and fall into blood-warm water where the colorful fish lived. She looked into his sparkling eyes and suddenly his dream seemed like her dream too. Why couldn't she live on a warm island and go diving in the sea every day? She could work in the shop wearing shorts and flipflops and find mangoes and local lobster in the grocery store every week. She could be one of those people that are envied by tourists with her year-round tan and sun-streaked hair. Not that her dark brown hair would turn blonde or anything but with enough sun encouragement her grandma's red highlights might shine.

By the end of their first date, she was ready to chuck her job at the dive shop, pack up her dive gear and her summer clothes, and head off for adventure, but Dan was made of sterner stuff. He had a plan and was going to stick to it. He made a spreadsheet with his earnings and expenses laid out and wasn't going to pack up and head south until certain things were ready. He had an amount of savings he wanted to be at before making the move and he'd priced living on various islands and chose Bonaire, one of the most expensive ones, "because that's where the dive tourist money is." A few days after their first date Ella went to the bank and opened a "moving to the tropics" savings account. She went over her spending habits and set up a budget so that she could pay her bills and still save for the future. Suddenly they were a team.

Six months after they started dating, Dan moved into her duplex so that they could share rent and save faster. Ella chafed at the wait, lobbying for a quick trip to the Bahamas, just to bleed off some of the anticipation, but Dan refused. "Why spend our money on a weekend trip when that money could get us to Bonaire a month faster?"

So, she waited through two years of cold-water dives and dreams of the tropics before they had enough money to go. It wasn't easy to sell all their belongings and pack their dive gear and a few clothes before saying goodbye to their families and flying away. Dan found them a sublet apartment and bought a faded green rattletrap car as soon as they got to the island. It was much more expensive to buy groceries than Ella thought it would be so they both lost weight. Dan found a job in a dive shop right away but none of the shops needed a clerk, not even part time. She didn't have a work permit since the government figured that islanders could do the job of dive shop clerk, and they could, but she needed a job. The only thing she could find was cleaning vacation homes after the renters left. It wasn't much fun, people left appalling messes sometimes, but it brought in a little money and that what was important.

Her boss, Mariette, was a Dutch ex-pat who came to the island twenty years earlier for a year and never left. Mariette said that whatever food and booze was left in the house was fair game, but Ella drew the line at taking home much of what was left behind. Things in the freezer like fish bought at the local morning fish market and never cooked when into the little Styrofoam cooler that she kept in the car for just such things, but not ice cream, although she loved it and thought she could live on it for the rest of her life. Ice cream melted fast in the intense heat of the southern Caribbean. So, she ate that standing at the kitchen sink. She kept fruit and vegs because she could always wash them and make stir fry with a little bit of meat from the butcher case in the market.

Only once had she gone into a house that was supposed to be empty and wasn't. She walked into the great room to find a man sleeping on the couch.

"Excuse me," she said, "aren't you supposed to be flying home today?"

"Mmph," said the man/boy lying there with his face smushed into the pillow. He reeked of rum and suntan lotion. "Wha..?"

She used her broom handle to prod him on the foot. "I said, aren't you supposed to be flying home today?"

His head popped up and he looked around. "Where is everybody?"

"Gone, like you're supposed to be." She put her cleaning supplies down and spied a note on the kitchen table. "Are you Anthony?" she asked.

"Yeah, why?" he said. "How'd you know my name?"

She waved the paper at him. "There's a note to Anthony on the table."

"What's it say?"

"It says, 'Anthony, we couldn't wake you, so we've left for the airport. Your ticket and passport are under this note. Sorry, dude, gotta fly."

Anthony groaned. "What time is it? Have I missed the flight?"

Ella checked her watch. "It's nine-oh-five. What time is your flight?"

Anthony sat up and rubbed his hand over his face. "I don't know. What's it say on my ticket?"

Ella looked at the paper ticket. "Eleven-fifteen. You have time to make it if you get moving now."

He looked at her. "But how am I supposed to get to the airport?"

Ella sighed. "Are you packed? I can take you to the airport right now, for a fee."

"Is there a bag around here anywhere?"

She looked at the overstuffed backpack on the floor by the kitchen table. "There's a backpack here that looks like it has someone's stuff in it."

"A green and brown backpack?"

"Yes, a green and brown backpack and, before you ask, I'm not checking to see if your belongings are in it. That's your job. Get up off that couch and check yourself."

He groaned and pushed himself to his feet where he swayed and nearly fell back onto the couch. "God, how much did I drink last night?"

She shook her head. "From the looks of you, all of it. Were you afraid of leaving anything behind? Come on, check to make sure you have your things and let's go."

He wavered and then made his way over to where she stood by the table. "Yep, that's mine. I guess someone packed for me. Let's go." He leaned down to pick it up and nearly toppled over.

"Geez, Anthony," Ella said, "get a grip on yourself. Go splash some cold water on your face and rinse out your mouth. Maybe that'll help you sober up."

"I doubt it," but he did what she said. He came back with water dripping off his chin and his hair standing on end.

She poured the soused young man into the passenger seat of her car and went around to the driver's side. "If you feel like you are going to be sick, let me know and I'll stop. I do not want you throwing up in my car."

He leaned on the passenger window. "Yeah, sure."

"And roll that window down so you don't get too hot."

She drove as fast as she dared down the island to the airport where she parked at the curb and went around to rouse the now-sleeping young man to get him out of her car. A rowdy group of equally young people rushed to the curb as she hauled him out of the passenger seat.

"Anthony!" they said, "we were sure you'd miss the plane. Come on, man, get checked in, it's almost time to board."

"Wait a minute," said Ella, holding onto the backpack, "he owes me gas money, at least. I can't afford to drive all over the island delivering drunks to the airport."

They pulled out their wallets and each handed a few dollars to her.

When she counted it there was twenty dollars. She nodded and handed over the pack. "Thanks. Get him some coffee before you board. He's still drunk from last night."

"Yeah, our Anthony's a real party animal." They surrounded him and bore him off toward the check-in counter.

"You mean, Anthony's a real alcoholic," Ella said to herself as she put the car into gear and drove back to start her cleaning over an hour late. Wait till she told Dan about this one. He was always interested in stories about her cleaning adventures.

It took her extra time to clean the house that the group of young people had spent a wild week in. She wondered if they had gone diving or windsurfing or done anything other than party. Oh well, it was none of her business. She got paid to clean up after them.

Dan had his share of dealing with drunks and the hungover. Too many people got "seasick" on the boat ride out to Klein Bonaire. The ride was short and relatively calm for there to be that many queasy tummies. He made note of who fed the fish on the ride out to the little island and kept a close eye on them. A few times there were enough seasick passengers on the early morning dive boat that he considered asking the captain to turn the boat around and head back to the dock. When that happened, he took his Divemaster aside and clued him in to be extra vigilant watching people's depth and air consumption. Dan didn't want any accidents on his watch.

When Ella and Dan compared notes that night it turned out that Anthony and his band of raucous pals were well known on the island. They had drunk their way from one beach bar to another for over a week. They had not been on Dan's dive boats, but their fame had spread among the dive professionals on the island. Dan and Ella shared a laugh over her having to get Anthony sobered up enough to get him to the airport.

"I can't believe that his pals just left his ticket and passport laying on the table in the house," Ella said. "There he was passed out on the couch, fortunately he was dressed, but they just left him there and took off for the airport."

Dan shook his head. "From what I hear the whole group of them never met a bottle they didn't like. It's a wonder none of them turned up at San Francisco Hospital in the decompression chamber."

"I'm only glad that he didn't upchuck in the car, which would have been the last straw. Did I tell you that I made them give me gas money before I handed over his backpack? It's a long way from Santa Barbara to Flamingo Airport and back. I wasn't paying for all that gas out of my measly pay. And they didn't leave a tip. They did leave a lot of food, though. I had the feeling that they shopped for food on principle and just drank their meals because there was enough food for six people for at least three or four days left in the kitchen and fridge. I almost didn't get it all into my cooler to bring home."

"Any liquor left?"

Ella laughed. "Are you kidding? All they left were empty bottles, bags and bags of empty bottles. I've said it before, Bonaire needs a glass recycling plant or at least a place to collect the stuff to ship off someplace to be reclaimed. There's just too much of it going into landfills."

Dan nodded, not willing to make a remark that would start Ella on a rant about waste and the environment. Ella was glad that they lived on an island surrounded by a marine preserve. The waters around Bonaire had been protected since 1972 and since there were no rivers on the island there was very little runoff. She spent part of their time at any dive site walking up and down with a mesh bag picking up any litter she found blowing around or tangled in cactus. Dan couldn't count the number of times he had endured her litterbug lecture or the times she had walked up to a group of people who left trash at a site and asked them to clean up after themselves. A few times she was met with glares and ignored but more often the people apologized and cleaned up after themselves. When she came up from a dive Ella's buoyancy control device's pockets were stuffed with any trash she had been able to pick up across the reef. She was careful to check that no creature had moved into a bottle or can before putting it into her pocket. Once on a dive in Anguilla she had been with a group of men who had gathered coral and shells on the dive as souvenirs and the Divemaster had lectured them and made them throw it all back into the ocean. Ella remembered that one of the shells had a hermit crab in it and she worried that the crab was traumatized by its trip to the surface in a pocket. She wanted to take it back and nestle it in a cranny of the reef, but the Divemaster said that there wasn't time, so he walked to the side of the boat and tossed it all overboard, including the shell with the crab cowering in it. Ella admitted to shedding a few tears over it. Dan teased her about her tender heart, but he was secretly pleased that she was so concerned with the state of the planet and her corner of it.

Now if they could only get themselves a little shop with a little boat so they could start working for themselves instead of for someone else. Dan kept his ear to the ground and networked with the dive shop owners on the island, but no one was interested in selling right now. Not that they had enough money to buy a dive operation outright, but he thought they had enough for a decent down payment. Ella could keep working for Mariette part time to augment the income from the shop and divers. He had never mentioned that part of his plan to Ella. He knew that she disliked cleaning up after messy tourists, but it was the only job she could get without a work permit. If he owned the dive shop, he wasn't sure that she could get a work permit even then. The Bonairean government was very protective of the native islanders, even Dutch expats had trouble getting permits to work if the government thought that an islander could do the job the expat did. He supposed that it made sense for them to look out for their own over the welfare of people from off island but it sure would be nice if Ella could get a job that she really liked. He had talked to Babs, the owner of the dive shop he worked for, and she sympathized with his frustration, but she couldn't do anything about it. She herself was a Dutch expat so she had to be extra careful who she hired and how many off islanders.

CHAPTER 2

Dan was glad to see that there was a new group on the dive boat. He got the signup sheet from Cecile in the office, put it into the clipboard, and went to check that his gear was set up and ready to go onto the boat. The shop guy, Reg, had the tanks lined up and was getting rental gear sorted out for those that needed it. Dan would hand out weights. That let him do a little pre-check of the divers before they got onto the boat. He liked to know how experienced they were before they left the dock. That way he could tell his Divemaster, Samuel, who to keep an eye on in the water.

"All right, divers, please line up and I'll hand out your weights. Let me know if you have integrated weights in your buoyancy control device or if you need a weight belt."

The next fifteen minutes were a blur of different voices and demands. One woman said she needed twenty pounds of lead, and she was small.

"With a thick, cold-water wetsuit maybe but not with a thin, warm-water suit," Dan said. "Let's try ten pounds and I'll make sure there are weights on the boat in case you need extra."

She tried to protest but he moved on to the next diver. Getting everyone on board with all their gear set up and safely stowed under the seats was a bit like herding cats.

Captain Bill and Samuel untied the boat from the dock, and they were off. It was a hot, sunny day and the winds were light, so the waves were small. The ride to Klein Bonaire was smooth. Since the water was so calm that Captain Bill took them around to the seaward side of Klein Bonaire where it was usually too rough for diving. Windy days and currents were the norm on that side of the little island nestled in the curve of Bonaire, so it was a treat to get to catch the buoy at Sharon's Serenity and see how the reef was faring. There had been a lot of coral bleaching over the last summer and Dan was anxious to check on a side of the reef he had not seen in a while. When they were tied up at the marker buoy, he called everyone to attention and briefed them on what they might find under the water.

"The bottom here at Sharon's Serenity is about one hundred twenty feet. I ask you to restrict yourselves to one hundred feet. Checking over the side it looks like there's a little current flowing north so start your dives facing into the current, that way you'll work a little harder at the beginning of the dive when you're fresh and can ride the current back when your dive is ending and you're a little tired."

He glanced around to make sure everyone was paying attention. At the stern of the boat the woman who had wanted all that lead was talking to her neighbor.

"Excuse me," Dan said, "I need you to listen to the briefing so we're all together on the dive."

She pulled her sunglasses down and glared at him over them.

"Thank you," he said. "Now you'll enter the water from one of the openings in the sides of the boat. Slip your buoyancy control device and tank on while you're sitting, Captain Bill will help you, put your mask and snorkel around your neck, and carry your fins to the side. He'll steady you as you put on your fins and get your mask settled on your face. You give him the okay sign and make a giant stride entry. Samuel will be at the mooring buoy waiting for you. As soon as you're in the water, clear the area by the entry, and swim over to Samuel. You can get your gear all settled while you wait for the rest of us to get in the water. I'll lead the dive; Samuel will swim at the rear. Please keep an eye on your air pressure and remember, do not go below one hundred feet. Any questions?"

The woman with the sunglasses raised her hand. "Can I wear gloves? My hands get cold."

"I'd prefer you didn't but if you do wear gloves, please don't touch anything. The waters around the island from the high tide line to two hundred feet deep are a marine sanctuary so all the corals, critters, and fish are protected so touching is prohibited, try not to land on anything, and don't stand on the bottom if you get there. We'll spend a few minutes at one hundred feet and then we'll start a slow swim up toward the top of the reef where there is the most light and life. If anyone gets down to one thousand psi in their tank let me or Samuel know, and we'll get you back to the boat for a safety stop and exit. All set?"

Everyone nodded and started to get into their wetsuits. Samuel got his gear on and did a giant stride entry off the starboard side of the boat. Dan watched to see his okay sign as he righted himself, cleared his mask, and swam off to the mooring buoy.

"Okay, divers, who's going to be first in the water?"

Hoping that the divers were self-reliant and experienced, he stood by the port entry ready to assist divers into their fins and into the water. Most of them were efficient, getting their gear on at their seat and then shuffling over to the entry point where they put on their fins, mask and snorkel, gave the okay signal, and stepped off into the water. Dan watched as each of them bobbed to the surface, cleared their mask, and gave the okay signal again, before swimming over to float by Samuel. The lady with the sunglasses was last. Of course. She needed help getting her gear on. She needed help walking over to the entry point. She forgot to take off her sunglasses until she was standing at the gunwale. Dan took them from her and put them on the camera table for safety. He held her fins while she adjusted her belts and buckles, then held her steady while she teetered on one foot after the other putting on her fins. She put on her mask. Finally, she was ready to enter the water.

She turned to Dan, "I've never done an entry like this. What do I do?"

Dan put a steadying hand on her tank valve. "Put your

regulator in your mouth. Hold it and your mask in place with your right hand. Use your left hand to hold your dive computer, then step off the boat, taking a giant stride, and draw your fins together as you enter the water. Your mask and regulator will stay in place, and you'll pop right back to the surface where you'll turn to me and give me the okay sign."

"Okay." She fumbled her right hand up to hold her regulator and mask and gripped her dive computer in her left hand. She took a deep breath and stepped off the boat. Dan was relieved when she popped right back up, her mask in place, and gave him the okay.

He hurried into his gear with Captain Bill's help and did his own giant stride off the boat. He took a moment to savor the swirl of silver bubbles that always delighted him when he entered the water. Then he oriented himself and swam to the mooring buoy.

"We're going to do a weight check first. Samuel will descend to the mooring, and you will follow him. If any of you have trouble descending let me know but be sure that you're emptying the air out of your buoyancy control device by holding up the inflator hose or pulling the rapid dump valve on your shoulder. Okay?"

He nodded at Samuel who slipped beneath the surface with barely a ripple and descended to the mooring set into the bottom. Samuel stopped and hovered about six feet above the sand and Dan watched to make sure he was ready for the divers to start down. At his okay Dan started the divers down in pairs. Everything went smoothly, the divers descended toward Samuel. He could see them putting little squirts of air in buoyancy control devices to slow their descent. The last diver floating next to him was the lady with the sunglasses.

Dan pasted a smile on his face as he turned to her. "Your turn. Got all your belts and buckles adjusted?"

"What do I do?"

He reached over and tightened the shoulder buckles and waist strap of her buoyancy control device, then he checked to make sure that her weights were secure in their pockets. "Ready. Now all you need to do is let some air out of your buoyancy control device and descend the mooring line down to Samuel." He realized that she was on the verge of panicking. "What's your name? Are you okay? Are you sure you want to do this? You can get back onto the boat if you're too nervous."

She shook her head. "I'm Ilsa. No, I am doing this. I didn't spend a month in a pool in Utrecht to miss my first ocean dive." She took a deep breath and lifted her inflator hose.

Dan heard air whoosh out of the hose and the woman began to sink under the water. He saw her lift her chin to keep her eyes above the water, so he purged air from his buoyancy control device and kept pace with her. As soon as she saw him in front of her, she let out a big breath and started to sink more rapidly. Dan reached out to slow her descent and put her finger on the inflate button so that she would remember to put in little spurts of air. Soon they were with the rest of the divers. Dan motioned for Samuel to lead the dive; he stayed in the rear with Ilsa.

Samuel turned into the current and the rest of the divers sorted themselves into pairs and finned off behind him. That left Ilsa and Dan to bring up the rear. He was happy to see that she stuck right close to his side, didn't go wandering off chasing pretty fish. There were plenty of those. Down at a hundred feet where they started the dive, the corals were plainer and there weren't any colorful sponges. Under the ledges lobster antennae waved in the passing current and little shrimp snapped their claws as the divers swam by.

Just a few minutes into the dive Samuel started angling up the slope of the reef and as they ascended more fish and sponges appeared. Dan pointed out a Damselfish tending its algae garden in the bowl of a coral head. Red Soldierfish peered out of their niches where they rested during the day, their big golden eyes marking them as nocturnal hunters. Along the reef Parrotfish of every color and variety swam, dipping down to munch a bite of coral and then pooping sand to replenish the beaches around the island. Dan wished that he could talk to Ilsa to tell her about the community of the reef, tell her to look for the white antennae of the red and white striped Banded Coral Shrimp that advertised their services as cleaners.

He kept his eyes moving, checking to make sure that none of the divers strayed from the group. A pair of divers had stopped and were staring down at the reef. One of them reached down into the coral and seemed to be digging out something. Dan hurried over to stop them. When he reached them, they pointed at a silver ball nestled in a crevice. He supposed they thought it was an ornament or some ball bearing when it was in fact the largest single cell reef creature called Sea Pearls. He wrote the name on his slate and motioned them to rejoin the group. Schools of Goatfish crossed the reef stopping in the sandy places to probe for morsels with the barbels under their chins.

Dan felt the way he always felt when he was diving, free. Free from earthly gravity and free from the stresses of life. Not that he wasn't paying attention to what he was doing and what the people he was in charge of were doing but the freedom of diving always came over him as he swam along the reef. Even when he and Ella were diving in the cold waters of the bay of Green Bay, swimming through murky green water, and trussed up in either a heavy wetsuit or a bulky drysuit he felt the same lift of the daily stress. But diving in warm saltwater was better. He didn't regret for a minute the years he spent learning to dive and diving for fun in the Great Lakes. He was convinced that people who got certified to dive in those harsh conditions turned out to be better divers than the people who did a three-day course at some tropical resort. Not that he was against teaching people on vacation to dive but he made sure they learned to be competent and self-reliant divers.

As the dive progressed and they got into shallower water Ilsa nearly floated away before Dan reminded her to remove bits of air from her buoyancy control device to keep herself neutrally buoyant. Too many new divers forgot to bleed little blasts of air so that they stayed on the reef. He couldn't count how many times he watched a newbie diver fly to the surface, vent their buoyancy control device, and then sink back to join the group. He was surprised that more people didn't get decompression sickness from that.

Now they were at the edge of the reef where the sandy shallows spread back to the shore of Klein Bonaire. This was where the tiny fish hid in little patches of coral that dotted the sand. Long streams of Calico Wrasse swam by in a ribbon of purple and navy. Dan liked to imagine that there was one enormous ring of them surrounding the island in a continuous loop. He checked Ilsa's air and found that she was below one thousand psi. Time to head back to the boat.

Samuel was already leading the group back to the mooring line where he paused them all for three minutes at fifteen feet to do the required safety stop to let the nitrogen start off-gassing from their systems. Most of the divers had to hold onto the mooring line to stay in position but a few of them could maintain that depth without holding on. Ilsa held on. When he saw the stinging crinoids on the mooring line, he was sure that most of the divers wished for gloves.

Captain Bill had put out a trailing line so that the divers could hold onto it and inch their way up to the boat without the risk of being carried away by the surface current. Samuel got out of the water first so he would be onboard to help Captain Bill get the rest of the divers on the boat.

One by one the divers handed up their fins and then climbed the boarding ladder and were escorted to their place by Samuel. He helped them settle the butt of their tank back into the rack behind the seats and got them out of their buoyancy control device. As the passengers dried off and got their gear shifted to the second tank, the talk was excited about seeing lobsters and barracuda patrolling the edge of the reef. One of them talked about how aggressive barracuda can be but Captain Bill said only if you have bait in your pockets or are dressed up like a fishing lure with shiny jewelry on. Everyone laughed at that, but Dan noticed that a couple women tucked necklaces into their cleavage.

Dan was the last to leave the water. He handed Captain Bill his fins and climbed the boarding ladder. Once he had his gear off and transferred to his second tank, he helped get ready to change sites by reeling in the trailing line while Samuel unhooked the boat from the mooring buoy. Dan felt a soft hand on his shoulder. He turned to see Ilsa standing there.

"Can I have my sunglasses?" she asked.

He pointed to the camera table behind her. "They're right there."

She put them on and said, "Thanks for buddying with me. It was my first ocean dive, and I was afraid when you said we were going to one hundred feet and that there was a current, but I did okay." She looked at him over her sunglasses. "Didn't I?"

"You did fine," he said with a smile. "All you need to do is remember to adjust the air in your buoyancy control device when you change depths and you'll be diving like a pro in no time. Our next dive is a shallower dive on the leeward side of Klein Bonaire. There will probably be less current, and it bottoms out at about fifty feet. You'll be good diving with the group."

He turned to hold onto the rail as Captain Bill put the boat into gear. The boat lurched and Ilsa stumbled right into him. He caught her upper arms and set her on her feet.

"Be careful. Why don't you go back to your seat? It can get a little rough out here now that the wind picked up a bit. Let me help you." He held her upper arm as they crossed the deck of the pontoon boat to the corner in the bow where her gear was set up. "Slide your fins under your seat and hang onto your towel. You don't want them blowing away."

She smiled, nodded, and did as he said.

Their second dive was at a site called Just a Nice Dive on the side of Klein Bonaire nearest to Bonaire. It didn't take long to get there from Sharon's Serenity and in no time, Samuel had snagged the mooring buoy and hooked the boat to it. Captain Bill cut the engines and let the boat drift in the waves. The divers, used to the program after the first dive, started getting their wetsuits back on and listened to Dan's briefing.

"This dive site is called Just a Nice Dive for a very good reason. It is an easy site to dive, the bottom slopes away from shore gradually with nice patches of reef and lots of nooks and crannies where fish and critters can hide. There usually isn't a current on this site and I can see by the sea fans and gorgonians that there is a little surge but nothing to worry about. We're going to let you all dive your own dives, no playing Follow the Leader on this one. Keep your depth above fifty feet and have fun. Be back onboard within an hour or when your tank gets below one thousand psi. Have fun."

With those words he turned to start helping the divers into the water. It went much quicker this time as everyone knew what to do. Even Ilsa got herself geared up and ready for the dive.

"Who should I dive with?" she asked.

Dan glanced around and noticed that everyone else had left the boat.

"I guess you're stuck with me again. This time you're going to lead though. Let me get my gear on and I'll follow you."

Within five minutes Dan was in his gear and standing at the entry point on the side of the boat opposite Ilsa.

"I'll meet you at the mooring buoy," he said as he fitted his mask to his face. He swung his arm down and back to catch his regulator hose, put it in his mouth, purged it, put his right hand over his reg and mask, grabbed his dive computer and stepped off the boat. Without his fins. He surfaced to see Samuel's laughing face.

"Forget something?" Samuel said as he handed the fins to the blushing man.

For a minute Dan was abashed at forgetting to put on his fins but then he chuckled. It was good to give Samuel, Captain Bill, and the divers something to tease him about. Dive instructors can be held up as gods, especially by new divers, so it's good for them to see their heroes make the same mistakes they make sometimes. It took him barely a minute to slip his feet into his fins, settle his gear, and turn to snorkel over to the mooring buoy to meet Ilsa.

"Did you forget your fins?" she asked, a big smile on her face.

"Yeah, I did. I was in such a hurry to get into the water that I just forgot. Even pros make mistakes, remember that."

"Okay," she said, and reached down to check her air pressure before the dive. "Three thousand psi on the button," she said.

Dan checked his. "I have twenty-seven hundred psi, so I'll have to keep my eye on my gauge, so I don't run out of air."

"Oh, I think I'll use air much faster than you will," she said.

"Yeah, probably, but let's go dive." He checked to make sure there was no hair under the skirt of his mask, asking Ilsa to look for him and he did the same for her. "Oh, there's a little hair in there. That will make an annoying drip all through the dive. Let's get that out of there." He fixed her mask and said, "Okay, you're the dive leader this time. Where are we going?"

She looked down to see the other divers spread out across the reef. "I don't know. How do I tell if there's a current?"

"Can you see any sea fans or gorgonians, those fuzzy stalks that look like weeds?"

"Yes, sea fans."

"Well, are they waving all one way?"

She looked down with concentration. "Not really, they're waving back and forth."

"That means there's surge, not current, so we can go either direction, but I'd recommend we go south," he pointed over her shoulder, "that way first since that's the way any mild current would come from. Sound good?"

"Sounds good to me," Ilsa said.

They put their regulators in their mouths, lifted their inflator hoses, and let air out of the buoyancy control devices to sink. As they descended, they put spurts of air into their vests to control their descent. Dan was pleased to see that he didn't have to remind Ilsa to add air. They stopped their descent at about forty-five feet and leveled off. Dan resettled his gear, checked the buckles and belts, and got ready to follow Ilsa. She looked at him, gave the okay sign, and started off to her left. Dan moved to swim at her left shoulder so that she would be closer to the reef. She started swimming fast, but he touched her arm and motioned for her to slow down. When she did, he began to point out critters in the crevices and holes in the reef.

In an anemone there was a tiny purple Pederson's Cleaner Shrimp that offered its services to the smaller fish that inhabited the reef. Where the reef met the sand a Spotted Moray Eel lay half out of a hole, moving its jaws up and down to wash water over its gills, hoping to catch an unwary small fish or shrimp. The Azure Vase Sponges looked like they were made of neon, they glowed lilac and turquoise in the filtered light.

While they swam along Dan gradually eased them into shallower water which is where more life is on the reef and would extend their air. Periodically as they swam, Dan asked Ilsa how much air she had in her tank. He taught her how to indicate it using the fingers of one hand.

A Stoplight Parrotfish swam by with a long silver Trumpetfish swimming right above it. Ilsa pointed at it and shrugged a question. Dan pulled out his slate and wrote "hunting" on it. When Ilsa indicated that she had fifteen hundred psi in her tank he motioned that they should turn around and swim back toward the boat. On the swim back they were more aware of the surge. They could feel the push of it and then the resistance when it reversed direction for a moment. Dan liked to mimic the swimming motion of a school of Schoolmaster Snappers that hovered over the reef top when the surge was strong. He would kick hard when the surge pushed him and then rest when it pulled him back. It was fun. He could see that Ilsa was struggling so he touched her arm and showed her how to make the surge work for her rather than against her.

The sunlight was bright on the top of the reef and Ilsa got good at spotting small fish that lurked around the patches of fire coral up there. It was harder to maintain buoyancy at that shallow depth and he was impressed how well she did since this was only her second ocean dive. She must have had a good instructor back in Holland. By then he could see that the other divers were clustered under the boat holding onto the mooring line to do their fifteen-foot safety stop. He checked his air, twelve hundred psi, and saw Ilsa do the same. She signaled that she had eight hundred psi. Time to end the dive.

They swam over to the mooring line as the last of the other divers released the line to drift up to the trailing line behind the boat. Dan adjusted his buoyancy so that he maintained the depth and watched Ilsa try to do the same. She kept sinking and rising despite her best efforts. He could see she was getting frustrated and motioned for her to hold the line to hold her position. She reached into her buoyancy control device pocket for a single glove, put it on, and then held the line. He knew she had gotten stung by the crinoids growing on the mooring line after their first dive and had obviously learned how to avoid it on the second dive. The three minutes passed slowly. Ilsa kept looking down to watch the life of the reef which left Dan watching the time on his dive computer. He didn't mind; it was his job to make sure the divers had a wonderful experience and if he got to go diving for work so much the better. Now if he and Ella could only figure out how to open their own dive shop so they would be working for themselves instead of someone else. He wanted Ella to get certified as a Divemaster so she could come along on dives and help but then who would run the shop. There was a lot to think about and a lot of money to be saved.

He tapped Ilsa on the shoulder and motioned with an upthrust of his thumb that it was time to surface. She made a sad face and nodded. They released air from their buoyancy control devices as they ascended, and their heads broke the surface at the same time.

Ilsa spat out her regulator and said, "That was amazing. I never thought I would see so much life on one dive on one little reef."

Dan laughed. "I learned from my first Instructor to slow

down and LOOK. He said any fool can zoom up and down the reef but that way you scare away all the fish so all you see are their tails. If you slow down, you're not as threatening, and the fish go about their daily business more readily."

"Thanks for a great dive," she said.

"You led the dive," he said.

"Yes, you say that, but I know that you were watching our depth and where we were much more than I was."

As they talked, they removed their fins, handed them up to the waiting hands of Samuel and Captain Bill and climbed the boarding ladder to the deck. Captain Bill escorted Ilsa to her seat and helped her rest the butt of her tank in the rack. Dan slipped his gear off and tucked it into his spot by the wheel. He wiped his face with his handy towel and turned to the group.

"How was your dive?"

Everyone smiled and nodded. One pair had seen a barracuda snatch a small fish and was the envy of the rest of them.

"Oh, that's so cool!"

"Were you afraid it would bite you next?"

Laughter. "No, I had no bait in my pockets."

"You'd better not," Dan said, "that's a rental BCD and I'm not cleaning dead fish out of the pockets."

Which made everyone laugh harder.

It was a short ride back to the dock across the street from the dive shop. Everyone groaned when Dan said that they had to haul their empty tanks back to the fill station and that there were rinse tanks on the right side of the entrance to the courtyard for everyone to use to rinse their gear.

"Be sure that the dust cap is secure on your regulator before dumping it into the rinse tank, please."

Poles and pegs for hanging gear to dry were in the room on the left side of the courtyard.

"I'll be happy to stamp and sign logbooks once all the gear is back in the shop and rinsed. Meet me at the table under the thatched chickee in the center of the courtyard."

Dan loved the after-dive time when the divers were all excited and telling each other what they had seen and felt. Everyone was happy and smiling and making new friends. As he sat amid the group signing logbooks and listening to tales of fish and eels and that one barracuda, he thought that he was exactly where he wanted to be.

The group started to break up. Two couples packed up their gear and went to a bright red pickup truck and drove off. A pair of middle-aged women took their time hanging the rental gear so it would dry, then spent time going through the Reef Fish, Reef Creatures, and Reef Coral ID books that lived on the table in the center of the courtyard. The women were interested in learning the names of the fish and creatures they saw on the dives and made notes in their logbooks. One of them went into the dive shop and bought a copy of Reef Fish so they could page through at night and learn about them so that they would be able to recognize them the next time they saw them.

"Maybe we should take a fish ID specialty course," one of the said and Dan offered them the opportunity to complete the Underwater Naturalist specialty while they were there on vacation. "That would be excellent. What do we have to do?"

"Just go into the shop and tell Cecile what course you want to take, and she'll get you signed up and give you the small book that goes with the course. Then all you need to do is three dives with an Instructor to get certified."

The women looked at each other and came to an unspoken agreement.

"We're already signed up to do three dives a day the rest of the week so we might as well."

They picked up their logbooks and went right into the shop to get signed up.

"I would like to learn more too," came a soft voice from across the table.

Dan looked up and saw Ilsa was still there. He smiled at her. "You could talk to the ladies and ask if they mind if you take the class too. Are you signed up to dive the rest of the week?"

She nodded, "And paid for too."

"That's great. Then the cost of the specialty course will be a little less since you've already paid for the dives."

She gave him a level look, nodded again, and went into the shop to see if she could join the class.

Three excited women came out of the shop a few minutes later. They were each clutching a thin course pamphlet.

One of the women sat right down and said, "Now what do we do next?"

Dan told them, "You need to read this little textbook, and we'll do the first dive tomorrow morning. You're scheduled to do the boat dive, right?"

They all said yes.

"Then come to the shop a half hour early and we'll get the classroom portion of the course taken care of. I'll see you in the morning."

He got up with a wave of his hand and went back to the office to fill out the paperwork from the day's dives and talk to the owner about the rest of the week. He was almost at the office door when he felt a hand on his shoulder. He turned around to find Ilsa behind him.

"Did you forget to ask something?" he said.

"Yes," she said, "I was wondering if you would like to have a drink with me when you get off work. I really appreciate all your help on my dives today. I know I wouldn't have enjoyed them as much with another dive leader."

"Uh, sure," he said. "I get off at four-thirty and can meet you at Karel's Beach Bar. Do you know where that it? It's in the middle of downtown across the street from the Pink Mall."

"Yes, I know where that is. I will meet you there… around five?"

"Sure," he agreed, "around five o'clock. See you there and thanks."

He went into the office and got his paperwork done then spent some time talking to Babs, the owner, about encouraging divers to take specialty classes when they were signed up to dive with them for a full week.

"It'd be a great way to make some extra money for both of us," he said.

She agreed that it was a good idea and to think about putting together some packages with dives and specialty certifications. Dan tried to call Ella to let her know that he would be late getting home from work, but she didn't answer her phone. Oh well, one drink wouldn't make him that late. She would understand. He didn't leave a message.

CHAPTER 3

Ella had another one of those houses to clean that day. The family that left that morning had obviously never cleaned up after themselves. The place was a mess. There were dishes and glassware all over the place and food everywhere. She had to get it all cleaned up or the bugs would take over.

She cleaned and cleaned all morning, tossing opened packages of food into garbage bags. Once she got most of the food cleared up and the first load of dishes in the dishwasher, she stripped the beds and got the sheets into the washer. Every step she took sounded crunchy there was so much sand on the floors. It's a good thing the floors are tile, she thought, I'd never get this much sand out of carpets. There were almost as many empty wine and liquor bottles as had been in the house where she found Anthony a few weeks ago.

This had been some family; they must have partied the whole week they were there. And how had they gotten peanut butter up there on the wall? She had to get the ladder from the carport to get up high enough to clean that mess. Did they have a food fight? She didn't even want to know. All she wanted to do was get home and have a quiet drink with Dan and maybe a salad for supper. Maybe they could get barbecue ribs from Bobbe Jan's, that would be excellent. She tried calling Dan's cell phone, but he didn't answer. He was probably on a dive, she checked the time, yes, he would be on the dive boat about now. She didn't leave a message. She would try later.

The dishwasher had finished its first cycle, so she emptied it and reloaded it for the second cycle. The family had used every glass and dish in the place and evidently had not known how to run the dishwasher.

All day she kept stripping beds, putting the sheets in the washer and dryer, and then remaking the beds for the next occupants who were scheduled to arrive early the next morning on the red eye from Houston.

She kept thinking while cleaning and looking out at the beautiful ocean view from every room in the house that this wasn't what she had in mind when she had agreed to move to Bonaire with Dan. She thought she would get a job in the same dive shop he did so they would see each other throughout the day. She missed the excitement of divers who couldn't wait to share what they had seen on their dives and the chance to share stories with Dan. True, she probably made more money cleaning for Mariette than she would have in the dive shop but that still didn't make her feel any better. Knowing how much it would cost them to open their own dive shop especially on an expensive island like Bonaire made her depressed. She didn't think they would ever get there but Dan, the optimist, assured her that they would.

"The guy that owns the shop down the beach from the Dive Inn is nearly eighty years old. He's bound to want to sell up one of these years and we're lucky to be in the position of being able to step in and take over. With my experience teaching and leading dives and your years working the retail side of the dive business he's got to see that we'd be the perfect people to take over his operation."

"I hope you're right," she said, "I'm getting dishpan hands from all of the scrubbing I do all the time and I hardly ever get to go diving. I miss diving with you. I miss diving with anyone. I even miss diving in the Great Lakes, that's how much I miss diving."

He pulled her into a big hug and kissed the top of her head. "We'll get there, just you wait and see. Let's plan to go diving on our next day off together. We can go down to the Hilma Hooker or maybe to Red Slave, that's one I rarely get to dive because the current is usually too swift for our divers and it's too far for the dive boat."

"It'd be a great drift dive, wouldn't it?" she said. "Too bad we don't have a boat."

He tightened his hug. "One of these days we'll have a boat, I promise." This time he kissed her on the lips, kissed her like he really meant it.

It had been a long day and she was running the vacuum under the bed in the master bedroom when her phone rang. She didn't hear it.

Dan left the Dive Inn and walked up the shore road to Karel's Beach Bar and saw Ilsa sitting alone at a table. He ran his hand through his hair and went over to her table.

"Hi, Ilsa, what can I get you?"

She looked up, smiled, and stood up. "No, I'm buying the drinks. What can I get you?"

"Are you sure? It feels wrong for the lady to pay."

"I want to thank you for all you did for me today. What would you like to drink?"

"I'll have an Amstel, I guess."

She touched his arm. "Okay, one Amstel coming up."

He sat down at the table and looked around to see if there was anyone he knew there. Everyone looked to be tourists on their way to being well and truly relaxed.

"Here you go," Ilsa said as she came back with a bottle of beer, a glass, and a tall glass of something that looked like milk.

"Pina colada?" he asked.

"Of course, I'm on vacation in the tropics."

They clinked glass and bottle and drank.

Ella decided to drive down the shore road on her way back to their little apartment in Belnem. After her day cleaning up that disaster in Santa Barbara, she needed to blow the cobwebs out and a drive along the sea would do it. She drove slowly along waving to people on their porches and dreaming of the day when she and Dan could live in a place with a view of the sea. As she came into Playa the traffic got heavier and she slowed down even more. People were crossing the street between cars and the Friday night revelers were starting to gather. She saw that there was a lineup at Bobbe Jan's which renewed her wish for barbecued ribs for supper. She was so hungry that she thought she could eat a combo platter all herself.

Traffic was moving at a snail's pace, so she inched along watching the passing people, looking to see if there was anyone around that she knew. She thought she spied a familiar back at Karel's Beach Bar and looked closer. It was Dan and he was with a blonde woman. They were leaning their heads together and she had her hand on his thigh. Ella's blood ran cold. Here she had spent the day slaving in someone else's mess, washing their dirty sheets and towels, and there Dan was flirting with some blonde bimbo right in the middle of town. She pulled out her phone and dialed Dan's number. She watched him pull his phone out of his pocket, look at the screen, and punch it to answer.

"Hey, babe," he said, "I tried to call you earlier. Where are you?"

She gripped her phone tight. "I'm on my way home from a long day. Where are you?" Lie to me and you're dead, she thought.

"I'm at Karel's Beach Bar with one of the divers from today's boat. It was her first time in the ocean, so I buddied with her, and she bought me a drink to thank me."

"That was nice. Anything else going on?"

He looked around but didn't see her car which was sheltered behind a truck parked in front of the bar. "Nope, I'm going to finish my beer and head home. Want me to pick up supper?"

She thought for a minute. "Why don't you call Bobbe Jan's and order us some ribs, I'll have a combo platter, and I'll pick it up since I have the car and you're on your bike."

"Great idea. I'll call right now. Pick it up in ten minutes?"

She nodded, but she wasn't going to let him know that she was right next to the bar. "Ten minutes works. See you at home."

"See you at home. I love you."

"Love you too," she said, but he had already hung up.

She watched him hit a number on his speed dial and assumed that he was putting in their ribs order. She inched forward past the parked truck and saw Dan see her. His hand started up to wave and then stopped. Ella waved at him. Just then the traffic opened, and she sped off. She went around the block and back up through town to the little ribs restaurant on a side street on the edge of downtown. She lucked into a parking place across the street and went to sit at the bar until their order was ready.

"Hey, Ella," said James the owner and bartender, "Dan just called in an order for you. It will be ten or fifteen minutes until it is ready. Can I make you a drink?"

She shook her head. "You know I'm not much of a drinker, I'll just have a soda."

"Diet or regular?"

"Oh, let's live a little, a regular cola, one with caffeine and sugar."

James filled a glass with ice, popped the top of the red aluminum can, and poured the soda over the ice. He slid the glass and the can across the bar to her and handed her a pasteboard coaster for the glass.

"How's the cleaning business?" he asked.

"Just dandy," she said, "I cleaned the worst mess I've ever seen today. The whole house was filled with sand and there were dirty plates and glasses all over the place. I swear the family that stayed there had never heard of a dishwasher or a broom. It took me an extra hour to get it ready for the next tenants who arrive in the morning on the red eye."

James shook his head. "I wouldn't want to be in that business. People are bad enough when they have too much to drink before and after a meal, I cannot imagine how they would be if they had a whole week's worth of drinking too much."

"I can tell you how they would be, they would be pigs."

She drank her soda and watched other customers come and go. She knew a few of them, said hello, and visited with James when he was between making drinks. It wasn't long before her order was up. She paid for it and her soda, took the bag, and went back to her car.

Once again, she drove down the shore road through town, but Dan and the blonde were no longer at Karel's Beach Bar. She kept going on the seafront road down past the Dive Inn where she noticed that Dan's bike was no longer chained to the fence on the side of the building. She wondered if she would pass him on the way home or if he had hurried up and left the bar to get home before she would.

Dan's bicycle was chained to the fence in the little yard of their apartment. She could see that their neighbors were eating out on their patio and Dan was standing visiting with them.

Ella left the car unlocked and the windows rolled down to keep from having them broken by thieves. It was becoming a big problem on the island. Cars and homes got broken into when the occupants were out or asleep and electronics and dive gear stolen. Ella wondered where the perpetrators thought they were going to sell or pawn the stuff. This was a small island, only six miles by sixteen miles, not a lot of geography to hide in.

Dan looked up when she stopped the car and came, smiling, to greet her. "How was your day?" he said. "Long?"

She handed him the bag of food. "Yeah, long. The family that spent their vacation in that house didn't clean up after themselves all week. The place was a pit. There was food all over the tables, all the dishes were dirty, there was even peanut butter on the wall in the kitchen. I had to get a ladder to clean it off." She followed him into the house. "I wonder if they live like that at home."

"I don't know, babe, that doesn't sound like a fun day."

She snorted. "It looked like you had a fun day. I noticed her hand on your leg when I drove by. What's up with that?"

He looked at her, his mouth hanging open. "Huh? Her hand was on my leg? Really? I didn't notice."

"Oh, right, you didn't notice her little hand creeping up your thigh. What, are you dead from the waist down?"

He put his hands on her shoulders. "Really, Ella, you know what I'm like. I never know if women are coming on to me."

She shrugged his hands off her shoulders. "Let me give you a clue. If a woman puts her hand on your thigh, she's coming on to you, big time. Didn't you notice her fluttering her eyelashes at you and leaning close to talk? Was she speaking so quietly that you had to lean in to hear what she was saying? All flirtatious, coming-on-to-you behavior." She took the containers out of the bag and set them on the table. "Come on, let's eat before it gets cold."

"What do you want to drink?"

"Just water. I had a soda while I waited for the food. I don't need any more caffeine."

"Yeah, I'll have water too. One beer is enough tonight."

"Yes, especially that beer," Ella said. "Dan, I wonder if we didn't make a mistake chucking everything and moving here."

Dan turned from the sink, a glass of water in each hand. "What do you mean? You think coming to Bonaire was a mistake?"

"I mean you're doing what you want to do and I'm cleaning up other people's messes. I don't like it and now I find you being mauled by some blond in the middle of town." She stood up from the table. "I'm going to take a walk."

"What about supper? It'll get cold." He set their glasses down at their usual places and sat down.

"I can reheat it. You eat. I'm taking a walk."

She left the room and walked out the front door before Dan could see the tears in her eyes. Ella walked the block to Bachelor's Beach and stood looking down at the waves swirling at the base of the small stairs leading to the sand. She stood crying until a pickup truck pulled up and a couple got out. She wiped the tears away before they saw.

"Are you diving?" the man asked, looking around for Ella's vehicle.

"Not nearly enough," said Ella and she turned toward home.

Dan was still sitting at the table when she went back into the house. Ella picked up her plate and slid it into the microwave without saying a word.

"Ella, are you going to be mad at me all week?" said Dan.

Ella looked at him. "Maybe."

"Ilsa is taking an Underwater Naturalist specialty course and will be diving with me all week." He looked down at his empty plate. "You didn't really mean that you think we made a mistake coming here, did you?"

"I guess not. I get tired of cleaning every day when you get to go diving every day." She took a bite of a rib and chewed. "Maybe I should take a day off and come on the dive boat. Stake my claim on you in front of Ilsa."

He set his glass down. "That's a great idea. It's been too long since we went diving together. Call Mariette and see if you can get one of the next few days off. You can be my Divemaster when I am leading the Naturalist certification dives. You're much better than I am at spotting critters and their behaviors."

He looked so enthusiastic that it was hard for Ella to stay mad at him.

"Okay, I'll call Mariette after supper, see what day I can have off this week." She took a bite of coleslaw. "I'll have to work a weekend day in exchange or go in extra early, but I think I can manage that."

It took Ella all evening to tamp down her mad over seeing Dan with that woman. And she still couldn't get it out of her head as she lay in bed that night. The worst part was Ilsa's hand on his thigh even though he swore he didn't realize it was there. How could he not have known that her hand was on his leg? She knew he wasn't dead from the waist down; she knew that because he got jumpy whenever she traced her hand over his thigh, so how come he hadn't gotten jumpy when Ilsa had done it? Ilsa, what a name. Wasn't that the name of Ingrid Bergman's character in *Casablanca*? I think so, her mother must have been a Humphrey Bogart fan.

Dan came into the bedroom from the bathroom. "You're not

reading?" he said.

"No," she said, "I'm not in the mood."

She was lying there flat on her back with her arms folded across her chest.

"I see. That must mean that you're still mad at me."

She rolled over to face him. "Yes, I'm mad because I can't believe that you didn't notice her hand on your leg. On your thigh, for god's sake. You nearly hit the ceiling when I touch your thigh. Why?"

He reached to pull her toward him, but she held back.

"Tell me why," she said again.

He squirmed a bit and looked away. "Well, when you put your hand on my thigh, I think it's a signal that you want to, you know."

"Have sex, you mean?"

He shook his head. "No, I mean make love. Sex is something other people do, you and me we make love. At least I always think we do."

Tears sprang to her eyes. "Oh, really? I always think we make love too." She slid her arms around his neck and pulled herself close to him. "I'm sorry I doubted you, Dan. Forgive me?"

"You had a tough day. Of course, I forgive you."

CHAPTER 4

The next morning Dan was at the dive shop early to meet with the three women taking the Underwater Naturalist class. He went through the little textbook with them and talked about the sorts of behaviors they should be on the lookout for on their dives. He sold them each a slate so they could write down the different things they saw as they swam along. He told them that they would be diving as a three-person buddy team so that they could help each other to find things.

"You're not going to be my dive buddy?" Ilsa said.

He shook his head. "No, that wouldn't be fair to Claire and Libby. I know what to look for, you need to train your eyes to see the behaviors and find the critters for yourself. We found some things on both dives yesterday that you should be able to find again today. You can do this."

"We were studying the Reef Fish book last night," said Claire, "we hope that will help us find more fish."

Ilsa said, "Well, Dan and I found tiny shrimp and now I know how to find them. I will show you."

"This is going to be fun," Libby said.

Leaving the women to talk about their upcoming dives Dan went out to see about the other divers on the morning dive boat. Many of the same people were back from the day before so they already had their rental gear and weights. Two of the men were carrying tanks down to the dock to put them on the boat and Captain Bill was onboard helping them get the tanks into the racks safely. Dan noticed that Ilsa waited for one of the men to offer to carry her gear bag down for her. He thought that if she had been his student, he wouldn't have let her get away with that. He was a big believer in self-reliance and that every diver should be able to haul their own gear, tanks included.

By then it was nearly nine o'clock and time for everyone to be on the boat. He herded the divers out of the classroom, across the road, and down the dock onto the pontoon boat tied up there.

"Before we shove off get your first tank set up, so you're not struggling to set it up on a rocking boat."

That produced a flurry of activity as everyone got out their buoyancy control devices and regulators to put onto their tanks. Those passengers who had their own gear and had integrated weights in their vests made sure that the pockets were secure. Dan went behind them and double checked.

"I lost a weight pocket on a dive once and I don't want you to have the same experience. I never did find that weight pocket and I had to cut the dive short."

No one wanted to cut a dive short, not on vacation, not in these pristine waters. Once everyone was set and Dan had made sure all the gear was correct, he nodded at Captain Bill and Samuel to shove off.

This morning they went up the coast of Bonaire to one of the dives below the cliffs on the north end of the island, Oil Slick Leap. After Samuel got the boat hooked to the mooring buoy Dan called for everyone's attention.

"This site is called Oil Slick Leap because it was once considered as a site for the oil terminal which is a mile or so to the north. There is a lot of wave action here so the corals are somewhat beat up but there are plenty of things to see. At the base of the cliff in about fifteen feet of water Damselfish tend their algae gardens and in the narrow terrace there are gorgonians and sponges where you might find Seahorses. You'll have to slow down and look closely to find them. If you do, let us know so that we can all enjoy seeing them. In the zone below the drop off you can see Tiger Grouper and Yellow Grouper. They like to hover in the orange barrel sponges. I have also seen many Filefish at this site. They're called Filefish because their skin is so rough sailors used to nail one up next to their stove and use the skin to light matches."

The divers laughed at the thought of a fish nailed to a wall and used as a striking spot.

"That's about all I have." He looked at his watch. "Maximum depth of one hundred feet, please, and be back on board in one hour or with no less than five hundred psi." He raised his hand to shoo them off. "Now, go diving."

Samuel geared up and did his giant stride off the gunwale of the boat. He swam to the mooring buoy to wait for the divers. Captain Bill and Dan helped the divers into their gear, then shuffle over to the side to put on mask, snorkel, and fins and make their own giant stride entries. It was a much more efficient operation than it had been the day before. Last to enter the water were the three students. Dan had overheard them making a dive plan and was impressed that they remembered to do that from their training.

"Have fun, ladies." He said as they gathered at the opening in the side of the boat. They all smiled at him and brandished their slates which they had clipped to the buckle of their shoulder straps, so they didn't get lost.

"Aren't you diving?" Ilsa asked.

"I'll drop in and kind of oversee the dive. I'll be there if anyone needs my help. Samuel is there too, he's a good Divemaster and is very familiar with this site. If anyone can find a seahorse it will be Samuel."

The three women gave each other excited looks and got themselves geared up and into the water. Plop, plop, plop. In they went one after the other. Dan watched them surface, give him the okay signal, and swim over to Samuel at the mooring buoy. The three of them submerged, met on the bottom, and swam toward the drop off where the big fish lived. He hoped they saw something big. Maybe a Nurse Shark or a Spotted Eagle Ray. He turned to put on his wetsuit and get his gear from his spot by the wheel. Captain Bill helped lift his tank and buoyancy control device unit and settle it on his shoulders.

"Thanks, Bill."

Bill nodded. Dan got his mask and snorkel out of the rinse bucket, picked up his fins, and walked to the side of the boat. He held onto the railing as he put on his fins and then settled his mask on his face. He checked his gauges, then asked Captain Bill to make sure his air was turned on. It was. He held his regulator and mask on his face with his right hand and secured his dive computer with his left hand and then stepped off into the ocean. That swirl of silver bubbles entertained him for the minute he entered the water and then he turned to see his charges scattered across the reef and sand, just the way they were supposed to be. He spotted the three women students, head down, examining the base of a cluster of purple tube sponges. Suddenly one of them pointed and they all crowded together. He could see their excitement. He cleared his ears and vented air from his buoyancy control device to head down to see what they had found.

They had found a seahorse. A tiny, red-orange seahorse with its tail curled around the narrow base of a purple tube sponge. It hung there, suspended like a helium balloon, swaying with the movement of the water and the flutter of its tiny fins. By the time Dan descended to join them, other divers had noticed the women's intense concentration and excitement and begun to gather. There was kind of a traffic jam as everyone tried to see the tiny creature at once. A couple of them had cameras and a camera tends to give a diver the idea that they have the right to butt in front of everyone to get their shot.

Dan sorted them out and gave everyone a chance to see and photograph the seahorse without disturbing it or harming it. Claire's eyes were shining, and she wrote "I found it!" on her slate. He gave her a big enthusiastic okay signal and grinned around his regulator mouthpiece to show her that he was excited too. Once everyone had a chance to look at the seahorse for as long as they wanted, he shooed them off to continue their dives after checking everyone's air to make sure that they were all over a thousand psi. A couple of them were getting close so he motioned them back into the shallow part of the site so that they would be near the mooring line when it was time to ascend.

The three Underwater Naturalist class women compared air and moved to the base of the cliff to see what lived in the coral rubble that the waves gathered there. Dan knew that lots of shrimp and lobsters lived in those nooks and crannies so he thought that the ladies would enjoy their time there. The trick would be for them to control their buoyancy in the surge as the water pushed them into the wall and then pulled them back. He kept an eye on them to make sure none of them shot to the surface. He was pleased to see that they all vented air from their buoyancy control devices so that they were more negatively buoyant and had more control over their position in the water. The rest of the divers had begun to hang at fifteen feet for their three-minute safety stops and then ascend to the surface to reboard the boat. Dan stayed hovering over the drop off to prevent anyone from escaping into the deep. He knew how easy it was to follow a fish or a turtle and forget to keep track of your depth.

Just as he had the thought a Hawksbill Turtle came slowing swimming up from the depths to graze on the algae in the shallows. He tapped on his tank with his knife to get the attention of the divers in the water. He didn't want the Underwater Naturalist women to miss seeing a turtle. One of the women turned to see what the noise was and spotted the turtle. She excitedly got the others' attention and the three of them turned to swim back to intercept the track of the swimming amphibian. All three of them also were scribbling on their slates, recording the sighting for their logbooks. As soon as the excitement of seeing the turtle abated Libby checked her air and motioned that she needed to go back to the boat. Dan was sure that they would all be close to five hundred psi when they boarded the boat, if not below. Critter hunting used up air and first-time critter hunting used even more. He trailed them back to the mooring line, his head swiveling to make sure that none of the other divers were left at the site.

No fins were visible, no columns of bubbles trailed up

from the bottom. All his chicks were safely in the nest. He hovered near the mooring line, watching the ladies compare notes on their slates. He was amused to see that none of them were holding the line, not thinking about their buoyancy but maintaining their depth with their breathing and the air in their buoyancy control devices. When they were all on board the women regaled the other passengers with their finds.

"I found the seahorse," said Claire. "I nearly spit out my regulator to call you all, I was so excited."

"Did you see that Damselfish with its algae garden?" Ilsa said. "There was a little crab that sneaked bites of algae when its back was turned. I laughed so hard I sucked in water and coughed and coughed."

Libby was looking at her slate. "I wrote down so many things I am going to have trouble fitting it all into my logbook. I'll be sitting at the table in the courtyard all through lunch just to get it all down."

"What about the turtle?" one of the other divers said. "Did you see the size of that thing? The shell had to be as big as a garbage can lid."

"Yes." Came from quite a few of the divers.

"It was great to see."

"It seemed to move so slowly but I had trouble catching up to it to take a picture," said the man with the big camera.

"It was a great dive. Thanks for bringing us to this site," Libby said.

Ilsa looked into Dan's eyes. "Yes, thank you, Dan. Today earned you another drink."

Dan gulped and wished that Ella had been able to get today off instead of tomorrow. "It's my job," he said. He would have to be careful to dodge Ilsa's invitation without giving offense.

The sea was getting rougher so he encouraged everyone to swap their SCUBA gear onto their second tank so that Captain Bill could slip the mooring and take them to their second site. It was a short ride down the coast to the site called Something Special which was just past the entrance to the Marina. Since there was no fixed mooring Captain Bill dropped an anchor in the sand and Samuel swam down to make sure it was secure. Dan called for everyone's attention for the short briefing.

"This is Something Special. The big attraction here is the colony of Garden Eels that live in the sand flat just where the slope meets the bottom at about forty feet. You might think that there won't be a lot to see in such a sandy site but there's a lot of action on the reef rubble in the shallows. You'll see Creole Fish, Mahogany Snappers, and Grunts. You might be lucky enough to spot a Tarpon hanging in the water just offshore from the reef. In the segment between the mooring and the entrance to the Marina you can see lots of Scorpionfish and Spotted Moray Eels. Be very careful not to cross into the entrance to the Marina. Boats come out of there and as soon as they hit open water, they put the hammer down. You could be shallow enough to be in grave danger. I have first aid training but would rather not use it today. Thanks for being careful. Now get your gear on and go diving."

The three Underwater Naturalist students were the first to have their gear on and be shuffling to the entry points on the sides of the boat.

"I'm glad we can write on both sides of the slate," said Libby. "I don't want to miss a thing."

Dan was holding onto her tank valve to steady her while she put on her fins. "Have a great dive," he said as she stepped off the boat.

He watched the group separate themselves into buddy teams and spread out on the site. Samuel was at the anchor line to keep an eye on the divers and to be there if anyone needed help. Dan stayed on the boat and watched from there. He was concerned that his students would stray into the entrance of the Marina, so he kept a close eye on them, ready to jump into the water and steer them back into safer waters. He knew how intently they were all looking down and not really paying attention to where they were in relation to the entrance. He was glad when a speedboat came roaring out of the Marina and caught everyone by surprise. That gave them all a shock and moved the trio of women away from the entrance. Good. That saved him having to go in and herd them away.

Soon the divers began filtering back to the boat. From the talk he overheard all the divers had been inspired by Claire, Libby, and Ilsa to slow down and really look at things. All of them had swum down to see the patch of Garden Eels, marveling at the coordinated way the tiny eels sunk down into their burrows as divers approached and then came back up at the same speed as divers passed. They all crooked their heads into the prevailing current the better to catch any plankton passing by.

Dan was busy helping people get back to their places to put their tanks into the rack when he heard a cry for help. Captain Bill had called out because Ilsa was caught in the trailing current line and couldn't keep her head above water. She had dropped her fins and gotten tangled in the line. Dan dived into the water straight at her and lifted her head above the water. He grabbed the inflator hose of her buoyancy control device and pressed as hard as he could to inflate her vest to keep her head above water while he untangled her.

"Oh, thank you," she said, "I panicked and forgot about inflating my BCD when I dropped my fins and couldn't keep my head up. What would I have done without your help?"

Dan untangled the line from around her, twirling her around in place, and looping the line in his hand so he didn't entangle her again. "You're okay now." He looked down into the water. "Samuel has your fins. Let's get you on the boat."

He towed her over to the boarding ladder and put her hands on it so she could find the rungs with her feet and climb aboard. Captain Bill was there to help her up the last few steps and then escort her to her seat in the bow of the boat. Dan treaded water until Samuel ascended and handed him Ilsa's fins.

"Thanks, man, I could have free dived down for them, but I'm glad you brought them up.

Samuel smiled and said, "No problem."

The two men climbed aboard, got the anchor pulled up, and

Captain Bill turned the boat toward the dock.

CHAPTER 5

Ella couldn't wait for tomorrow to arrive. She had the day off, and she was going out on the dive boat with Dan and the blonde woman that had been flirting with him. Ella intended to subtly give the impression that Dan was her private property, in the nicest sense of the word, and not available for a vacation fling. She knew how clueless Dan could be about women.

According to his mother, his dad had been the same way, a traveling salesman that genuinely liked women and never knew when they were coming on to him. Mom told about one time Dad came home and said that he didn't know what was wrong with the cosmetologist in the Osco Drug in Wausau.

"Why? What did she do?" Mom had asked.

Dad scratched his arm. "Well, she kept rubbing her breast on my arm all the time I was showing her the selling sheets."

Mom said, "She had a rash."

"Really?"

"No, you goofball, she was coming on to you, letting you know that she was available for a little fun and games. You had no idea, did you?"

Dad shook his head. "Nope, I was wearing my wedding ring. What did she think?"

Mom had patted him on the arm. "She thought that you were like a lot of married men, and especially married traveling salesmen, always ready for a little on the side. I am glad you don't get it when a woman flirts with you because I know you flirt with them."

"I like women."

"I know you do, sweetheart." Mom pulled him into a hug.

"That's why whenever I lose you at a party, I go looking for the biggest group of women and that's where I find you."

Dan had grumbled that was one attribute of his dad's that he wished he hadn't inherited. Ella was just as glad that he had.

The house that she had to clean that day was a big, two-story home on the seashore. It had four bedrooms, five bathrooms, and a pool. Luckily, the cleaning company had a pool man, so she didn't have to deal with cleaning the pool. There was a car in the driveway that she didn't recognize. She knew it wasn't Mariette's car and it didn't belong to the pool man, he had a rusted out, pale blue pickup truck. She hoped that all the guests had left. She didn't want another Anthony sleeping it off on the couch. Ella gathered up her cleaning supplies and let herself into the house through the car port.

"Hello?" she called when she stepped into the laundry area and mud room.

There was no answering voice and no TV or stereo sound, so she stepped into the kitchen. She was relieved to see that the counters and the sink were clear of dirty dishes and her steps didn't crunch on tracked in sand like they had at the last house. Opening the dishwasher, she saw that it needed to be run so she made a sweep of the downstairs and the patio to check for any dishes or glassware left behind and started the machine. Then she went upstairs to the bedrooms to strip the beds and gather the towels so she could start the laundry. With a house this big the laundry would take most of the day to wash and dry. She had stripped the beds in three of the four bedrooms and was walking into the fourth bedroom when she realized that the bed was occupied. She took a picture with her phone.

"Oh, excuse me," she said. The shape in the bed didn't move. She raised her voice, "Excuse me."

A man's voice said. "What?"

She stayed in the doorway and spoke loudly. "I'm the maid, sir. You were supposed to be out of here this morning. I need to clean the place for the next guests."

He rolled over and stretched and yawned. "No, I decided to stay another week. I called the rental office, but no one was there so I left a message." He sat up and the sheet fell away from his bare chest. It was obvious to Ella that he was naked, so she started to back out of the doorway. "Don't go away, sweetie," he said, "I'll get dressed and we can work this out."

Ella backed farther. "I'll take these sheets and towels down and start the laundry. You come down when you're decent."

She hurried down the tile steps with the heaped basket of sheets and towels. She sorted them on the laundry room floor and got the first load in the washer. When she turned around the man, fully dressed, was standing in the door, his hand braced on the jamb.

"You're awfully pretty to be a maid, awfully white too. What are you doing being a maid when there are locals who can do the job and probably cheaper."

She swallowed a sharp retort at his racist remarks and said, "It's my job, the only one I could find. Non-natives have a hard time getting a work permit. I can clean on the side and don't need a permit." She stepped around him. "Excuse me. I'll call the office to clear up the misunderstanding."

She pulled her cell phone from her pocket and dialed the number of Playa Palms rental. She stood in the middle of the living room gazing out at the sparkling sea as the phone rang.

"Hello, Gina, it's Ella. I'm at 25417 Santa Barbara Shores and there's a gentleman here who says he's staying another week. Mariette told me to clean the place because a new rental is arriving tomorrow. Did I get it wrong?"

"No, Ella, you're not wrong. I had a message from a Bert Champeau saying that he wanted to stay an extra week, but he didn't leave a callback number. I drove by the house on my way home last evening, no one was there so I planned to come again this morning. Tell him we're sorry, but the house is rented for next week. I can come over and help him find another accommodation for next week, but he must leave 25417 so you can clean."

"I'll tell him, but he's not going to be happy."

Bert took a few steps toward her. "What did she say? Why am I not going to be happy?"

Ella tucked her phone in her hip pocket and turned to face him. "I'm sorry, but you can't stay here for another week. Another party has reserved it. Gina is happy to help you find another place to stay but I must clean this one, so you'll have to leave."

Bert reached over and took her wrist with his right hand. "Can't you talk to her, sweet talk her, so I can stay here? I don't want to have to pack up and move. I like it here."

Ella shook her head. "I'm sorry, I can't. I don't have that kind of authority. I'm just the cleaning lady."

He pulled her closer. "Sure, you do. You can flutter those big brown eyelashes and make people do what you want. I bet you can." He had pulled her hard up against his chest, twisting her left arm behind her back.

"Stop. You're hurting me." She put her right hand on his shoulder and pushed.

He was strong, too strong for her to make him move.

Ella lifted her leg to try to knee him in the groin, but he twisted away and pulled her arm up tighter behind her back.

"Uh-uh-uh. You can't hurt me like that. I'm too fast for you."

As he spoke, he was moving forward, forcing Ella to back up. Soon her calves hit the edge of the couch, she overbalanced, and he landed on top of her. She heard her shoulder pop, and she cried out.

"Oh, you're not hurt." His left hand wormed between them, grabbed the edge of her tee shirt, and reached under it.

"No, don't touch me. I'll scream."

His face was right above hers. "Go ahead and scream. I like it when my women scream."

She inhaled to scream, and he covered her mouth with his. She tried to bite his lip, but he squeezed her breast and made her gasp. Ella bucked her hips trying to dislodge him, but he was too big for her to move. He ground his hips into her, and she could feel his rigid manhood through her shorts.

I'm going to be raped, she thought, terror making her mind race. He still had her left arm twisted behind her and his hand up her shirt. His knee was forcing her legs apart and she could feel her strength waning. Gina said she would come right over and help find him another place to stay. How long until Gina arrived? Would Ella be able to fend him off?

She heard a car on the gravel street and hoped it was Gina come to the rescue, but it went on past. Maybe the pool man would be here soon. She could see the pool from the couch so he would be able to see what was happening. Oh god, please, Gina, hurry.

"Hello? Ella, are you here?"

Bert let off the pressure on her left shoulder and lifted himself off her.

"What is going on?" Gina said.

He stood Ella up on her feet and dusted her off, straightening her shirt and patting her on the shoulder. "Oh, we were just playing," he said. "No harm done."

At that Ella burst into tears. "No harm done?" Ella moved to stand next to Gina. "Gina, he tried to rape me. I think he almost dislocated my arm. I'm calling the police."

She reached into her pocket for her phone and started to dial.

Bert stepped forward, reaching out toward her. "Now there is no reason to get the police involved. I was just being friendly."

Ella backed up and kept the phone at her ear. "If you call that being friendly, you're one sick man." The phone was answered. "Hello, police? I want to report an attempted rape."

Bert Champeau stood looking in disbelief as Ella spoke with the police department reporting his attempted rape. "Yes, thank you, Officer. 25417 Santa Barbara Shores. Yes, I'll be here." She hung up and looked at Bert.

He held out both hands. "I was just being playful. You don't have to get the police involved. Can't we just say sorry and move on?"

Ella rubbed her left shoulder which ached from being twisted the wrong way. "No, we can't just say sorry. You hurt me and you assaulted me. You had your hand on my breast and your knee between my legs. You were headed somewhere, and I couldn't stop you."

He turned and ran up the stairs. In a very few minutes he was back down with his suitcase and car keys were jingling in his hand. "I'm out of here," he said, and went around the two women through the laundry room and out the door to the carport.

Gina turned to look at Ella. "Too bad I parked him into the carport. He cannot get away and I hear a siren very nearby. He will not get away with hurting you."

Gina's words were prophetic. The police car pulled in just as Bert came back into the house insisting that someone move their car so he could leave.

The police officers were efficient and handcuffed him as soon as Ella pointed out that he was the one who assaulted her. "We do not tolerate men hurting women on this island, sir. You are under arrest."

They kept him standing there while one of them questioned Ella about what had happened. He yelled that he was just being playful but the growing bruises on her wrist and swollen mouth said otherwise.

Ella was relieved when they took him away. She agreed to come down to the police station later that day to swear out a complaint.

After they left Ella looked at Gina and said, "I'll finish cleaning up this place and then I'll take the rest of the day off, if you don't mind."

Gina stared at her. "Are you sure? You can leave, go get checked out and go to the police station to make your statement. I can finish up here."

Ella shook her head. "No, I need the money from cleaning today and I want to scrub Mr. Bert Champeau out of this house. I'll be okay."

"Then I am helping you. With two of us working we can get done faster and chase his spirit from the house." She laughed.

"Maybe we should have a witch doctor or a priest in to do an exorcism."

Ella gave a mirthless laugh. "That's not a bad idea. I'll call the priest at Saint Michael's and ask him about an exorcism. I'll do it today."

The women got to work and finished cleaning the house within a couple of hours. Gina put Bert Champeau's suitcase in his rental car and called the rental company to come pick up the car. Mr. Champeau could get his belongings from them. She wasn't going to have anything further to do with him. She was especially glad that the rental fee for the house was already paid because she suspected that he would try to get out of paying it if he could.

By the time they had finished cleaning the house, Ella's hands were shaking, and she was shivering.

Gina took one look at her and said, "Shock. I am taking you to the doctor and then home. I will pick up Dan and bring him back to get your car. We will put it off to the side so it will not be in the way when the rental car company picks up Mr. Champeau's car."

Ella nodded. "Okay. I do feel a little shaky, too shaky to drive."

She got checked out in the emergency room at San Francisco Hospital and then Gina took her to the police station and held her hand while she gave her statement. The police took pictures of her bruised wrist, her swollen mouth, and the scratches on her midriff. She was relieved to say that Champeau had not gotten into her shorts so neither the emergency room doctor nor the policewoman had to ask her to take off her clothes.

After the police station Gina drove Ella home, made her take one of the pain pills the doctor had given her and a sedative he had insisted she take as soon as she got home.

Ella lay down in bed and was soon asleep. Gina drove to the Dive Inn where Dan was just getting back from the morning dives. She took him aside and told him what had happened to Ella. He turned pale at the news and then red with anger. He was ready to charge over to the police station and beat up Bert Champeau, but Gina stopped him.

"Ella does not need you to be in jail for assault. It is enough that Mr. Champeau is there. She has had a rough day and needs you to take care of her. Get your belongings and I will drive you up to Santa Barbara Shores to get your car and then you can go home and take care of Ella.

"Okay, if you say so but I'd like to get my hands on that guy."

Gina put her hand on his shoulder. "Yes, I know you would. Anyone would feel the same way, but you can help Ella by being gentle and worrying about her feelings because she's going to have a lot of them to deal with."

On the drive back up the island to fetch the car Dan asked Gina to retell the story over and over, to tell him what she saw when she walked into the house, what the police said, and how Ella was right now.

"Right now, Ella is sleeping. The doctor gave her a sedative that I made her take. She may sleep the rest of the day, but you should be there in case she wakes up and is frightened."

Dan nodded and stared out the windshield, his hands were clenched into fists that he kept opening and closing. When they got to the house the rental car was gone. Gina was relieved not to see it there.

She handed Dan the keys to Ella's car and said, "Now do not drive like a maniac because you are angry. Just get yourself home and do something like make soup for Ella. Stop at the market if you do not have any soup makings at home. Soup is a good healing meal and Ella will need healing."

"Fine, I'll do that. Thank you for the ride and for showing up to save Ella from that predator."

He slammed the car door too hard and stomped through the gravel to Ella's car. It's hard to stomp on gravel in sandals and Dan ended up getting rocks between his feet and shoes. He had to stop and shake them out before getting into the car. He heeded Gina's warning and kept it at a reasonable speed.

He stopped at More for Less market and picked up some oxtails, an onion, a can of mixed vegetables, and beef broth to use to make soup. His mom had made oxtail soup when he was a kid, and it was one of his favorite things to eat. It had been too long since he had eaten it. The house was quiet when he arrived home. He carried the soup makings into the kitchen and peeked into the bedroom to make sure that Ella was sleeping.

She wasn't, she was awake and terrified. "Oh, good, it's you," she said in a faint voice, "I was afraid Bert Champeau had gotten away from the police and come to find me."

Dan went into the room and sat on the edge of the bed. "No, it's just me. Gina came and got me at work, took me up to get the car, and now I'm going to make some oxtail soup for supper. Hopefully, I can make it half as good as Mom used to make."

"Soup will be good." She rolled over and fell back to sleep. "Later," she said as she drifted off.

Dan leaned down and kissed the top of her head. He went back into the kitchen and got busy chopping the big onion and some celery and carrots they had in the fridge for his soup. Ella slept for a few hours more. It was getting dark when she shuffled out of the bedroom into the kitchen where Dan sat reading.

"You're up," Dan said, "how are you feeling?"

Ella ran her hand through her hair. "Groggy. I don't know what was in that sedative, but it sure knocked me out."

He chuckled. "I think that is the point of a sedative." He pushed his chair back, the legs squeaked across the tiles, and stood up. "How about a bowl of soup?"

She inhaled. "It smells wonderful. How much onion did you put in?"

"A lot. Mom always doubled the amount of onion called for in any recipe and especially soup. She said it accented all the other vegetables and gave the soup a sweetness that she liked. Mom loved cooked onions but couldn't eat them raw. Too hot, she said."

Ella sat down at the table. "I never thought of raw onions as being hot." She reached across to touch his book. "What are you reading?"

Dan was standing at the stove ladling out two bowls of soup. He looked over his shoulder. "Reef Fish Behavior. I'm trying to

51

learn more that I can teach the three Underwater Naturalist women tomorrow. It's their last certification dive and I want to give them each a slate with behaviors and creatures listed on it and see how many of each they can find in one dive. Kind of like a final exam and scavenger hunt rolled into one."

She ran her hand over the colorful fish on the cover. "That's a good idea. I'm coming along tomorrow remember."

He set the bowls of soup in their cotton bowl cozies down on the table and turned to pick spoons out of the crock they kept them in and pull the crackers box down from the shelf. "Are you sure that you should?"

"No, not at all. I might not be able to bear the weight of a tank on my left shoulder, but I took the day off to go diving and I will go diving."

When they got into bed that night Dan was afraid to reach out and touch Ella. What if she thought it was that man? What if she stopped wanting to be touched? Dan didn't know what to do. As soon as the light was out Ella scooted over and tucked herself into Dan's shoulder the way she always did when she had a bad day. He let out a sigh and wrapped his arms around her, holding her but not too tight. He felt her shake and figured out that she was crying. He kissed the top of her head and started rubbing her back.

"It's okay now, I'm here, I'll keep you safe."

She sniffled. "I know you will, that's why I'm crying, because I finally feel safe." She rubbed her nose on his tee shirt. "Oh sorry."

"That's okay."

"Thanks for the soup, it was good. How did you know that I would need soup?"

He kept rubbing her back. "Gina told me to stop at the store on my way home and get a can of soup. I knew that wasn't good enough. A day like today called for actual homemade soup. I'm glad that Mom made soup all those years so that I know how to make it too. It was rather good if I do say so myself." He could feel her smile.

"It was, and it will be even better tomorrow. We can stop at the bakery for a baguette to go with it. I think we have some gouda cheese in the fridge too. Supper tomorrow is solved." She gave a big yawn. "And now I think I can sleep again. Thanks for being you. I love you," she said as she drifted off to sleep still wrapped in his arms.

"I love you too, babe."

He closed his eyes, but it took a while for him to fall asleep.

CHAPTER 6

Ella wasn't in bed when Dan woke up the next morning. He was on the verge of panic when he smelled coffee. If she made coffee, she must be all right, he thought, so he didn't hurry out to the kitchen but went into the bathroom to brush his teeth like he did every morning before kissing her.

He took an appreciative sniff as he walked into the kitchen. "Do I detect the aroma of Tanzanian coffee?"

She turned from the counter where she was fixing a bowl of yogurt and granola with fruit. "Yes, I decided to break out the Mt. Meru coffee that Neil and Abby gave us for Christmas. I saw it in the freezer when I was looking for some fruit and thought 'why are we saving it?' so here you are." She handed him a steaming mug of coffee.

He dipped his nose into the steam and inhaled. "Oh, that smells so good, like citrus and coffee mixed. Thanks, babe." He leaned into the refrigerator and took out a couple slices of whole wheat bread that he slid into the toaster. "Do we have any of that guava jelly left?" he asked.

"Yes, it's behind the six kinds of mustard you bought the last time we were at Cultimara."

"I didn't buy six kinds of mustard; it was only four kinds and I like mustard."

"I do too but not all at once."

He emerged from the fridge with a jar half filled with jelly in his hand. "Hey, sometimes they run out and mustard doesn't spoil. It won't go bad."

Ella realized that they were having a normal morning conversation, that her world hadn't turned over due to the events of the day before. Yes, her shoulder was a bit sore, but a shower had helped her wash off the feel of that man's hands on her and sleeping in Dan's arms had made her feel safe. She was looking forward to spending the day on the dive boat, swimming in the silky warm saltwater and spending the time looking for small, interesting things to show Dan's students.

The toast popped up and Dan tried to take it out when it was too hot. "Ouch, oh, hot, hot," he said.

"Be patient and you won't burn your fingers."

He sucked his burned fingertips. "But I'm hungry."

"Eat more than toast. Do you want some yogurt and granola?"

"No, I don't like birdseed or spoiled milk."

Ella laughed at him. "Philistine," she said, "How about a scrambled egg?"

"Yeah, good idea." He stood up and took a small frying pan off the wall behind the stove. "What time is it? Do I have time for an egg?"

She looked at the clock. "It's just after seven. You have plenty of time for an egg and more toast." She reached over to the counter. "Have one of these bananas before they go bad." She laid a brown speckled banana on the table.

"Yuck," he said, "it's too ripe. Time to make banana bread."

She took another look at it and admitted he might be right. "I guess it is a little aged. I'll put them into the fridge and make banana bread when we get home this afternoon."

"Hooray," Dan said, "then I can have banana bread for breakfast. We should get some cream cheese to put on it."

She nodded. "We can stop at the mini mart on our way home."

They cleaned up their breakfast dishes and Ella packed her dive gear. She put on her swimsuit under her shorts and tee shirt. When she reached over her head to slip into the shirt her left shoulder let her know that it was still hurt. She couldn't expect that to heal overnight but she was glad it wasn't worse. I thought he had popped it out of the socket, she thought, so I guess I'm lucky. She made sure that she had her sunscreen. She put on the first layer before leaving for the dive shop. It was a good idea to let it soak in.

Despite living in the tropics for a year she still could very easily get sunburned. She had her Northern European ancestors and her red-haired grandmother to thank for her pale, sun-sensitive skin. Part of her wished she got a decent tan but another part of her was grateful that she had to be careful in the sun. Maybe she could avoid skin cancer that way. A hat, she thought, can't forget a hat. She dug around in her dresser and found a canvas boonie hat with a wide brim and a string that she could tighten to keep it on her head when she was in the wind and put it into her dive bag.

"Ready?' Dan called. "It is time to get rolling."

She picked up her bag. "I'm ready and on my way."

Dan took her bag and stowed it in the trunk of the car. She spread out the ratty beach towel that they left in the car to cover the sunbaked vinyl passenger seat. She didn't want to sear the backs of her thighs sitting on it.

They got to the Dive Inn early enough that Dan got a parking place next to it. "I'm glad we didn't have to park around the corner. I always hate leaving the car there where no one can keep an eye on it."

Ella nodded. "I wish whoever is breaking into cars would just stop it."

"Wouldn't that be great?" Dan said.

The three Underwater Naturalist women were sitting around the table in the courtyard with their logbooks and the Reef Fish guides spread out, talking about all the things they had seen on the previous day's dives. "And more today, right, Dan?" said Ilsa with a wink.

"That is right, ladies, and I brought along someone who is a master at finding interesting and unusual things." He put his hand on the small of Ella's back. "Ladies, this is my partner, Ella. Ella, this is Ilsa, Claire, and Libby."

Ella smiled and held out her hand to shake. "Good

morning, Ilsa, Claire, and Libby." She shook their hands in turn. "I'm glad to meet you. Dan told me that you're getting good at finding things underwater. I know he has a fun challenge for you today, so I hope that I'll be able to help you meet that challenge."

Claire and Libby smiled and looked excited; Ilsa folded her arms across her chest and looked irritated.

Dan came out of the office where he had stashed his briefcase and said, "I'll carry your tanks down to the boat, babe. We don't want you injuring that shoulder any more than it already is."

Libby looked up. "What happened to your shoulder?"

Ella rubbed her left shoulder and said, "I clean houses for a rental company, and I slipped on wet tiles and bashed my shoulder into a wall yesterday. No actual harm done but it hurts a bit today. I need to give it a rest."

"Will you still be able to dive?"

Ella smiled. "I think bathing it in warm saltwater and sunshine will be just what the doctor ordered. Never fear we will have fun critter hunting."

Dan came up to the table with three big slates in his hand. "Okay, ladies, here's today's challenge. You each have a slate with critters and behaviors listed on it. Each one is worth a point. You'll have both dives to find as many items on the list as you can."

Claire raised her hand. "Is there a prize for the one who finds the most?"

Ilsa piped up. "A date with Dan."

Everyone laughed.

Dan said, "I don't think that would be appropriate. Ella might object, but there is a small prize, and it is not your certification card. May the best woman win."

He handed out the slates and motioned Ella to follow him to the boat.

Dan put his arm around Ella's waist as they walked across the street and down the dock. "Man, that Ilsa is persistent, isn't she."

Ella leaned into him. "She sure is. You'd better watch out, so she doesn't catch you someplace and get her hands on you."

Dan looked down at her. "You know that I'm not interested in anyone but you, right?"

She stepped onto the deck of the dive boat. "I know, I hope so. Just watch yourself. You have your dad's flirtatious way with women." She patted him on the back, kissed his cheek, and went to set up her SCUBA gear.

The rest of the divers came down to the boat in twos and the three Underwater Naturalist women came together, their heads bent over their new slates.

"How can we hope to find all of this stuff on two dives?" said Libby.

Claire said, "We keep our eyes open and spread out. That way we'll cover more reef than if we stick close together. We may not all see the same things, but I bet we'll all see more than before we took this class."

Ilsa didn't say anything. She was determined to be the winner and even more determined to wrangle another drink with Dan, even if he had Ella there to deflect her. She wasn't easy to avoid.

By now all the divers knew each other, they had dived together for three days and were starting to form friendships. Claire and Libby had invited Ilsa to have supper with them the night before and the ladies had gone to Karel's Beach Bar afterwards and danced the night away. All three of them were a little tired and a tiny bit hungover today so they were a little slow getting their gear set up and pulling on their tight wetsuits. They were also all wearing dark glasses to keep the blazing sun out of their eyes.

Ella enjoyed the scent of the sea as the wavelets rolled under the boat and hissed on the sand at the head of the dock. She also detected the aroma of coconut sunscreen which reminded her to put on another layer. She rummaged in her bag and got out the tube. Dan came over just in time to be put to work putting lotion on her back.

"Thanks, sweetie," she said over her shoulder. His hands were especially gentle as he rubbed the cream over her sore left shoulder.

"Anytime," he said.

"Can you check my gear set up?" Ilsa said from her seat at the bow of the boat.

Dan rolled his eyes, said, "Coming," and went up to do as she asked. It was his job as the main instructor of the Dive Inn to make sure that all the customers got the service they desired. It wasn't his job to be preyed upon by lonely women on vacation, but that often happened. He was getting good at deflecting that sort of attention while not giving offense. He had to lean over Ilsa to check her gear setup. She didn't move when he came up but swung her knees aside, so he had to lean over her shoulder to reach the tank.

"All set," he said, "You have it right."

"Thank you, Dan," she said with a purr.

Yikes, he thought as he walked back to where Captain Bill stood at the wheel, I had better keep my eyes open or she'll snag me for real.

Ella looked at him and grinned at the sheepish look in his face. "Go get 'em, tiger," she teased.

Dan cleared his throat and said, "Everyone got their gear set up for the first dive?" Receiving nods from all the divers he told Samuel to untie the boat and Captain Bill fired up the motor, then eased away from the dock. Captain Bill took the boat around the south shore of Klein Bonaire, around the point, to a dive site in the middle of the north side of the island. Samuel leaned from the bow of the boat, hooked the mooring buoy, and got the boat attached on the first try. He was congratulated by the pair of guys seated in the bow. They had watched him struggle in rough waters the day before and were impressed by his skill at getting hooked up today.

"All right, listen up," Dan said. "This site is called Carl's Hill or Punta P'abou. This is a very lush site with lots of gorgonians, sponges, various kinds of coral, and even black coral. There are

Tiger Grouper and Rock Hinds that frequent a cleaning station. They are so used to divers that you can get close, within about five feet, before they move away, and if you back off, they'll come right back. At this cleaning station the cleaners are Neon Wrasse instead of the shrimp you've seen at other sites. From the mooring if you swim east," he turned to point that way, "you cross a field of Staghorn Coral, then you come to the edge of the wall. It bottoms out at about seventy feet and there are lots of types of coral on the wall.

"For you Underwater Naturalists be sure to check the holes and niches of the wall. You'll find many of the items on your lists there but also keep an eye on your air consumption. Don't stay too deep for too long as there are even more things to find in the shallows, especially in the Elkhorn Coral forest near the shore. Watch the blue off to your left as you swim along the wall, you might see Tarpon or even Dolphins or Sharks patrolling there, if you're lucky."

There were excited murmurs from the divers. Libby called out, "Should we be wary of sharks on this dive?"

Dan shook his head. "Most sharks are just cruising by, not looking for divers to chomp on. We're not on their menu." A few people laughed at his weak joke. "Okay, let's get geared up and go diving."

Dan turned and lifted his SCUBA unit, swung it over his shoulder and onto his back. There was a possibility of a current at this site, so he wanted to be in the water.

"Watch for a current," he said as he buckled the belt of his BCD. "Remember to swim into it at the beginning of the dive if there is one."

Samuel was the first in the water and swam over to the mooring buoy. He knew that he didn't have to guide these divers, but he liked to be there if anyone had an issue at the beginning of the dive. Too many times a diver lost a mask or a camera on a giant stride entry and being already in the water let him retrieve it right away.

Pairs of divers entered the water on either side of the boat then swam over to the mooring buoy to meet up and start their dive. Some of the buddy teams planned their approach now that they could look down into the water and see the site. Samuel was always willing to help them figure out the best way to get the most out of the experience. The three Underwater Naturalist women were the last divers to reach him. They had their slates buckled to their shoulder straps and were discussing the best way to find all the things on the list.

"Can you help us, Samuel?" said Claire. "Which way should we go to see the best things on this site?"

"Like Dan said, swim over the Staghorn Coral to the drop off and then down the wall to the bottom. Work your way back up toward the shallows and check in every hole. I know that there are a lot of lobsters and eels that live in that wall. When you get back to the shallows check in every sponge and anemone for Brittle Stars and those little purple cleaner shrimps. I forget their name."

"Thanks," Libby said.

Ilsa was looking at her slate as if she were trying to memorize it. She wasn't listening to the advice. "Ready?" Ilsa said. She cleared her mask and asked Claire to check to make sure there was no hair under the skirt. On such an important dive she didn't need water dripping into her mask the whole time. "I am going my own way but will stay in sight," she said to Claire so that Samuel didn't hear.

"That's not safe, you should stay with us," Claire said.

"I won't go far but I want to stay apart so that we're not all looking at the same things."

"Okay, just be careful and watch your air."

The three of them vented air from their buoyancy control devices and sank under the surface. Ilsa jackknifed and swam down the drop-off right by the mooring, not bothering to swim across the Staghorn Coral under the mooring buoy. She went straight down the wall.

Samuel could see her pinching her nose to equalize the pressure in her ears as she went but he thought that he better follow her. Ella swam over to him, and he pointed at Claire and Libby for her to join up with them.

She nodded, cleared her mask, pinched her nose to equalize, and vented air from her buoyancy control device to descend and join the women. Claire and Libby followed Dan's recommendation to swim over the shallows to the wall and then drop down. They looked around and saw Ella swimming toward them and waved. Ilsa was nowhere in sight.

When Ella reached them, she held up three fingers and shrugged to ask where the third member was. Libby pointed behind them and down the slope. Ella knew that Samuel had gone that way so she gave the okay signal and motioned that they should swim on down the wall. Libby and Claire were careful divers, they stayed close together, and checked each other's air regularly. They were good at finding items on Dan's list. They found three types of eels and two different kinds of lobsters. The wall was alive with the claw clicks of the shrimp that lived in the crannies of the wall. Libby found a lush stand of Black Coral jutting out from the wall.

Ella gave Libby a big okay and applause when she showed Ella the Black Coral. Both Claire and Libby were grinning around their mouthpieces, so Ella knew that they were having a good time. She hoped that Samuel had caught up with Ilsa and would keep her out of trouble.

By this time, the women's air was below fifteen hundred psi, so it was time to head into the shallower water to conserve air and extend their dive. They swam slowly over the Staghorn Coral pausing to find Brittle Stars and Bristle Worms. Ella shook her finger at Claire who had reached down to touch a Bristle Worm. Ella wrote 'stings' on her slate and Claire jerked her hand away. Both women pointed at the place where the wall dropped off. There was a Tarpon hovering there. The big scales of the three-foot-long fish looked like silver dollars in the bright sunlight. In unison the women picked up their slates and placed a check mark next to 'tarpon' on their list.

Now they were in Ella's favorite part of a dive, the shallows where baby fish and little eels hid in the patchy reefs and stands of Fire Coral. Some of the fish they found were no bigger than a thumbnail and Ella pointed out a baby Spotted Cowfish no bigger than a pea. No sooner had she pointed it out to the other women than a Yellowtail Snapper swam up and gulped it down. Both women had round, sad eyes in their masks but Ella just shrugged. 'That's life on the reef' she wrote on her slate.

They were swimming along and Ella noticed the sparkle of glass in a sandy area near a patch of coral. She swam over and showed her dive partners. There was a row of empty beer bottles in front of a hole in the reef. Ella reached down and rearranged the bottles, messing them up, and then moved back. She motioned the others to stay still and soon a gray-brown tentacle came out of the hole. The tentacle was followed by the whole octopus that came out of its hole and put its front porch bottle decoration back the way it had been.

Ella heard one of the women beside her giggle in delight at the sight. As soon as the bottles were back in order the octopus went back into its hole but not before giving Ella a dirty look from a surprisingly knowing eye.

The rest of the dive was spent looking for little shrimp living among the polyps of sea anemones. In one of them they spied a little shrimp that popped out of the niche where the anemone was and menaced them with its claws. Claire motioned them to come look at a red sponge she was hovering over. Beneath the sponge was an Arrow Crab that looked like a handful of toothpicks with a frowny face and little purple boxing glove claws. By now their tanks were getting empty and it was getting hard to maintain buoyancy in the shallow water that kept moving them toward shore.

The three women swam back to the mooring buoy and did a three-minute safety stop before climbing back onto the boat. In the sand under them Ella spotted a Peacock Flounder. It was almost perfectly camouflaged. It had turned the same brilliant white as the sand and only its swiveling eyes were visible. It took Claire and Libby some time to see it but eventually they did and happily marked it on their slates. They were almost the last ones aboard. Ella looked and saw that neither Dan nor Samuel was on the boat. She looked around in the shallows thinking that she would see Dan's neon yellow fins in the clear water, but she didn't see him or Samuel's bright green fins either. Where could they be? Then she saw Dan's head break the surface. He took the regulator out of his mouth and called for help.

Since Ella was still in her dive gear she slid her feet back into her fins, put on her mask, and went over the side. She swam as fast as she could over to where Dan was holding onto Samuel. Samuel, in turn, was holding onto Ilsa with his hand cupped under her chin to keep her head above water.

Ella swam up to them. "What happened?"

Dan shook his head. "I'm not sure, but I found Samuel wrestling with Ilsa down at the bottom of the wall, then she went limp, so I helped him drag her to the surface."

"Is she out of air?"

Samuel panted out, "I don't know, but I think she had a blackout. She was pretty narced."

As they talked, they were swimming back toward the boat, Ella and Dan towing Samuel who kept Ilsa's face above the water. Ella could hear him talking to Ilsa all the time.

"Come on, lady, wake up. It will look bad on our record if you kick it while you're diving with us. Come on, wake up. You can do it."

But Ilsa remained limp. They got back to the boat. Dan threw his fins up to Captain Bill and clambered up the boarding ladder.

"Here, Samuel," Ella said, "give her to me. I'll keep her afloat while you get on the boat so you can help get her up there. I'm not strong enough to lift her."

Soon hands reached down and took Ilsa's SCUBA unit that Ella had removed from her inert form. Then Dan and Samuel worked together to get Ilsa onto the boat. They laid her on the deck in front of the camera table and checked her breathing.

"She's breathing but very slowly. Roll her onto her side in

the recovery position and grab a towel to cover her."

Ella scrambled onto the boat and got her tank settled in the rack behind her seat. She checked Ilsa's air pressure gauge and looked at Dan. "Empty."

"Dammit," Dan said, "I told them to stay together and watch each other's air."

He looked at Claire and Libby. "How did you guys get separated?"

The women looked ashamed. "She swam away from us at the beginning of the dive saying that she would be all right on her own. We let her go and should have followed her."

"Damn right you should have followed her."

Samuel spoke up. "I was with her, Dan. I should have checked her air more often. Do not blame them, blame me."

By then Captain Bill had radioed into the dive center for them to have the ambulance meet them at the dock. One of the divers had unhooked the boat from the mooring buoy and they were racing back to shore. Everyone was quiet and looked scared.

When they got to the dock the paramedics were there with a stretcher. They took the lines when they were thrown and quickly secured the boat. Everyone stayed seated while the paramedics came on board and carried Ilsa to the stretcher, strapped her on, and carried her up to the waiting ambulance.

Dan looked around. "Okay, everybody, get your gear up to the shop, get it rinsed and hung up to dry. There won't be a second dive this morning. You're welcome to join the afternoon dive to make up for it if you'd like. Thank you."

Dan hoisted his SCUBA unit onto his shoulder, grabbed his gear bag, and hurried after the stretcher. Ella saw him dump his things at the rinse tank and hurry into the office to report the accident. It was a subdued group that left the dive boat. Not much talking and no laughing. Claire was crying and Libby was trying to console her.

Ella went over to them. "Don't beat yourselves up over this. You didn't know that she was going to be so reckless.

Samuel was with her, and he's a Divemaster and still she got herself in a mess."

Libby looked at Ella. "We know. Ilsa was determined to impress Dan with all she found. She said on the ride out to the site that she was going to stay the deepest she could and to find the most there was to find. I guess she found more than she bargained for."

"Dan is more impressed with good diving than a list of critters on a slate," said Ella.

She turned and started packing up her dive equipment in preparation to taking it up to the shop. She slid her SCUBA unit over her shoulders and stood up to walk it up the steps to the rinse tank.

"One day," she said to Captain Bill, "I'm going to dive on a level site where I don't have to carry this stuff up and down hills or over coral boulders. One day."

Captain Bill nodded.

When she got up to the shop there was a crowd at the rinse tank, so she unhooked her regulator and buoyancy control device from her tank, laid it off to the side, and took the tank back to the fill station. She could hear Dan in the office talking to Babs.

"Samuel was diving with her. She swam away from her buddies, so he followed her."

Ella couldn't hear what Babs said next.

"No! I don't know what happened. Samuel said she stayed at depth at the bottom of the wall peering in all the nooks and crannies to find things and then she just collapsed. I guess you can say that it is my fault for dreaming up that little scavenger hunt as the last dive of their certification dives."

Babs raised her voice. "It wasn't your fault. You set them up as a buddy team and she left the team. Samuel went after her and stayed with her. Something must have gone wrong. Something that you couldn't control."

Dan's voice was low and sad. "Thanks for saying that, Babs, but I still feel like it was my fault."

He walked out of the office, head down and shoulders slumped. Ella put her arms around him and just held him, not saying anything. She knew that anything she could say wouldn't remove his feeling of responsibility for the accident.

He picked his head up. "I'm going over to the hospital. Do you want to come or stay here?"

"I'll stay here and help Samuel sort out the divers and get the gear taken care of. You go on and see how she's doing."

He pulled the car keys from his pocket and left. Ella put her gear in the rinse tank and helped people fill out their logbooks. Dan might not be there to sign them but at least she could help them get the dive entered.

Dan realized that he was strangling the steering wheel. He loosened his fingers as he made his way through Playa toward San Francisco Hospital. He kept going over in his mind if there was anything he could have done to stop Ilsa from running out of air and getting decompression sickness. Probably not, he decided. Samuel was with her, and he was an incredibly good Divemaster and dive guide. Dan was sure that Samuel had tried to get Ilsa to ascend but knew that she was stubborn enough that if he had begun to swim to a shallower depth she would have stayed where she was. At least Samuel was with her when she ran out of air and could bring her to the surface safely. Who knew what caused her to black out on the ascent? She had air; he had seen Samuel's safe second regulator in her mouth as they popped to the surface. Samuel had held it in Ilsa's mouth as they were towed to the boat. Dan saw all that. So why had Ilsa blacked out?

He found a parking place a block from the hospital and jogged over to the Emergency Room entrance. The ambulance was still there so he slipped into the cool interior and went over to the desk.

The receptionist looked up at him. "Can I help you?" she said. Her nametag said Noreen.

"Yes, I want to know how the woman diver who was just

brought in is doing."

Noreen looked down at a clipboard. "Her name?"

"Ilsa, uh, Ilsa… I don't know her last name. I'm the dive Instructor at Dive Inn and oversaw the dive. Can you tell me how she's doing?"

Noreen flipped a page over on her clipboard and shook her head. "I do not have anyone named Ilsa registered."

Dan pointed out the door. "But she just came in that ambulance. You had to see them race by here with a woman on a gurney. How is that woman?"

"Oh, I do not have her name." She flipped the page back. "I am sorry, sir, but unless you are a relative, I cannot release any information."

Dan reached down and picked up Ilsa's purse that he had brought along and held it up. "This is her purse. I am certain that there is identification and insurance information in it. Does this give me the right to know how she is, Noreen?"

She reached out and took the purse from him. "I will give this to the nurse."

Just then the paramedics came out of the Emergency Room rolling their empty gurney. Dan turned to them. "How is she?"

They looked at each other and shrugged. "She's still unconscious. The doctor is on the phone with the Divers' Alert Network for assistance in making a treatment plan. I think she will spend some time in the decompression chamber soon."

Dan reached out and clapped him on the shoulder. "Thanks, man." He turned back to Noreen. "Will you please call the Dive Inn when you know more? Our liability insurance demands it."

Noreen nodded and went back to studying her clipboard.

Realizing that he would get no more information there he went back to his car and drove back to the dive shop. He was surprised to see that all the divers from the boat were still sitting around the table in the courtyard under the chickee's thatched roof. It was obvious that Claire had been crying. The others were all talking quietly, and Ella was trying to get them to leave.

"How is she?" Ella asked as Dan walked in from where he parked the car around the corner.

"The same. The doc is talking to Divers' Alert Network, and they're making a treatment plan together. The paramedics said they thought she would be in the decompression chamber soon."

One of the men spoke up. "Is there room for all of us on the afternoon dive?"

Dan looked like he couldn't remember how to find that out. Ella stood up. "I'll check with Cecile in the shop." She was gone only a few minutes. "There are only two people signed up so there is room for all of you if that's what you want. You need to go in and get your name on the list, then I suggest we all go find some lunch and meet back here at one-thirty to get ready for the afternoon dive."

Everyone except Libby and Claire got up and trooped into the shop to get their names on the afternoon dive list.

Libby looked at Dan. "Claire and I aren't sure we can dive again. We feel responsible for Ilsa going off by herself and getting hurt."

Dan shook his head. "It wasn't your fault. She swam away from you and went her own way. Samuel was with her and even he couldn't keep her from hurting herself. She must have had a bad case of nitrogen narcosis and lost track of where she was."

Libby and Claire looked relieved. "We never thought of that. Do you really think that's what happened?"

"I do. Her tank was empty, and she blacked out at depth. It was a good thing that Samuel was with her. He took his safe second regulator, pushed it into her mouth, and purged it to force air into her lungs. That kept her breathing while he brought her slowly to the surface." Dan looked them both in the eyes. "This wasn't your fault. Ilsa did something you learn not to do in class. She ditched her buddies and went off on her own. There's a good reason they teach you never to dive alone, it's just not safe. Come diving with us this afternoon. It's a good idea to get back in the water today, so you don't stop diving altogether."

"Okay," they said in unison, and they went into the shop to sign up for the afternoon dive.

Ella stood up and went over to put her arms around Dan. "Are you okay?" she said.

"No, but I'll get there. I need to find Samuel and see how he's doing."

He squeezed her upper arms and stepped around her to go into the fill station and repair shop. Samuel was filling tanks.

"Thanks, man," said Dan, "you saved her."

"No, if I had saved her, she would be here and not in the hospital."

"You didn't know that she was narced and was breathing her tank dry."

"She signaled that she had air, and I didn't check for myself."

Dan touched Samuel's shoulder. "You did your job, man, what any Divemaster would do. You got her to the surface alive."

"How is she?"

Dan folded his arms over his chest. "When I talked to the paramedics, they said she was still unconscious and that she was headed to the decompression chamber. That should put her to rights, but she may have to have a few sessions. Stupid scavenger hunt I devised made her want to win at all costs. I feel like it's my fault that she did what she did. I should have dived with her. I knew that was what she wanted. I should have done it."

Now it was Samuel's turn to touch Dan on the shoulder. "I saw what she was like. She had her sights set on getting you on a date. You couldn't dive with her; she would have thought that meant you were interested in her. Foolish woman."

"Yeah," Dan said, "but we were responsible for her safety, and we blew it."

Samuel nodded. "We blew it."

Babs, the dive shop owner, went to the Windsock Deli and brought back crab salad and a loaf of Italian bread for lunch for the staff. "A good lunch will make everyone feel better," she said.

They were all starving, so they washed up and sat around the courtyard table eating crab salad sandwiches and potato chips for lunch. It did make them all feel a little better.

By then it was time to start getting ready for the afternoon dive. Ella realized that she had left her dive gear in the rinse tank since she came up from the boat, so she got it out and hung it up. Even though she hung it up inside out she knew that her wetsuit wouldn't be anywhere near dry, but it was hot enough that putting on a wet wetsuit might feel good.

Dan was carrying filled tanks to the rack and asked, "How's your shoulder?" as he passed her.

She put her right hand on her left shoulder and rubbed. "It's not too bad. A little sore if I reach up but not too bad. I can do another dive with it today, never fear."

Dan grinned. "You put your name on the list too?"

"I did. I'm not going to waste a day off cleaning and on the dive boat because some predatory woman nearly did herself in because she wanted to impress you."

Dan raised his eyebrows. "Oh yeah? You figured that out, did you?"

Ella snorted. "I'm not blind. I saw the way she looked at you, and the way she looked at me. I was surprised that she didn't push me overboard when you said that I would be diving with them today. She wanted you and she wanted you bad, bad enough to nearly kill herself to win that stupid scavenger hunt."

"Well, I'll never do that again."

Ella reached out and took his hand. "Don't give up on that. It's a clever idea. It's a fun way to get people to slow down and really look at what's around them. Too many divers want to go deep and swim fast and they miss all the small, interesting things about the civilizations under the water. Don't give it up, please."

He squeezed her hand. "Okay, I'll think about it."

CHAPTER 7

Dawn was just breaking when the aroma of brewing coffee woke Dan. He reached across the bed, but Ella wasn't there. He pulled on some shorts and a tee shirt that he picked up off the floor and went out into the kitchen. Ella sat at the table in her robe, her hands wrapped around a steaming mug of coffee.

"How come you're up so early?"

"I couldn't sleep," she said.

"How come?"

She took a sip and put her mug back down on the table. "Today is court day, remember? Today I have to go and face Bert Champeau and tell everyone what he did to me and what he tried to do to me. They're going to show pictures of the marks he made on me, and I don't know if I can endure it."

Dan sat down next to her at the table. "Oh, babe, I'll be right beside you and I will hold your hand the whole time."

She smiled a sad little smile. "I know you will, but you won't be able to hold my hand when I'm on the stand testifying and answering questions from his lawyer. I just know that they are going to try to make this my fault somehow, that he was an innocent bystander." Tears seeped from her eyes and rolled down her cheeks to drip into her coffee. "And what am I going to wear?"

Dan sat back. Trust a woman to worry about what she was going to wear. "Who cares what you wear? You're there to tell them how that creep assaulted you, tried to rape you."

She nodded. "Yes, but I have to make a good impression. I can't go in there dressed in clothes that are too revealing. I have to look like an innocent woman but not a victim."

"Why shouldn't you look like a victim? That is what you are, a victim of an assault."

She looked up from her mug. "Do you want some coffee?" She started to stand up.

"I'll get some," Dan said. "Do you want a refill?"

"No, I'm jittery enough. I don't want to have too much caffeine."

From the counter where he poured coffee into his own favorite Zambaldi Beer mug, he said, "What time do you have to be there?"

"At nine o'clock. What time is it now?"

He looked at the clock on the coffee pot. "It's seven-thirty."

Ella finished her coffee and stood up. "I'd better get in the shower. I know it will take me time to figure out what to wear. I wonder if I have a decent skirt." She walked out of the room mumbling to herself about skirts and pants.

Dan sat down in the chair she just vacated and watched her walk into the bedroom where she took off her robe and nightshirt and slid her robe back on. He liked to watch her walk from the bedroom to the bathroom for her shower because she never tied her robe shut when she put it back on, so he got a little peek at her breasts. Guess this isn't the day to tell her that, he thought.

She was starting to go through her clothes when he went in for his shower after she was done and he waited for the water to heat again, and she was still rejecting outfits when he came out. "I didn't know you had that many clothes," he said.

"I don't," she said, "and that's the problem. Nothing is right. I've tried things on two or three times, and nothing looks right."

Dan could tell that she was about to cry and wanted to say something that would help but he didn't know what. He was hopeless when it came to ladies' clothes and what kind of impression they made.

She finally settled on a pair of khaki slacks and a pale pink button-down shirt. That meant getting out the old ironing board that had been in the apartment when they rented it and digging her iron out of the boxes on the top shelf of the linen closet. It was eight-thirty when she was finally dressed and pressed to her satisfaction.

They left as soon as she was ready so they could find a parking place and not have to rush into court. Dan was lucky and got the last parking place in the courthouse lot. He had to tell the attendant that they were going to court to be let into the lot and the attendant checked them off on a list in the guardhouse. Ella saw her attorney when they walked into the courthouse. She was glad to have a female attorney, she felt a woman would be a better advocate in her case.

"I am glad that you are on time," said her lawyer, "and that is the exact right thing to be wearing."

Ella introduced Dan. "Sarah, this is my partner, Dan Martinson. Dan, this is my attorney, Sarah Richards.

"How do you do?" Dan said and put his hand out to shake Sarah's hand.

Sarah led them down the hall and into a small courtroom with tall windows that let in a lot of light and had ceiling fans turning lazily to keep the cool, air-conditioned air moving. Sarah indicated a table with two chairs near the front of the room. "You and I will sit here, Ella. Mr. Champeau and his attorney will sit over there. Mr. Martinson you can sit right behind Miss Thomas in the front row on the other side of the barrier."

"Oh," said Dan, "I was planning to hold Ella's hand."

"That will not be possible. Miss Thomas needs to be sitting here by me and you must stay in the gallery with the other observers."

Ella squeezed Dan's hand and leaned her chin on his shoulder. "I'll be all right knowing that you're right behind me."

"How about I sit off to one side so that you can turn your head and see me? Will that work?"

Ella let out a breath. "That'll be great, as long as I can turn my head away from Champeau."

"Don't worry, I'll sit where you can see me without seeing

him." And he sidestepped down the front row of observer's seats and sat where Ella could see him if she just turned her head a little bit.

"That's perfect," she said. She turned to Sarah. "Why are you calling me Miss Thomas instead of Ms. Thomas? I prefer Ms."

Sarah shook her head. "We do not want you to appear as a hardheaded modern woman, we need you to be soft and ladylike. They are going to try to say that you approached him, and we want you to look and sound like the kind of person who would never do that."

"I would never do that," Ella said.

Sarah patted her hand. "I know that, but we need the judge to know that. There will be no jury, so we only need to convince the judge that you're a decent upright woman who was just doing her job."

The courtroom door opened, and Bert Champeau came in followed by his lawyer, a sharp looking man in a black suit with a shiny blue tie. Champeau gave Ella a glare and then looked away. Ella was glad that Sarah Richards was sitting between her and the defendant's table so that there were two people between her and the man who attacked her.

In a very short time, a door in the front of the room opened and the judge walked in wearing billowing black robes. He was so dignified that Ella was surprised that he wasn't wearing a white wig but then she remembered that Bonaire was a Dutch island not a British one.

"All rise," the bailiff said, and everyone stood up until the judge was behind the bench. "Be seated."

The judge didn't waste any time. He opened a manila file on the bench and said, "Mr. Champeau, you are accused of assaulting Miss Thomas and attempting to sexually assault her on Sunday, April twenty seventh of this year. How do you plead?"

Champeau's lawyer stood up. "Mr. Champeau pleads not guilty, Your Honor."

The judge looked up. "I need to hear it from Mr. Champeau."

"Not guilty," Bert Champeau said in a low voice.

"You need to speak up so that everyone can hear you, the court reporter included."

"Not guilty," he said again in a loud angry voice.

Ella looked over her shoulder at Dan. There were tears in her eyes. He gave her a little smile and a thumbs up. She turned back to the front as the judge called on Sarah Richards to present her opening argument. Sarah was very precise in laying out what had happened that Sunday when Ella went into the house at 25417 Santa Barbara Shores to find Mr. Bert Champeau lying in the master bedroom asleep. She outlined Ella's call to Gina at Playa Palms Rentals and Mr. Champeau's reaction to being told that he would have to move. Sarah was clear that she would prove that Ella had been a blameless cleaner preyed upon by a disgruntled renter, that she did nothing to bring on the attack.

Ella was happy with the way Sarah laid out her argument and was confident that the judge would believe her.

Then the defense attorney got up and started talking. He said that Mr. Champeau had been asleep when Ms. Thomas came into the room and tore the sheet off him, that she had seen that he was undressed, and put her hand on him to rouse him. In his sleep-induced stupor Mr. Champeau thought that Ms. Thomas was going to attack him or ask him for money, so he went on the offensive to fend her off. Ella realized that this wasn't going to be as easy as she thought.

Ella sat listening to the lies that Champeau's lawyer was spinning about what happened that day and the pit of her stomach got cold. She could smell Champeau's aftershave, and it took her right back to the time when he was pinning her down and had his hand up her shirt. She clasped her hands together as tight as she could and had to concentrate on staying in her seat. She wanted to run.

Dan cleared his throat and she turned to look at him. He held her gaze for a minute and gave her a look that told her he knew what she was feeling.

The lawyer went on and on, outlining every moment

of his fabricated story, until the judge interrupted. "That is enough, Mr. Bailey. You are not trying the case right now."

"Sorry, Your Honor."

The judge turned to Ella's side of the court.

"Mrs. Richards, call your first witness."

Sarah stood up. "I call Miss Ella Thomas to the stand."

Ella knew it was coming but it still jolted her. She stood up, smoothed her hands down the sides of her slacks, and walked to the witness stand. The bailiff approached her with a Bible in his hand.

"Place your left hand on the Bible and raise your right hand. Do you swear to tell the truth, the whole truth, and nothing but the truth?" he said.

Just like on TV, Ella thought. "Yes, I do."

He took the book from under her hand. "You may be seated."

Sarah Richards stood at the Prosecution table looking down at her files. Then she looked up at Ella and gave her a small smile. "Please tell us your name and where you live."

"I am Ella Thomas. I live at 1368 Liberty Street, Belnem."

"Where do you work, Miss Thomas?"

"I work for Playa Palms Rental as a cleaner."

Sarah had told her not to volunteer any information other than exactly what the question asked. "How long have you been working at that job?"

"I have been a cleaner for one year and three months."

"How did you happen to meet Mr. Campeau?"

Ella twisted her hands together in her lap. "I went to clean the house at 25417 Santa Barbara Shores with the understanding that it had been vacated by the tenants. I went up to strip the sheets off the beds and Mr. Champeau was asleep in the master bedroom when I got to it. I stopped in the doorway and called out to try to wake him."

Sarah Richards said, "Did you go into the room? Did you touch Mr. Champeau?"

Ella shook her head vehemently. "No, I did not. I stayed

in the doorway and called out 'excuse me' a couple times to wake him. He awoke and sat up asking what I was doing. When I saw that he was undressed I excused myself and said that I would meet him downstairs when he was decent. Then I left the doorway and went down to start the laundry."

"What happened next?"

Ella looked up at Sarah and then at Dan. Dan nodded at her to go on.

"I was in the laundry room when he came down in shorts and a tee shirt. He told me that he had called the rental company the night before to say that he wanted to stay another week, but no one was there so he left a message. I said that I was told that the house was rented to other guests starting the next day so he would have to move. He, Mr. Champeau, said he didn't want to move and said that I should call Playa Palms Rental and fix it. So, I called Gina to ask if I had made a mistake."

She stopped talking and took a sip of water from the bottle the bailiff had put on the side of the witness stand for her.

Sarah said, "And what did Gina say?"

"Gina said that I had not made a mistake and that she would come over to work with Mr. Champeau to find him a different place for the next week. When I told him that he grabbed my wrist and twisted it behind my back, telling me that I should fix it so he didn't have to move. Then he pulled me into his chest and kept pushing my left wrist up behind my back. It hurt and I couldn't get away." Ella stopped talking and looked down at her lap.

"What happened next?" Sarah said.

It helped Ella that Sarah's questions were straight and unemotional. "He, he kept walking toward me, forcing me to back up, until my legs touched the edge of the couch and I fell backwards. He fell on top of me." Tears started to flow down her cheeks. "He was too strong, too big for me to move him off me. He said horrible things about liking his women to scream. When I tried to scream, he mashed his mouth down over mine until I couldn't breathe. I was squirming, trying to get away but he was too big."

Now tears were streaming down her cheeks and dripping off her chin. "It is all right, Miss Thomas, take your time," Sarah said. "And then what did he do?"

Ella gulped and cleared her throat. "He was grinding himself into me and trying to wedge his knee between my legs. He slid his hand up under my shirt and bra and was squeezing my breast. It hurt. I was sure that he was going to rape me, and I tried and tried but I couldn't get away." Ella took another drink of water.

"And that is when Gina arrived?"

Ella nodded. "Yes, Gina finally got there and came into the house. Mr. Champeau got off me and pulled me up after him. He dusted me off, straightened my shirt, and told her that we were just playing. I hurried over to stand by Gina and told him that I was calling the police. So, I did."

Sarah Richards turned to face the judge, "I have no further questions, Your Honor."

The judge looked at Mr. Bailey, "Cross examination?"

The lawyer in the sharp suit and tie stood up and shot the cuffs of his long-sleeved shirt out of his suit coat sleeves. Why was he not melting, Ella thought. It's like an oven in this room even with the air conditioning. She felt her blouse sticking to her back and sweat gathered at her temples. Would it look like she was lying if she wiped her brow? She decided it would, so she resisted the urge; she took a long drink of her now lukewarm water instead.

"Ms. Thomas, would you say that you are an adventurous woman?"

Ella looked at him as if she didn't understand the question. "I guess I am."

"You came down to Bonaire without a job and with a man who is not your husband over a year ago on a whim."

"It wasn't a whim; we planned our move together. We're not ready to be married yet."

"So, you are cohabitating with a man who is not your

husband and working as a cleaner for a local vacation rental company. Are you in the habit of having a sexual relationship with any man that you find in the houses you clean?"

"No, I am not."

"You are not overly friendly with Carlos the pool man?"

"I barely see Carlos. He works only at houses with pools, and I work at any house they need me to work at."

"Is it not true that you and your partner are trying to save money to open your own dive operation on this admittedly expensive island?"

"Yes, we hope to have our own business someday so we're saving money as much as we can."

"So, earning a little extra on the side would be a good thing."

Ella saw Dan move as if he would stand up. She shook her head and Sarah Richards waved a hand at him; he subsided.

"Earning a little extra would be a good thing it's true but not at the expense of my self-respect. I would never... well, I would never do that."

"Is it not true that you pulled the sheet off Mr. Champeau as he lay asleep in the master bed? That you touched him inappropriately. And when he followed you to the main floor great room to pursue your invitation you pressed yourself against him in a provocative manner?"

Fresh tears ran down Ella's cheeks. "I didn't. When he sat up in bed, the sheet fell to his hips and I realized that he was nude so I excused myself, asked him to dress, and meet me downstairs to discuss how we could find him a place to stay for an extra week."

"Is it not true that you asked him for money to secure another week's stay and when he refused to pay you called for help that you were being assaulted?"

"No. None of that is true."

Mr. Bailey turned back to the Defense table. "No further questions, Your Honor."

The judge turned to Sarah Richards. "Redirect, Miss

Richards?"

Sarah stood up. 'Thank you, Your Honor."

She turned to Ella. "Miss Thomas, how long have you been in a relationship with Mr. Dan Martinson?"

"Three years," she said trying to control her voice to keep from sobbing.

"And in all that time have you ever been unfaithful to him?"

"No, I haven't."

"Ever been tempted?"

"Not even a little. Dan is the man that I want in my life."

"And you wouldn't compromise your self-respect for a little extra money to fulfill your dream of owning a dive business?"

"No. It's hard to wait, to work so hard and have your goal be no nearer, but I would never debase myself for money. I have too much respect for myself and for Dan."

"No more questions, Your Honor," Sarah Richards said.

The judge turned to Ella and said, "You may step down."

Ella was never so relieved to hear four words in her life. She felt as though she had gone through the assault all over again.

The judge turned to the Prosecuting attorney. "Miss Richards, you may call your next witness."

Sarah stood up. "Thank you, Your Honor. I call Mrs. Gina Nolan to the stand."

There was a shuffle at the back of the courtroom and Gina walked confidently up the aisle, through the gate in front of the gallery, and to the witness stand. The bailiff swore her in, handed her a bottle of water, and offered her the seat.

The judge had her state her name and address into the record and then nodded at Sarah Richards to begin.

Sarah led Gina through the phone call from Ella when she asked if she had been mistaken that the house was supposed to be empty. Gina confirmed that it had been rented to Mr. Champeau's party for the previous week and they were to have vacated the premises by nine o'clock in the morning. She acknowledged that she had gotten a telephone message that Mr. Champeau wished to remain in the house for another week but that he had not left a callback number. He had been out when she stopped by on her way home from work and she intended to go there again the next morning to help him find another place to stay as there was already a family with a reservation for the house at 25417 Santa Barbara Shores. Before she had a chance to get there, she received a phone call from Ella Thomas saying that Mr. Champeau refused to leave and would Gina please come over to resolve the issue.

"Where is your office, Mrs. Nolan?"

"It is in downtown Playa, so it took me about twenty-five minutes to close up the office and drive to the house in Santa Barbara Shores."

Sarah Richards consulted the file lying on the table in front of her. "What did you observe when you went into the house?"

Gina looked at Ella. "I saw Mr. Champeau getting up off the couch where he had Miss Thomas pinned down."

"Were they both clothed?" Sarah asked.

"Yes, they were but he had his hand up her tee shirt. I saw scratches on her stomach."

"And then what happened?"

"Mr. Champeau pulled Ella up to her feet, dusted her off, and said 'no harm done' or something like that. I could see that Ella, uh, Miss Thomas, had been crying and she hurried to stand next to me rubbing her left shoulder as she did."

"What did you do?"

"I did nothing, just stood next to her as she accused him of trying to rape her and saying that she was calling the police. Ella reached into her pocket for her phone and dialed nine-one-one and told the officer who answered that she had been assaulted and she wanted to press charges."

"What was Mr. Champeau doing at the time?"

"He tried to talk Ella out of calling and when he heard her

on the phone he hurried upstairs and, in a few minutes, came downstairs with his suitcase. 'I am leaving,' he said, and he tried to leave but I had parked behind his car and just then the police car arrived. They believed Ella that he had tried to hurt her. She had a swollen lip and he had wrenched her arm up behind her back. Her shoulder was sore, and he had scratched her stomach when he shoved his hand under her shirt."

Bert Champeau jumped to his feet and said, "I didn't hurt her that bad. It was just a friendly little tussle."

The judge banged his gavel and his lawyer pulled on his arm to make him sit down.

"That will be all, Mr. Champeau," said the judge. "You will have your opportunity to rebut this testimony in your turn."

"Yeah, but you shouldn't let those women lie about me like that."

The judge frowned down from his bench. "One more outburst and I will have you removed from court."

Champeau subsided into his seat and whispered into his attorney's ear.

His attorney put a consoling hand on Champeau's shoulder and Ella heard him say, "We will get our turn after the Prosecution is finished."

"But you're not objecting to anything they say. I thought lawyers objected to things they didn't like hearing."

His attorney said, "Patience."

Champeau folded his arms on the table and frowned at the witness stand. "I don't like this," he said to no one.

The judge gave him a stern look and turning back to Sarah Richards, he motioned her to continue.

"What did you do once the police arrested Mr. Champeau and left with him."

Gina said, "I took Ella to the hospital to get checked out and then to the police station for an interview with a police officer. I think they had a policewoman take pictures of her injuries."

Sarah smiled at her. "Thank you, Mrs. Nolan, I have no

further questions."

The judge turned to the Defense attorney. "Cross examination?"

The attorney nodded and stood up. "Mrs. Nolan, how long were you in the room before Mr. Champeau got up off the couch?"

"He was standing up as I entered the room."

"So, you didn't see him pinning Miss Thomas under him?"

"Well, he was getting up off of her when I came in."

"But did you see him lying on her?"

"No, I didn't."

"Did you see him help her to stand up?"

"I did. He tried to arrange her clothing, but she pushed him away and came over to stand by me."

"Did Mr. Champeau pay for his rental in full and on time?"

"Yes, he did but..."

"No further questions, Your Honor." He walked back to the Defense table and sat down.

The judge turned to Sarah Richards. "Redirect?"

She shook her head. "Nothing more, Your Honor."

By then it was nearly eleven-thirty, so the judge rapped his gavel and called for the lunch recess. "We will reconvene here at one-thirty. Do not be tardy." He glared at Mr. Bailey and Mr. Champeau, stood up from the bench, and left the court room.

Ella felt a hand on her shoulder and turned to see Dan standing behind her. "Are you okay?" he said.

"I'm fine, I think, it was just as bad as I thought it would be, but I survived."

"Are you hungry?"

She shook her head. "Not really but I'll go with you so you can eat."

She turned to her lawyer. "Sarah, would you like to come to lunch with us?"

Sarah smiled. "I would like that very much. Give me a moment to get these files into my briefcase and we can go."

Dan was glad to get out of the stuffy courtroom and into

the breezy sunshine.

"Where would you like to go?" he said.

"There is a local café about two blocks back from the courthouse. It is often quiet in there at this time of day. We could go there."

"Sounds good to me," he said. "Lead the way."

He took Ella's hand in his and they walked, three abreast, down the sidewalk and around the corner.

Ella said, "Do you think Mr. Bailey and Champeau will be in the café?"

Sarah laughed. "Matthew Bailey go to a local café for lunch? He would rather starve than eat in a place like this." She held open a screened door and ushered them into a clean dining room with ceiling fans lazily turning over mismatched tables and chairs. Ella could smell baking bread and something savory that she couldn't identify.

"Three for lunch, Emile" Sarah said to the smiling man behind the cash register.

"Sit anywhere," he said with a wave of his arm.

Sarah steered them to a table under the breeze of one of the fans and sat down. Dan looked at the napkin holder, salt and pepper shakers, and bottle of hot sauce in the middle of the table and then up at Sarah.

"No menu?"

"No, no menu. You get what Emile cooked today. There is usually soup and a salad of some kind and a plate of something good. You eat what he brings out for you. It is all good."

They had not been there for long before Emile came out bearing a tray with three glasses of water and three bowls of soup on it. "Today we have kabritu soup with pumpkin."

Ella looked up at him. "I'll just have the soup. I'm not very hungry."

He smiled at her. "That is okay, my darling, you eat my soup, and your day will be much better. Let me bring you some good brown bread to have with it. I will be right back." And he was back within a few minutes with a small plate with two slices of bread and a pat of butter on it.

"Thank you," Ella said.

Emile patted her on the shoulder. "You are always welcome here."

Ella was surprised to feel tears spring to her eyes when he said that.

"I'm too emotional today. A man brings me soup and bread and I burst out crying."

Dan reached over and squeezed her hand. "You had a trying morning. Eat your soup, it'll make you feel better. It's delicious."

Ella glanced at his bowl to see that it was half empty already. "Wow, you were hungry."

"When I get angry, I get hungry," he said. "And that Defense attorney's questions made me angry."

Sarah hushed him. "Do not talk about it. Let us just enjoy our lunch."

So, they did. Emile brought plates of breaded fish with slices of cucumber and tomato on the side, then he wheeled Ella into trying his bread pudding for dessert. It was spiced with nutmeg and had a buttery sauce over it. It was a magnificent lunch. Dan insisted on paying the very reasonable tab and left a generous tip.

As they left the café Emile said, "Come back anytime."

"Oh, we will definitely be back," Ella said.

They were at the courthouse in plenty of time for the afternoon session. Sarah Richards called the police officer who had answered Ella's call for help to testify to her state of mind when he had arrived at the scene. She also asked him about Mr. Champeau's demeanor.

"He was trying to downplay the seriousness of what she was saying and then he got angry when we put him under arrest. He threatened us with lawsuits and demotions, but we arrested him anyway. He has been a cooperative prisoner in the jail."

The Defense attorney, Mr. Bailey, again established that all the police had to go on was Miss Thomas' contention that Mr. Champeau had assaulted her. There was no hard evidence. The officer disagreed.

"There was Miss Thomas' swollen mouth and wrenched arm and her general state of upset. We do not take assault lightly," he said.

"But couldn't her mouth have been swollen from passionate kissing, consensual kissing?"

The officer nodded. "It could have been, but she was shaking, and her clothing was rumpled, and she had scratches on her abdomen she said were inflicted by Mr. Champeau."

Bailey pounced. "You said 'she said' meaning you have no proof that he inflicted those scratches on her. She may have done them herself to discredit him. Her paramour could have done it the night before."

"I do not know. All I know is what I saw and what she said."

When it was Sarah Richards' turn for redirect, she went back and established the officer's years of service, his citations for excellent work, and his rate of closure of cases.

"This is not a rookie officer on his first call," she said. "This is an experienced officer with years of police work under his belt."

After the officer was excused from the stand, Sarah Richards said, "I rest my case, Your Honor," and she sat down.

It was late enough in the afternoon that the judge adjourned court for the day. "We will begin again tomorrow morning at nine o'clock." He banged his gavel, got up, and left the courtroom. The bailiff followed him out the door.

Ella turned to Sarah. "How do you think it went?" she said.

"I think we did all we could," Sarah said. "Tomorrow will be hard because Mr. Bailey will try his best to play up Mr. Champeau and downplay you and your reputation. It will not be pretty or easy to hear. Be prepared." She gave Ella a serious look. "It will be hard but try not to cry. He will pounce on that as a sign of weakness and deception. I know him and I know his tactics."

Ella nodded. "I'll try."

"Have a nice dinner and get a good night's sleep. Try to put this out of your mind for a few hours."

Ella laughed. "Put it out of my mind? Right. There's nothing else on my mind right now. But I will try," she said again.

Dan met her at the gate in the bar between the gallery and the court. He put his arm around her and led her out of the court room and outside.

She looked around. "I don't remember where we parked, do you?" she said.

"Yeah," he said, "we got the last spot in the courthouse parking lot. It's right across the street."

They waited for a break in the traffic and crossed the street to their car. Because they left the windows down it wasn't baking hot in the car although they needed the ratty beach towel they left in the car to keep from burning the backs of their legs when they sat down.

Dan turned to Ella. "Do you mind stopping at the Dive Inn? I'd like to find out how Ilsa is doing."

She smiled at him. "Of course, we should stop. I completely forgot about her with all this crazy court stuff. I want to know how she is too."

They got lucky and got a parking place right next to the dive shop. The afternoon dive boat had just come in, so the courtyard was full of people rinsing and hanging their gear, chatting about their dives, and filling out their logbooks.

"There's Dan," Claire said. "Thank you so much for teaching us Underwater Naturalist. We're seeing so much more on every dive. It has changed the way we dive forever. Thanks again."

Dan smiled at both Claire and Libby. "I'm so glad that you enjoyed the class and that it has made a difference."

"Have you heard anything about Ilsa?" Libby asked.

Dan shook his head. "That's why I am here. I'm hoping that there will be word from the hospital. If I learn anything I'll let you know."

"Thanks, Dan, and thanks again for the class."

"I'll sign your logbooks when I get back from the office." He went down the short hall and into the office where Babs greeted him.

"How was court today?"

"Brutal. They're not going to go down without a fight. The defense attorney twisted every word that Ella said and is trying to make her out to be a floozie. It's hard on her, but I think she's bearing up okay." He leaned on the door jamb. "Have you heard from the hospital? Any word on Ilsa's condition?"

"Yes, I got a call this afternoon that she has had three sessions in the decompression chamber and is responding nicely."

"I wish I knew why she stayed down there so long."

Babs picked up a note from her messy desk. "She told the doctor that she was determined to win the scavenger hunt and lost track of her air and her depth until it was too late. It sounds like Samuel was the only thing between her and the grave."

"Man, I'm glad he was with her, but I wish he had been able to lure her to a shallower depth so that she wasn't so narced and kept her wits about her. I wonder if she'll ever go diving again."

"I do not know but I will have to refund her the fees for her remaining dives. I hate giving money back." She laughed, "But I guess it is better than having to use the money to pay for someone's funeral on vacation."

"Way better. Did they say when she would be safe to fly home?"

"No, only that she's responding to treatment."

"I can't decide whether I should go to visit her in the hospital or not. I kind of feel like it is a little my fault for her being in the state she's in."

"Do not think that way. You cannot keep everyone safe and ensure that everyone follows the rules. She chose to dive alone, you sent Samuel to watch over her, and she was already in trouble when he got to her. He saved her life." She handed him a short stack of paper. "This is the incident report you need to fill out for the Professional Association of Diving Instructors. Get it filled out in the next few days and give it back to me. I will fax it in for you. Is the trial finished?"

"No, not finished. Tomorrow it is the Defense's turn to call witnesses and ask questions. Today was brutal for Ella. She had to go over the assault in minute detail over and over and then his attorney insinuated that Ella was immoral and had put the moves on him. I ask you; it was all I could do not to jump over that fence thing and punch his lights out."

She laughed. "That would have impressed the judge."

"Yeah, I guess it would have meant an assault charge for me, but it was hard to listen to. I'm hoping that tomorrow is the last day. There's no jury, so it's up to the judge to make the decision. He didn't set bail because he said the island was too small and it would have been too easy for Champeau to find Ella and intimidate her."

Babs looked shocked. "Do you think he would have done that?"

"In a heartbeat. He looks like that kind of guy to me. And from what Ella said about him he's kind of a predator."

"Then I am glad that he's locked up. I wouldn't want my daughter anywhere near him."

He reached out and touched Babs' arm. "Thank you for giving me the time off to be in court with Ella. I'm hoping that I can be back on the dive boat day after tomorrow. I'm not used to being cooped up inside all day."

"I know Ella needs you with her, but I will be glad to have you back. The season is heating up and we need all the Dive Instructors and Divemasters on the job."

"We're on our way home. I am hoping to get Ella to eat something and get some sleep. I don't think she slept at all last night."

Babs turned back to her computer. "Take care. Let me know how things go."

"Thanks, Babs."

Dan went back out to the courtyard where he signed off on Claire and Libby's dives so that they could get their Underwater Naturalist certification cards. He assured them that he would be back at work before they left for home the next week. "You're going to be dived out with two straight weeks of diving under your belts."

Libby laughed. "Oh no we won't. We're trying to figure out how we can get in more dives every day. As it is we do three boat dives, one shore dive, and one night dive."

"Every day?" Dan said.

They nodded. "Every day. We're determined to get in as much diving as possible before we go back to work and home. You're lucky that you get to live here year-round and dive every day if you want to."

"Yes, this is a lucky life," Dan said.

CHAPTER 8

Court the next day was just as horrible as Ella and Dan thought it would be. Mr. Bailey put Bert Champeau on the stand, and he told a completely fabricated story of what happened that day when he assaulted her.

"I was asleep, and she ripped the sheet off me leaving me naked in bed. Then she touched me on the, well, um, on my manhood, saying that she knew how to have fun on a cloudy Sunday."

Mr. Bailey turned toward the Prosecution table. "She touched you on your penis?"

"Yes, right on it and it jumped right up to say howdy, too." Champeau grinned looking around the courtroom, but no one laughed.

"What happened next, Mr. Champeau?"

"Well, I invited her to join me for a little slap and tickle but then she backed away, telling me to get dressed and meet her downstairs in the living room. I was a little disappointed, she's not bad looking and I am a friendly guy, but I got dressed and followed her downstairs figuring maybe she didn't like it in bed. Or wanted to undress me or something. I was willing to play along."

"Yes. What happened when you joined her in the living room?"

"When I got down there, she was on the phone asking if she had made a mistake and I was staying another week. She said, 'he's not going to be happy' or something like that and hung up. Then she told me that somebody named Gina was coming over to help me find a different place to stay so I thought 'whoopee, a threesome' and took her hand to get started but she had other ideas."

'What were those ideas?"

"Well, she wanted money to arrange another place. I told her no way, but she insisted. She pushed herself up against me and hooked my arm around behind her back, so we were even closer. She started to walk backwards and ran into the couch and fell on her back. With her grip on my hand, I lost my balance and fell on top of her. I probably hurt her a little, but I didn't mean it."

Mr. Bailey kept his eyes on Ella. "And that is how you ended up lying on top of her when Mrs. Nolan arrived on the scene?"

"Yeah, that's how it happened."

"Did you have your hand under her shirt?"

Champeau scratched his head. "I might have. I was trying to get my arm back from under her and might have accidently gotten my hand under her shirt when I was trying to get up."

"How did your knee get between her legs?"

"The same way. I was trying to get up and used my knee to lever myself off her."

"Did you kiss her?"

"My lips might have brushed hers, but I didn't mean to kiss her."

Bailey's eyes finally left Ella's face and he turned to his client. "Are you a married man, Mr. Champeau?"

Champeau's face grew solemn. "Not anymore. My wife died six years ago last month. I miss her every day."

"Thank you, Mr. Champeau, no further questions."

The judge turned to Sarah Richards. "Cross examine, counselor?"

She stood up. "I just have one question, Your Honor." She stayed behind the table and looked at the defendant on the stand. "Mr. Champeau, if Miss Thomas pulled the sheet off you how do you explain the fully made bed with you in it in the picture on her phone?"

"I, uh, I guess she must have taken the picture first?"

Sarah Richards smiled. "No further questions."

The judge nodded and looked at Bert Champeau. "You do know that there is a penalty for perjury, do you not?"

Champeau looked startled and nodded his head.

"You may step down." The judge looked at Mr. Bailey. "Do you have any other witnesses to call, Mr. Bailey?"

Bailey stood up. "No, Your Honor, the Defense rests."

The judge looked at the clock. "Even though it is a bit early," he said, "I suggest we break for lunch and reconvene at one o'clock." He banged his gavel once, gathered his papers, stood up, and left the courtroom. The bailiff followed him.

Ella looked at Sarah Richards. "That was all lies. I never did any of the things he said I did. I certainly never touched his manhood."

Sarah was glad to see that Ella was more angry than hurt. Anger would get her through faster than tears would. Sarah, Ella, and Dan went back to Emile's café for lunch. That day's offering was pumpkin soup, kabritu stoba or goat stew, and banana cake for dessert. All three of them, even Ella, ate every morsel.

In the afternoon both Sarah Richards and Mr. Bailey gave their closing statements. Sarah went over everything that Ella had said and done, everything she said that Bert Champeau had done, and what she thought the punishment should be.

Mr. Bailey painted Ella as a scheming liar looking for an illicit love affair for an afternoon and some extra money to further her wish to own a dive shop on the island. He said that Bert Champeau was the victim of Ella and should be exonerated.

The judge nodded at every point each lawyer made and when Bailey was finished, the judge looked at Mr. Bailey and Bert Champeau. "Mr. Bailey, I know you think that island justice is easily manipulated but I must tell you that even a blind man could see through the lies that you and your client have told today. I do not believe that Miss Thomas is a scheming woman who would make unwanted advances to any man, much less Mr. Champeau. Therefore, I sentence Mr. Champeau to time served, one thousand dollars fine, and he will pay Miss Thomas' legal fees and court costs. If you need to set up a payment plan, you can see the court office down the hall. Court is adjourned." He banged his gavel on the desk, gathered his files, and moved to leave the courtroom.

As he was leaving, Bert Champeau leaped up. "No, Your Honor," Champeau said, "I wasn't lying, and I will not pay her costs. You can't make me."

The judge turned back and said over his shoulder, "On the contrary, Mr. Champeau, I can make you do that, and I could have done much more but took pity on you because you are such a bad liar. Good day."

He went through the door into his chambers in a swirl of his robes. The door clicked shut behind the bailiff.

"He can't make me pay all of that, can he?" Champeau asked his attorney.

"He can and he has ordered it. You will need to pay it in full or make payment arrangements before you will be allowed to leave the island."

"Son of a bitch," he said and glared across the aisle at Ella and Sarah Richards. "I'm not paying no bills sent by a... by a... a woman, much less a Black one."

Bailey looked at his client. "You will pay her bill and you will pay my bill, sent by a Black man, if you ever want to be done with this little mess. And next time you are on an island, Mr., Champeau, keep your filthy hands to yourself."

Mr. Bailey slid his files into his briefcase, snapped the latches, picked it up, and left the courtroom, leaving his client sitting open mouthed and gaping at the Defense table.

"Wait," Champeau said, and he got up and followed Mr. Bailey out the door.

Dan was standing behind Ella. "Well, that was interesting," he said. "I guess Mr. Champeau doesn't have respect for anyone but himself."

Sarah was loading her files into her briefcase. "It sounds like it is a good thing that I have my bill prepared. I will just walk it down to the court financial office so that Mr. Champeau can decide how he wants to pay it." She put out her hand to Ella. "Thank you for being an excellent client, Ella. I am certain that I will see you at Emile's one day again soon." She turned to Dan. "I hope that your dive shop dream comes true soon, Dan. Take care of Ella."

Dan shook her hand. "Me too and I will. You take care of yourself, Sarah. You were the right lawyer for Ella in this case. You made it easy for her to get through this." He put his arm over Ella's shoulders. "Come on, babe, let's go home and get outside. I'm sick of being cooped up inside all day."

Ella smiled up at him. "Maybe we can take a picnic to Pink Beach. We can swim, eat supper, and then watch the sunset."

"That sounds like a great idea," he said.

There was a cruise ship at the Town Pier, so the downtown streets were filled with passengers walking from shop to shop. They didn't watch where they were going so traffic was moving slowly as people crossed in front of cars with very little warning.

"I am glad we don't live downtown, "Ella said. "I would hate all this traffic and activity when ships are in port. If we hadn't had to be in court today, I would have avoided Playa at all costs."

Dan nodded. "Yeah, but I bet they could have used me today with all of the divers and snorkelers off the boat."

Ella reached to touch his hand on the steering wheel. "I appreciate that you took the days off to come to court and be my moral support. I know that Babs probably could have used you today, but I am glad that you were with me."

In just a few minutes they were out of the crowd of people and could speed up. The wind coming in the car windows lifted Ella's short hair off her face and dried the perspiration at her hairline. "Can you believe that Champeau got away with lying in court?"

"He didn't, not really. I suspect that the judge upped the fines because he knew that he was lying through his teeth."

"I'm just glad that I don't have to pay attorney's fees and

court costs."

"Me too. That would have made a big dent in our savings."

Ella put her arm on the edge of the door. "Let's stop talking about today and get our picnic organized. I'm hungry."

Dan and Ella were glad to get home and even happier to get out of their courtroom clothes and into their swimsuits under shorts and tee shirts. Ella went into the kitchen and surveyed what was in the refrigerator to use to make a picnic. There wasn't much.

"How about we finish the coleslaw and I make us some ham and cheese sandwiches?"

"Sounds good to me," Dan said. He was head down in the broom closet searching for the little cooler that they used as a picnic basket. "Found it. I hope we have some ice I can bag up to keep things from getting too warm while we drive down there."

Ella opened the freezer. "We have plenty of ice. Remember we bought that bag of cubes when we planned to have everyone over for drinks and then over half of the staff got food poisoning from that bad salt cod? I was ever so glad that neither of us had any of that revolting fish."

"Me too." He got out a gallon zipper plastic bag and filled it halfway from the big bag of cubes in the freezer and tucked it into the cooler. He grabbed a couple Amstel beers from the fridge and nestled them between the ice and the side of the cooler. "What do you want to drink, babe?"

She looked up from spreading mustard on bread. "Is there any ginger ale?"

He looked in the fridge and said, "Yep, one left. I'll put in a bottled water for you too, how's that?"

"Sounds just right."

She put the sandwiches into some plastic sandwich boxes she had brought from home. She would rather use reusable containers than plastic bags that they use once and throw away. The island was too small to have a recycling operation and all the trash from the island got burned in the island incinerator. She hated the stinky, smoky pollution that caused but thought that a landfill might be worse for the environment.

"You about ready?" Dan came back into the kitchen with their beach duffle. He had put in towels and sunscreen and their hats.

"Just about." Ella put the sandwich boxes into the cooler, put the container of coleslaw on top, and slid two forks down the side. "Do you want some chips?" She held up a cylinder. "We have a few Pringles left."

Dan held open the duffle. "Chuck them in here, then they won't get soggy from the ice."

"Good thinking."

While Dan went to put the cooler and duffel bag in the back of the car, Ella pulled down her old beach blanket from the top of the linen closet. A patter of sand fell as she pulled it off the shelf.

"Hm," she said, "we must not have shaken out all the sand from our last picnic. Oh well, we'll do better this time."

She followed Dan out to the car, and they set off. There was still plenty of day left when they got to Pink Beach. Dan parked the car next to the giant dune that backed the beach, slung the duffel over his shoulder, and picked up the cooler. "I have the food and the bag. You bring the blanket and let's go. I'm ready for a swim."

"Me too."

Ella made sure that the windows were open and there was nothing worth stealing left in the car. She followed Dan over the side of the dune and down onto the wide expanse of pink sand that gave the beach its name. There were a few couples scattered across the sand on blankets and towels. Dan picked a spot off to one side and put everything down. Ella spread out the blanket and moved the cooler and duffel onto the blanket to hold it down in the wind that was ever present on the island.

Dan was taking off his shirt. "Swim?" he said.

"Yes, I can't wait."

She slipped out of her shorts and tee shirt and joined Dan to walk down into the warm saltwater. They waded out until they were about hip deep and then simultaneously dived underwater.

The warm water felt great as it washed away the cares of the day. Ella felt the silky caress on her skin and sighed. She dived down to the sand and opened her eyes to see if there were any fish around. Everything was blurry but she saw colorful shapes darting around the small patches of coral that dotted the area off the beach. She surfaced to see Dan swimming strongly out to sea. She knew that he would turn around soon and swim back. He was a real swimmer; she was more of a paddler. She swam around a bit more and then walked back to the blanket to stretch out in the warm, late day sunshine.

"You look good in a bathing suit, but you should wear a bikini," a man's voice came from overhead.

She squinted up to see Bert Champeau standing over her blocking out the sun. "What are you doing here? Get away from me," she said.

"I just wanted to tell you that you might have won the case, but you will never forget me. I will never forget you, Miss Thomas."

"Hey," Dan's voice came from the shallows. "Get away from her."

Bert Champeau looked at Dan over his shoulder, looked back at Ella, and winked. "I'm leaving but try to forget me. Just try." He turned away and walked toward the parking area. "Gotta go, my flight leaves in an hour. I just wanted to say goodbye, Ella." He made a kissing sound and turned away.

Ella sat up and hugged her knees to her chest.

Dan dropped onto the blanket on his knees. "Oh my god, Ella, are you all right?"

She nodded but she didn't look all right. She was curled into the tightest ball she could manage and was rocking back and forth. "How did he find me?" she said. "Do you think he followed us?"

Dan pulled her to him, pressing her against his wet chest. "He had to have. How else would he have known where to find you." He was rocking her and rubbing her back. "What did he say to you?"

She took a deep shuddering breath. "He said he wanted to say goodbye and that I should try to forget him. Dan, I don't think that I'll ever forget him."

"I know, babe, I know but the memory will fade after a while. I'll always be here for you."

She looked up at him. "I don't know if I can go back to cleaning houses. I don't know if I can ever go back into a house that is supposed to be empty again."

He kept rocking and rubbing her back. "Talk to Mariette. Maybe you and she can work together for a while. Two people must get the job done faster. Maybe that would work."

She nodded. "Yeah, maybe that will work. I'll call her tomorrow." She pushed away from him. "Ugh, you're wet."

"Sorry, I didn't take the time to dry myself off before charging to your rescue."

She smiled up at him. "That's okay, I don't melt." She pulled her towel up and dried off her face and chest. "I'm going to make sure that he has left the island like he said he was. Mariette's husband works at the airport. He might know if Champeau left. Or maybe the police will know. I'll find out somehow." She put down her towel and reached for the cooler. "Now who's hungry? I sure am." She got out the sandwiches and coleslaw, digging down for the forks. "I thought we could just eat out of the container," she said.

"Works for me." Dan twisted the cap off one of the Amstels and popped the top of her ginger ale. "I am proud of you, babe. You've held up like a trooper through all of this."

"Thanks, sweetheart, you were a tremendous help."

They sat side by side facing the ocean watching as the gulls and frigatebirds wheeled overhead. When the sun got near the horizon a long skein of flamingos flew past on their way to their nighttime roost in Venezuela.

"They look so ungainly on the ground with their backwards knees, but they sure can fly," Dan said. "I love watching them."

She looked at him as he gazed up at the birds streaming overhead. Soon they were done with the food. Dan opened his second beer, and they sat watching the sun sink below the horizon.

Ella nudged him with her shoulder, "Do you think we'll see the green flash tonight?"

Dan nudged her back. "That's a myth brought on by alcohol and the power of suggestion."

"No, it's not. I saw it once on a boat from this very island."

"Was there liquor involved?"

"I had a drink, yes."

"That proves my point. You don't have a head for spirits. If you had a drink, I would bet that you saw a little green man dancing in the flash."

She laughed and shoved him. "I didn't. I wasn't the only one who saw it that night. It's a real thing, you nonbeliever." She looked back at the horizon, but the sun was already below it. "Aw, man, now you made me miss it."

"Sorry."

"It's all right. I'll make you take me on a picnic again soon and won't let you distract me."

"Okay, it's a deal." He leaned over and kissed her. "I love you, you know."

She kissed him back. "I know, I love you too."

He put his arm around her. "Listen, I am going to go talk to old Jack Slater again and see if he's thinking of selling his dive operation. We have enough saved to make a decent down payment and the season seems like it's going to heat up fast this year. He has a perfect location at the Sunset Beach Resort. We could step right in and hit the ground running. I'm sure I will have to work extra hours for the next few days to make up for being off but the first chance I get I'm going to go talk to him. I want you working with me not cleaning houses with creeps in them."

"Wouldn't that be great?"

As brave as Ella tried to be she couldn't fall asleep that night. Every time she closed her eyes, she was back on Pink Beach with Bert Champeau standing between her and the sun. She kept seeing his silhouette looming over her and hearing his nasty words.

"Just try to forget me," he had said.

The words rang in her ears and scrolled past her eyes like the crawl on the TV. Every time Dan put his hand on her breast, she wanted to push him away. It took all her resolve not to do it. She couldn't imagine how she would feel if Gina had not arrived and interrupted the assault. If Champeau had gotten her clothes off her and had raped her. Even so would she ever be able to share affection with Dan again? He was being cautious now but soon he would forget, and he would turn to her in bed, and she couldn't be sure that she wouldn't scream or cry or at the very least push him away.

Ella knew how attractive Dan was, how much women on vacation appreciated a handsome, charming dive guide. She had seen how Ilsa had lured him out for a drink and then had her hand on Dan's thigh. Dan was too innocent, too unaware of his allure and how forward a lot of women were. Maybe she could find a woman therapist. On this island? Yeah, she thought, good luck with that. But she would ask Mariette and Babs if they had heard of a woman doctor or therapist who could help her deal with this assault. Better to do it now rather than wait until she was so afraid that she could never have a normal relationship again.

She rolled over and snuggled up to Dan's warm broad back. He sighed and took the hand of the arm that she wrapped around him.

The next morning, she called Mariette who said that she was happy to clean together. "It gets lonely working alone. We can probably do more together than separately," she said.

Ella was grateful that Mariette understood that she would need some time to get her confidence back. Ella also got the phone number of Mariette's airport gate agent husband and called him to double check that Bert Champeau had left the island the day before like he said he was going to do. He was able to check on his computer that Champeau had flown out on the six o'clock flight through Aruba to Houston and back to whatever hole he had crawled out of. That made Ella feel a lot better. She put on a brave, happy face when she kissed Dan goodbye when he left on his bike to pedal to the Dive Inn.

"Have a good day," she said, "I hope you see a lot of cool fish."

"Oh, I will," he said. "You have a good day too."

"I'll try," she said. "Mariette and I will be working together. That makes me feel better."

She made sure she had all her cleaning supplies in the car, and she set off to meet Mariette and get back to work. The two women were a little more cautious than usual when they arrived at the house on Habitat Row. They called out "Hello!" loudly and together went through every room before they split up. Mariette took the bedrooms and left Ella to clean the great room and kitchen and first floor bathroom. The Habitat Row places were two story townhouses with two bedrooms and a bath upstairs and a great room, half bath, and laundry and mud room on the first floor.

Ella appreciated not having to do the bedrooms her first day back. She cleaned out the refrigerator and freezer, putting a few things in her little Styrofoam cooler. She would ask Mariette if they should split the food but for now it was safest in the cooler. The group that had vacated the house this morning had not left too big of a mess. They had even loaded and run the dishwasher so all she had to do was unload the clean dishes and put them away. There was the usual scattering of sand all over the floors and the bathroom showed signs of hard use. Ella didn't mind the cleaning. She pulled on rubber gloves and attacked the dirty house with a lot of energy. She found that if she stayed busy, she didn't flinch each time she heard a footfall and reminded herself that she wasn't alone. Those footfalls were Mariette upstairs as she stripped and remade the beds and cleaned the full bath up there. Mariette threw the dirty towels and sheets down over the stair railing so that Ella could get the laundry started. It didn't make sense for Mariette to have to go up and down the stairs when Ella was right there to take care of the linens. There were a lot of towels. The people must have taken lots of showers or spent a lot of time in the pool.

She had a moment of panic when a vehicle pulled into the gravel drive, but it turned out to be Carlos the pool man. He waved at Ella as he carried the vacuum hose and handle to suck up all the sand that was swirled at the bottom of the pool. The hot tub looked like it needed a refill. They must have had a lot of people in there to slosh out that much water, she thought.

Ella swapped the wash into the dryer and folded the towels ready to carry them upstairs for the next guests to use. She was glad not to be working alone.

CHAPTER 9

Dan was having a good day. He was so happy to be back at work that he wanted to hug someone. He didn't but he was extra nice to Cecile in the office, which put a big smile on her face and made her happy all day.

There was a full boat for the morning dives and a full boat for the afternoon dive. People had also signed up for the evening's night shore dive. The dive shop hosted a night dive one night a week most weeks, sometimes if the demand was great, they did it twice. Dan was a huge fan of night diving, Ella was too. Maybe she would like to come with him tonight and dive. He would call her at lunchtime to see how her day was going and to ask her if she wanted to dive that evening. Libby and Claire stopped in to have their logbooks signed and to thank the staff for making their vacation so memorable.

"We would never have had so much fun if we hadn't taken Underwater Naturalist," said Libby.

"Yes," Claire said, "you changed the way we'll dive forever."

Dan shook their hands and they each pulled him into a hug.

"Thanks for being good students," he said. "I hope you come back to see us again."

"Oh, we will," they said in unison.

Claire touched his arm. "Ilsa flew home to Holland yesterday. We went to see her in the hospital, and she was recovering nicely but I don't think she'll ever dive again. She really got scared and the sessions in the hyperbaric chamber were torture because she's claustrophobic."

"Ouch," Dan said, "that can't have been fun."

"No, she said it was all she could do not to pound on the walls and scream to be let out."

It was time to get the divers on the boat and get the morning dives started. "Thanks again for diving with us, ladies. Have a safe trip home."

Dan picked up the clipboard with the names on it and called the divers to head for the boat. Once on board he checked to make sure that everyone had all their gear and tanks and weights before giving Captain Bill the signal that he could shove off. Samuel untied the lines and they backed away from the dock. Dan smelled the scent of the sea that was churned up by the outboard motor and the faint aroma of coconut from someone's sunscreen. He was so glad to be back on the boat and outdoors. The last two days stuck in that courtroom were hard on him. He had spent over a year working outside on the dive boat and in the water so sitting on a hard chair in a stuffy room for two days was a kind of torture.

He spread his arms wide and inhaled the wind and sunshine and diesel fumes. They had left the dive shop early enough that he asked Captain Bill to take them down the coast to see if they could tie on to one of the three moorings at the Hilma Hooker wreck out between the double reef so rather than puttering out to Klein Bonaire they were racing down along the shore.

Someone called out, "Look!" and he glanced up just in time to see Flying Fish gliding over the water away from the boat. They were lucky enough to snag the last available mooring over the wreck.

"Listen up, everyone," Dan said. "We're tied up to the wreck the *Hilma Hooker* which is a drug smuggling ship that was confiscated in the summer of 1984 here in Bonaire. Drug enforcement agents found twenty-five thousand pounds of marijuana behind a false bulkhead and detained the captain and crew. The owners were never found and never came forward to claim her."

One of the divers said, "Can you blame them?"

Dan laughed. "No, I can't. I wouldn't claim that load of weed either. The hull began to leak so she was towed to an anchorage here and in September 1984 she had taken on enough water that it started pouring through her lower portholes. The ship turned on its side and sank where she was anchored. She lies at one hundred feet and is two hundred forty feet in length. The cargo holds are wide open and there is little to no opportunity for penetration of the wreck."

There were a few disappointed groans at that news. "Sorry, people, but there is no place to get in, the holds are wide open to the sea and the openings are big enough to drive a Hummer through. Time to get into your wetsuits, check your air, and get diving." Dan turned to ready his own gear. "Oh, and Dive Inn is painted on the underside of this boat so you won't get on the wrong boat by mistake. We hope."

More laughter and excited chatter as the divers got ready for the only wreck dive on the island.

Dan and Captain Bill helped the divers enter the water from either side of the boat. They held them steady while they put on their fins, then surreptitiously checked that their air was on while they put on their mask. One by one they did a giant stride into the sea, turned to give an okay signal when they emerged, and swam off to meet their buddy at the mooring where Samuel was stationed. Dan was happy to don his SCUBA gear and step off into the warm saltwater. He settled his gear, equalized his ears, and dived under the surface to make sure that his clients were diving safely. He would be extra cautious today after what happened last week to Ilsa, and he was sure that Samuel would be on his guard too. Dan looked around at the swarm of divers around the wreck. Three boats full of divers meant a packed site but the blue tanks of the Dive Inn divers made them easy to differentiate from the red and yellow tanks of the other dive operations. He kept an eye on the resident tarpon that hung nearly motionless over the high side of the wreck and wondered why it had not taken off when the large groups of divers descended on it. Maybe it was enjoying having its picture taken. There seemed to be a lineup of photographers waiting for their turn to snap a portrait of the prehistoric looking fish.

A couple of the Dive Inn buddy teams were at the bottom of the wreck, checking in the sand for garden eels, and other bottom dwellers. Dan slowly descended to be nearby in case someone had a problem at depth and to remind them not to stay so deep for too long. He could see that a couple Dive Inn buddy teams were already slowly swimming across the upper side of the shipwreck headed toward the reef wall behind the keel of the sunken ship. There was a lot more life to be seen on the reef than on the ship. Dan didn't know why but the *Hilma Hooker* wasn't festooned with sponges and corals like other wrecks he had seen in other parts of the Caribbean. Maybe the ship's paint had some chemical in it that repelled sea life. He heard a gurgling shout behind him and turned to see a pair of divers gesturing and pointing at the deep blue. He followed their pointing fingers to see a pod of dolphins swimming by. One of the dolphins paused and looked at the divers swarming around the shipwreck as if it couldn't figure out what kind of creatures they were, then it gave a small shake of a shrug, turned its head, and swam away with its pals. A few divers with cameras started trying to head them off to get better pictures but the dolphins were too fast for the terrestrial mammals flailing in their wakes. Soon the photographers gave up and swam back to the ship and reef.

Dan guided the deepest pair of divers up to the top side of the wreck and encouraged them to start exploring the reef. He indicated his air pressure gauge and had them both check their air and let him know where they were. Both were nearing fifteen hundred psi so it was time for them to swim up the reef to a shallower depth where their air consumption would slow down. He swam down around the wreck again, checking in the open holds to make sure none of his divers were in there and had lost track of time and depth but everyone evidently was already working their way up the reef wall, so he swam to join them.

When he reached the edge of the drop off where the sand flat stretched to the shore, he surprised a Spotted Eagle Ray flying over the sand and rapped his tank with his knife to call people's attention. A few of them looked up and were able to see the beautiful creature as it flapped its wings and made its way over the bottom. It dipped down to the sand and churned it up hoping to find something to eat. A school of Yellowtail Snappers hurried to swim over the ray to catch anything that the ray missed. Two of the camera toting divers got into a shoving match trying for the best angle on the ray. Dan was dismayed to realize that they were both divers from his boat so he knew that there would be an argument when they got back on board. He didn't want to have to deal with that. Why couldn't people just take turns? All that fuss served to scare the fish off faster and then no one got a decent shot. Maybe he could get the two divers to sign up for the Underwater Photographer specialty course, then he could teach them manners, but he bet neither of them would agree. People who were that aggressive underwater were convinced that they knew what they were doing and didn't need some dive instructor to tell them how to take pictures. Oh well. He would at least try.

One after the other, the buddy teams made their way back to the mooring. He saw more than one pair swim under the boat to make sure they were getting on the right one. Good, at least they had listened to that part of the briefing. Dan scanned the site to see if there were any more blue tanks swimming around but all he saw was Samuel at the mooring, so he finned over to join him for a three-minute safety stop. He watched the last buddy team pull themselves along the trailing line behind the boat, their fins over their wrists ready to hand up to Captain Bill. He hoped that the two photographers that had tussled over the Spotted Eagle Ray managed to hold their tempers when they got on board.

CHAPTER 10

As easy as cleaning the first house of the day was, that was how much of a mess the second house was. Both she and Mariette were glad that they were working together when they saw the condition of the place. Once again, they called loudly when they entered the house, then when they saw the mess, they agreed not to split up.

"What did they do?" Mariette asked when they stood in the doorway of the first bedroom.

"I don't know but I'm glad I wasn't here for it," said Ella.

The mattress was half off the bed and the sheets were draped over the louvered closet doors. The smell of marijuana was strong in the room.

"I think we had better air the place out," Ella said. "Somebody had a wild party."

Mariette nodded. "Mm-hmm." And she went over to the French doors and swung them wide open.

It took them twice as long to clean this house as it had the townhouse on Habitat Row, and it was the same size. Dishes and glasses were all over the place, under the beds, in the closets, in the shower.

"Someone was eating in the shower? Now that is a case of the munchies," said Mariette.

"I'll say," Ella agreed.

There were Doritos bags shoved under the couch pillows and empty pickle jars in the bathrooms.

Ella walked around the house with a garbage bag and as she picked up the third pickle jar, she said, "I don't even want to know."

For all the mess nothing appeared destroyed. They had the washing machine and the dryer working all day to clean the linens. The dishwasher ran all day too.

"I didn't know that there were this many dishes and glasses in these houses," Mariette said.

Ella just shook her head. They carried the bamboo couch and chairs out onto the patio so that the breeze and the sun could clear them of the aroma of weed. Ella sprayed everything with Febreeze hoping that would take care of the smell. They did the same with the bed pillows, Febreeze-d them, and then left them in the sun while they reorganized everything. When Carlos the pool man came to tend the pool and hot tub, he spent some time diving into the pool and bringing up bowls and plates that he brought into the house for them.

"In the pool?" Ella said. Carlos nodded. "Thank god for Corelle dishes. They're tough to break."

They worked hard and it was full dark when they finally finished. "It is a good thing that the next guests are not arriving until tomorrow morning on the flight from the Netherlands." Mariette said. She looked at her watch. "It is nearly six o'clock. I am exhausted. How about you?"

Ella wiped her brow with her forearm. "Yes, I am exhausted too. I don't think I have ever seen a place as trashed as this place was, although nothing was broken or ruined, just thrown all over. I guess the company won't refuse to return their security deposit because they made a mess."

"No, they must destroy things for that to happen. We just had to work all day and half the night to clean up after them. Good thing we get paid by the hour," said Mariette with a grin.

Ell picked up her broom and bottle of Febreeze. "Let's get packed and get out of here. I'm starving, lunch was a long time ago."

"Agreed. Let's go."

It didn't take them long to pack up their cleaning gear, lock the house, and go their separate ways.

Dan was pacing in front of the house when Ella drove up.

"Where have you been? I've been worried sick," he said before she even turned off the key.

"I'm sorry, I should have called you." She got out of the car and hugged him. "The second house we cleaned was totally trashed. I mean, like the mattresses were off the beds and the sheets were draped over the ceiling fans and the closet doors. There were dishes everywhere, even in the pool, and it all smelled like marijuana. Someone had one whale of a party before they left for home." They walked into the house. "It was a good thing Mariette and I worked together today because a lone cleaner would still be there. It was a disaster. I'm starved. What do we have for supper?"

Ella felt like she was back to normal after her long exhausting day of working with Mariette. She thought maybe she could get back to working alone in the next few days.

Their supper of fish fillets baked with homemade salsa on top, couscous, and a salad was quick to make and delicious. Dan was a genius at sautéing the vegetables for the salsa, adding the fresh tomatoes at the last minute so all the juice didn't cook away, and it kept the fish moist and tender. Ella had to keep him from adding too much jalapeno pepper. If he had his way, he would add the whole pepper and the fish would be too hot for her to eat.

"Moderation, that's the key," she said.

He rolled his eyes and put three quarters of the diced pepper in a zipper bag to freeze. "One of these days I'll have it as hot as I want it."

She stood her ground. "You can add all the sriracha to your serving that you want but I can't tolerate things as hot as you like them. Think of my poor tender taste buds."

"Taste bugs," he said, "That's what my little sister used to call them."

"That's cute," said Ella.

"Yeah, but not when you're a grown up." Dan laughed and stirred the sautéing vegetables, so they didn't burn. He wanted them just a little brown before adding the diced tomatoes.

Ella greased the casserole dish and laid the rinsed and dried fish fillets in the dish ready for Dan's salsa to be spooned over the top. She sprinkled a little salt and pepper on the fish. The house smelled of frying onions and bell peppers with a little tang of jalapeno.

Dan inhaled deeply. "I love the smell of frying onions."

"Yes, it smells great."

While Dan finished the salsa and got the fish into the oven to bake for a few minutes, Ella made the couscous and assembled the salads. They tried to cook together as often as possible. Both liked to cook, and it was a good way to wind down from the day. Dan usually had a beer and Ella had a small glass of wine if there was wine in the house, otherwise she just had fruit juice with 7-Up. Their supper was ready in fifteen minutes, and they sat down to eat on the patio. The sun was setting and there weren't very many bugs to bother them. Ella lit a bug coil and slid it under the table to chase away any mosquitoes that might be sheltering from the breeze under there. Dan held up his beer bottle.

"Here is to a good day," he said.

"A good day," Ella echoed.

They clinked glasses. "Cheers."

While they ate, they talked about their days. Ella told of the total state of mess that the second house was in. Dan talked about the Spotted Eagle Ray at the *Hilma Hooker* and how the two photographers had nearly come to blows trying to take its picture.

"The funny thing was there was a school of Dolphins that swam by and neither of them noticed it."

Ella laughed. "I guess they missed an opportunity."

After the meal was finished Ella rummaged in the freezer and found a carton of mango sorbet with just enough to share while Dan cleared the plates to the kitchen counter. Ella spooned up her first bite.

"Mm, now if we had some coconut to go with this it would be perfect."

Dan reached for her bowl. "Well, if you don't want this without coconut, maybe I'll just finish it for you."

Ella swatted his hand with her spoon. "Get away from my dessert." She laughed and pulled her bowl closer. "Eat your own."

He tipped his bowl toward her. "But mine is all gone."

"I can't help it if you ate yours too fast. Stay away from mine."

It was Dan's night to do the dishes while Ella put away the leftover couscous. They had learned the hard way that you do not leave dirty dishes out overnight. They had done that when they first moved to the island and had been greeted by an army of ants and cockroaches in their kitchen the next morning. It took them weeks to rid the place of them and they had been diligent dish washers ever since. They spent an hour watching the fruit bats swoop in the night sky before turning in. Both had to be up and at work early so they went to bed early.

In the middle of the night Ella woke up screaming. She struggled to get out of the covers and leaped out of bed.

"Wha…?" Dan looked around confused to see her standing in the darkened room silhouetted by the window where the streetlight seeped through. "What's the matter?"

Ella was shaking. She said, "He… he was holding me down. I couldn't get away."

Dan got out of bed and went around to her. "No one was here. No one was holding you down. It was just a bad dream."

"A bad dream," she sighed. "I don't have bad dreams."

Dan eased his arm around her. She was wet with sweat and shivering. "Let's find you a dry shirt to wear."

He helped her change out of the sweat-soaked shirt and into a dry one. He turned her pillow over to the dry side and tucked her back into bed. He went around to his side and eased up beside her.

"Would it help if I held you?"

She shook her head. "I don't think so. I think your arm over me is what triggered the dream. I'm sorry."

"Don't be sorry. How about you snuggle up to my back, so

you know that you're not alone?"

She sniffled. "Okay."

Dan turned over and she molded herself to his back, throwing her left arm over his side. He reached up to touch her hand. "I'll keep you safe, babe," he said as he drifted back off to sleep.

Ella lay awake for a while thinking she would never be free of Bert Champeau. She said a little prayer that Jack Slater wanted to sell his dive operation sooner rather than later.

Ella kept having bad dreams every night. She was exhausted when she awoke in the morning.

"I don't know how long I can do this, Dan," she said. "I'm afraid to fall asleep."

He put his arms around her. "Have you had any luck finding a therapist?"

She nodded. "Mariette has a friend who is a therapist. I am going to call her this morning and see if I can't get an appointment next week."

"See if you can get an appointment today," Dan said. "We need our sleep."

Ella was in luck. The therapist had an opening that very day in the late afternoon. When she told Mariette about it her co-worker was happy for her and encouraged her to go even if they were not finished with the last house of the day.

"I can finish up on my own. You go see about getting yourself better. You cannot live in fear the rest of your life."

Ella was grateful to have such a good friend and someone who knew just about everyone on the island. The therapist was in a strip of offices off the main road at the edge of Playa. She was a middle-aged woman with a motherly look about her but with a sharp mind and good insight into what Ella needed. She took Ella through her experience with Bert Champeau and Ella was glad to have someone acknowledge how difficult it was to get over such an experience. The therapist validated that Ella did the right thing by calling the police and pressing charges. She said that Ella probably should let the police know that Champeau had followed her to Pink Beach on his last day on Bonaire just to say goodbye and scare her one more time. Recounting the court experience was uncomfortable. Ella kept breaking down and crying over the lies that Champeau told, how his version was the exact opposite of what really happened.

"How did that make you feel?" the therapist said.

Ella dabbed at the tears that streamed down her cheeks. "It made me feel like I wasn't in my right mind. It made me question my own memory of the assault, but I knew that what I had said was the truth and what he said was a pack of lies."

The therapist looked at Ella. "I suspect that was his intent. Predators like Mr. Champeau need to have their own version of their despicable deeds, to convince themselves that what they do to women is not criminal, that you were asking for it."

Ella sat upright and looked at the therapist. 'That is exactly what he said in court, that I was asking for it. I'm not a flirt, I don't think I'm a flirt, and I know that I didn't flirt with Mr. Champeau. He was too old and too mean. I don't like mean people."

The therapist suggested that Ella take an herbal supplement that was supposed to enhance sleep to see if she couldn't make it through a night without bad dreams. She made another appointment in two days. Ella felt better as she drove away from the therapist's office.

Dan had texted her that he was leading the night dive from the Dive Inn that evening and did she want to come along. She texted back that she would love to, so she drove home to pack her SCUBA gear and check the batteries in her flashlights. By the time she had her equipment packed it was nearly time for the dive, so she drove back into town past the airport just as the evening flight from the Netherlands was landing. She always felt like she needed to duck when the planes flew so low over the road. She knew it was silly but still she couldn't help but bend her head down and hunch her shoulders as the big white airplane thundered overhead.

When she got to the Dive Inn there wasn't a parking place

in front for her, so she went around the block and parked there. She hated to leave the car there in the dark but had no choice. Leaving the windows down and the car unlocked she shouldered her gear bag and walked around the corner to the dive shop. The courtyard was a buzz of activity with divers renting gear, setting up gear, and carrying tanks. Ella found Dan in the middle of the confusion.

"Hi, babe," he said, "how was your day?"

"Good, busy, interesting," she said, "I'll tell you all about it after the dive."

He put her name on the bottom of the list of divers and told her to grab a tank and get her gear set up.

"I need you to help keep an eye on the divers. I hope you don't mind. A few of them have never done a night dive so I'll be busy with them. If you and Samuel can share the divemaster duties, I would be grateful."

"I don't mind. I'll just swim above the throng and watch for strays."

He leaned down and kissed her cheek. "That's perfect. Thanks, babe."

He turned to the crowd. "If you have your gear set up, go ahead and get your wetsuit on. We will be crossing the street and going down to the beach in about five minutes."

Ella said, "Then I had better get a move on."

She grabbed a tank from the rack and got her buoyancy control device and regulator assembled on it. She made sure that her integrated weight pockets were secure in their mounts and laid down her SCUBA unit to prevent it from getting knocked over. She went around and reminded others to lay their unit down, there were too many people milling around for it to be safe to leave a tank unattended. She was getting into her wetsuit when Dan called for everyone's attention and asked them to gear up and follow Samuel across the street and down to the beach.

Looking like a row of hunched old people the group trailed the Divemaster across the road and down to the beach. Playa Chachacha was a great site for a night dive, especially for first timers. It had a shallow sand entry with patchy reefs out to about thirty feet where the reef dropped off to bottom out at one hundred feet. Getting everyone's attention Dan gave the pre dive briefing.

"This site is called Playa Chachacha after the woman who used to live in the house next to the dive shop. The top of the reef is about thirty feet deep and drops to a hundred feet, but we're not going down there. Forty-five feet is the maximum for this night dive. Do not go chasing a fish down too deep. Watch your depth gauge. Stick with your buddy. One way to stay together is to keep your light beams together, and don't shine your light in anyone's eyes." Everyone laughed at that. "Any questions?"

One female voice called, "Will we see any sharks?"

Dan shook his head. "Probably not. Sharks are rare on Bonaire. You might see a Tarpon or a Snook out hunting. They like to hunt on shallow reefs at night and there is one Tarpon that likes to hunt in divers' lights so don't be too scared if a silver fish flashes past you. Those of you who have been night diving before will be mostly on your own. Samuel and Ella will be nearby if you have a problem. I will be diving with the two buddy teams that are doing their first night dives."

Ella raised her voice. "Can I add something, Dan?"

"Sure."

She motioned to the riprap slope to the right. "On your way back to shore at the end of your dive try to swim along these rocks. Lots of lobsters, shrimp, and other small creatures live in the rock spaces. Your light will shine in many little red eyes, and you will hear shrimp claws snapping to warn you away. Enjoy your dive," she said.

The next few minutes were spent checking people's gear and making sure that their air was turned on before they entered the water. Ella could tell that a few of the people were nervous to be out in the ocean in the dark and she tried to identify them by their mask so she could keep an eye on them.

"Oh, just man up," she heard a guy say to his partner.

"Trouble?" Ella asked him.

"My wife is getting cold feet." He sounded disgusted.

"Don't be afraid," Ella said. "It's shallow enough here that you can walk back to shore if you need to. Keep your light beam with your husband's and hold hands if you really feel nervous. I predict that soon you will be comfortable enough to let go."

The wife's voice was small when she said, "Will you hold my hand?"

"Of course, I will," said her husband. "I want you to enjoy this, not shake yourself apart."

Two by two the buddy teams walked into waist deep water, put on their fins and masks, and submerged. Ella watched the lights swing all over the reef as she got herself ready to get into the water. She felt the day's warmth in the sand under her feet and smelled the salty fishy aroma of the sea. Dan and his quartet of newbies moved down the beach a little and he was giving them a bit of extra instruction in night diving techniques. Ella settled her mask and tightened her buckles. She fell forward and felt the warm water trickle down between her skin and her wetsuit. It made her shiver a bit but then she warmed up, adjusted her buoyancy, and kicked to follow the crowd of divers. Ella kept her light off as she swam toward the edge of the reef. She could see the buddy teams spread out along the coral heads. A lot of the divers were head down peering into holes and crevices of the reef. She could see the red Big-eyed Soldierfish out hunting. These medium sized fish hid in the reef during the day and came out at night to slurp up tiny fish and there was a big school of little fish hovering over the reef for them to hunt.

One of the divers jumped back as if startled and Ella glided over to see that a big Green Moray Eel was out of its hiding place looking for prey. The eel paid no attention to the divers or their lights and went on its way. The divers that had found it were excited to see it, she could tell.

Swimming over a coral head she glanced down to see a Scorpionfish hunkered down on the coral waiting for something to swim by. She pointed the fish out to a pair of divers who had trouble seeing what she was pointing at, but they finally did, and the fish extended its pectoral fins like orange and black fans and swam off to a quieter place to sit in wait for its food to swim by.

Ella came up to the husband-and-wife team, still holding hands. She gave them the okay signal and received it in return. Ella waved her hand in the dark water to show them the bioluminescence. At first, they thought she was just waving to them, but she had them cover their lights and they saw the blue green fire that moving their hands through the water excited. The wife was especially entranced by the spectacle and turned off her light so that she could make glowing trails in the water.

One buddy team had gotten too deep, so she took off to herd them back to a shallower depth. When she reached them, she saw that they were following an Octopus out for its evening hunt. They were not happy when she urged them away from the creature and back into the shallower water, but she showed them her depth gauge, seventy-five feet, and they agreed to abandon their friend and follow her.

By then all the divers were trailing along the drop off toward the riprap wall for the swim back to shore. Ella could hear the snap of shrimp claws, it sounded like popping corn, and see their tiny red eyes in the lights. Lobster antennae waved from holes in the rock wall and one or two of the crustaceans were out on the sand where they could be easily seen. One of the lobsters was a Slipper Lobster which looked like an armored submarine with its plates covering its head and body. Soon the water got shallower and shallower, and it was possible to stand up, take off her fins, and walk out of the water.

There was excited chatter all around as the buddy teams came out of the water and told each other what they had seen.

"We saw the Tarpon just hanging at the edge of the drop off. It was huge and bright silver like stainless steel."

"Cool. We followed an Octopus down too deep, but it was cool to see it change colors as it changed where it was. It turned from white and smooth to brown and bumpy in the blink of an eye."

"Did it ink you?"

The diver shook his head. "No, I guess we didn't irritate it enough and then she came and made us get back to shallower water."

"We saw a gigantic Green Moray Eel. It must have been six feet long."

"She showed us a, a..."

Ella overheard and said, "A Scorpionfish."

"Yeah, that. It was so camouflaged that we couldn't see it at first but then it spread its fins and swam away. I guess the spines on its back are poisonous."

Ella said, "Yes, they are. You don't want to get your hand punctured by one of those. You'll regret it for a long time."

"Have you ever gotten stung by one?"

She shook her head. "No, I haven't but I know people who have, and they said it was excruciatingly painful. That's why I learned to spot them."

The divers laughed and began drifting back across the street to the dive shop. They clustered around the rinse tank and Dan came up and opened the gear locker so that they could hang their gear to dry overnight to be ready to dive in the morning.

Dan came over to Ella. "Good dive?"

She nodded. "A very good dive. I only had to chase down one team that were following an Octopus and lost track of their depth. Otherwise, it was an easy one."

"I really appreciate you coming along and helping to divemaster. It was a lot of people for me and Samuel to keep an eye on."

"Anytime."

It took over an hour for the crowd of night divers to get their dives logged, get their logbooks signed, and get their gear rinsed and hung up. Everyone had seen something amazing and had to recount it a few times to make it real.

Ella enjoyed the buzz of after dive excitement that kept the group talking. She missed the camaraderie of the dive community. There was no excitement after a successful house cleaning. She said as much to Dan when they drove home. Dan left his bike locked in the gear locker at the dive shop and rode home with Ella. "I miss that."

He turned away from looking out the car window. "What? Diving?"

"No. Well, I do miss diving as much as we used to when we were in Green Bay, but I miss the after-dive excitement of the customers." She slowed down to let a wild donkey cross the road. "I miss people coming into the shop excited or nervous, telling me about their dives, asking questions about classes, needing reassurance that they can learn to dive." She laughed. "I always loved it when educated people, women especially, came into the shop bemoaning the fact that they were having trouble learning the information. I would ask them if they had learned physics or bubble mechanics in their university days and they would say no. Then I would ask why they expected to already know such specialized things. A light would go on in their eyes and they would feel better about themselves. I would feel better about myself too, that I had helped them get over a hurdle to enjoying the underwater world."

By then they were pulling into their parking spot in front of the apartment. Dan carried in the bags with their wet swimsuits and towels. Ella went into the kitchen to see what there was to eat while Dan went out the back door to hang the wet things on the clothesline to dry overnight. He came back into the kitchen and said, "I am starving. What do we have for supper?"

Ella stood with her head in the fridge surveying what was on offer. "Well, we have some leftover chicken shawarma and rice or some salsa fish with couscous. I think there is a single serving of each, pick which you want, I don't have a preference. There's also some fruit salad and I bought ginger windmill cookies to go with it."

Dan hummed as he decided. "I will have the chicken shawarma, if you don't mind, although I wish it was steak."

"Oh, dream on. Have you seen the beef in the market? It costs an arm and a leg, and it doesn't look very good."

He put his arm around her and whispered in her ear. "Maybe we can go to the Mona Lisa restaurant for supper one night this week and I can order a real steak."

She smiled up at him. "Maybe. If there isn't a cruise ship in port, we can go. It would be cheaper if we didn't order a drink before dinner."

Dan sighed and let her go. "All right, if you say so, but I like to have a beer with my beef."

She was pulling containers of food out of the refrigerator. "True, but it will cost close to fifty dollars to eat there as it is. Adding drinks would take it up to seventy-five. If you're going to talk to Jack Slater about buying his dive operation soon, we need to watch our spending."

Dan sat down at the table. "I have been thinking about that." He started shredding a paper towel that was lying on the table.

"Yes?"

"Well, what if we waited a while before buying a dive operation? I feel some loyalty to Babs and would hate to leave her in the lurch in the middle of the season."

"It is almost the end of high season," Ella said. She watched his nervous fingers making the paper towel into scraps. "What else were you thinking?"

"I was thinking that we would need a boat for a dive operation so what if we bought a boat now with our savings and did some side charters. We could earn extra money that way."

She put a fist on her hip. "Yes, we could earn money that way and then will have the expense of finding and paying for a mooring and boat repairs and gas, plus buying a decent boat would take at least half of our savings. When exactly would you do these side charters? You already work six days a week."

"On my days off. I'm tired to living on a shoestring. I'm tired of saving and not spending on things that I want. I want a new regulator and I need a new dive computer. Mine is out of date. It doesn't look good for a representative of a dive operation to have obsolete gear."

"So, you want to spend our twenty-thousand-dollar savings on a boat and new SCUBA gear?"

Dan stood up and folded his arms over his chest. "Some of it, not all of it. Geez, Ella, you sound like my dad. He was always so cautious. 'Make do with what you have,' he would say all the time. I want new things. I want a new wetsuit, mine is faded and getting holes. I am tired of being on a budget."

Ella sat down at the table and looked at her hands. "I thought we had a plan."

Dan flung his arms out. "A plan? We had a dream; a pipe dream it seems to me. I want to go out with the divers after a night dive. Go out for a burger and a few beers at City Café. I want to have a car when I want a car and not have to pedal all over the island frying myself on a bike. Why do you get the car and I get a bike?"

She looked up at him. "Because I can't carry my cleaning supplies on a bike. I suppose Mariette could pick me up at the Dive Inn some days if you want to have the car but then it would just sit parked at the dive shop while you worked. What's the point of that? So, you can drive somewhere on your lunch break?"

"I don't know what the point is. I just don't want things to stay the way they are." Dan picked the car keys off the hook by the door. "I'm going out."

"I thought you were hungry, starving you said."

He turned away and walked out of the kitchen. "Turns out I am more thirsty than hungry, and we're out of beer." He let the screen door slam behind him as he left.

Ella looked after him. "No, we're not out of beer. I brought some home this afternoon and put it in the fridge so it would be cold when we got home."

But she was talking to herself. She heard the car's tires crunch on the gravel and then squeak as they hit the asphalt street. Ella reheated the salsa fish and couscous, then had a bowl of fruit salad with a couple windmill cookies for dessert.

CHAPTER 11

Dan didn't come home before she went to bed. He didn't come home before she fell asleep, but he was home when she woke in the night with another bad dream. Dan was sacked out on the couch snoring. She had not heard him come in. She looked to make sure that the keys were on the hook, but they were not. She put on her shorts and shoes and went out to make sure that they were not in the car but there they were. We're lucky no one stole the car, she thought. I wonder how long he has been home. I wonder how much he had to drink.

The living room smelled like a barroom--beer and smoke. Ella leaned over and sniffed Dan's clothes. Smoke, cigarette smoke, something that Ella thought she would never smell on him. Dan hated smoking, griped about smokers in bars and especially at the dive shop. Had he been smoking or just been around smokers? And was that a skunky hint of weed mixed with the beer and cigarette smell? She sat down in the chair and looked at him. How had he gotten so unhappy so fast? Not a week ago he was talking about how excited he was to buy Jack Slater's dive operation; how happy he was that they were able to save so much money because of her good money management. And now he was so unhappy that he would go out, get drunk and smoke weed?

Ella left him sleeping on the couch and went back to bed, her bad dream forgotten for the moment. Had her experience with Bert Champeau been the catalyst of Dan's discontent? She lay watching the moonlight spread its blue light across the ceiling. Was it her fault for needing to spend money on a therapist and that made Dan want to spend some of their money on himself? Was he that juvenile?

"Oh man," Dan said from the living room.

She heard him get up from the couch and hurry into the bathroom where he was thoroughly sick. I just hope you made it into the toilet, she thought, and curbed her impulse to go see if he needed any help. When her alarm went off the next morning, she wasn't surprised to see Dan sleeping on the bathroom floor.

She leaned over and shook his shoulder. "Dan? It is time to get up for work."

He groaned and rolled away from her hand. "Let me sleep."

"I can't leave you to sleep on the bathroom floor. I need to get ready for work."

Dan opened his eyes just a bit. "Going to bed. Tell Babs I'm sick." He rolled over on his hands and knees and used the edge of the sink to help him stand up. "Oh, my head's pounding. I'm going to bed."

"Fine. I will tell Babs that you poisoned yourself last night."

"Whatever. Going to bed." He reached for the door jamb and ricocheted down the hall to the bedroom.

Ella stopped at the Dive Inn on her way to her first cleaning job of the day.

"Dan's sick," she told Babs, "Throwing up sick, but I think he'll be better tomorrow."

Babs looked at her over her reading glasses. "Sick or hung over?" Babs said.

Ella looked away. "Hung over," she said.

"Well, tell him not to make a habit of it. Luckily, we have a slow day today. No cruise ships in port so the staff can cover his absence. Thanks for stopping to tell me."

Ella waved and left to go to work. Mariette was waiting for her at another house in Santa Barbara Shores.

"Right on time," Mariette said when Ella pulled up. "You look a little tired."

Ella shrugged. "Dan went out and got drunk last night so I

was awakened when he got sick and had a hard time going back to sleep. The alarm felt too early today."

"Dan went out and got drunk? Does he do that often?"

She shook her head. "Hardly ever. He'll have a beer or two in the evening, but I think he did a good job of it last night."

"What set him off?"

"I'm not sure. He was talking about buying a boat and a bunch of new dive gear and when I questioned him about it, he grabbed the keys and stormed out."

They gathered up their cleaning supplies, Mariette unlocked the door, and they went in.

"That's funny," said Mariette, "the door wasn't locked."

Ella's eyes got big, and she looked at her friend. "Do you think someone could be in here?"

Mariette cocked her head. "It does not feel like there is anyone here but let's go around and check each room together."

They walked through the whole house calling "hello" at every doorway, but the house was empty. No one was in a bed or a bathroom, no one was asleep on the couch or laying out by the pool.

"That's a relief," Ella said.

Mariette nodded and they got started cleaning. This time Ella took the bedrooms.

"I have to stop being afraid of cleaning the bedrooms if I am ever going to be comfortable cleaning alone again," she said.

"Okay but come get me if you get nervous."

"I will."

It didn't take them long to clean this house. It looked like the departing guests had cleaned up after themselves thoroughly. They had even stripped the beds and piled the towels in the bathroom, so all Ella had to do was carry them downstairs and start the washer. Mariette was emptying the dishwasher when she came down to start the first load.

"They ran the dishwasher?" Ella said.

"Yes, they did."

"They stripped the beds and piled the towels up, so I didn't have to do it. Nice people."

"Rare people," Mariette said.

They were done cleaning long before noon, so they went up the hill to the next house in Santa Barbara Crowns, the row of houses up on the edge of the bluff behind the main road. These houses had sweeping views of the island and the sea and were highly prized as vacation rentals. A few of the houses were owner occupied but many of them were Air B&Bs listed online and hard to get a reservation in. The house they were to clean was a small, modern house with all glass across the front and loft-style bedrooms over the kitchen area. The two of them worked quickly and were done cleaning before the last load of towels was out of the dryer.

"I guess we will have to sit out by the pool until the laundry is finished," Mariette said.

"What a pity," said Ella smiling and pulling off the scarf she had tied over her hair. "Let's go."

They sat in companionable silence for a while and then Mariette turned to Ella. "I have a proposal for you."

Ella turned her way. "What?"

"Gina said that Playa Palms Rentals is thinking of selling off their cleaning business and I was thinking of buying it. Would you be interested in going in with me?"

"Oh, Mariette, I don't know. We're saving our money to buy a dive operation. Jack Slater is getting old, and Dan thinks that maybe he will be ready to sell up soon."

Mariette laughed. "Jack Slater will die in SCUBA gear, he's not going to sell, he thinks he will live forever."

Ella looked stricken. "Do you really think so?"

"I know so. I heard Jack say that he likes it when Dan comes sniffing around looking to buy the business, but he is not ready to sell. He says will leave that up to his heirs."

"So, Dan has good reason to be frustrated. Darn it. It's mean of Jack to string Dan along like that and I know that Dan won't believe me when I tell him what you said."

Mariette turned to face Ella. "They want ten thousand

dollars for the cleaning business, which means only five thousand each. We could hire more cleaners and get contracts with other rental agencies. We could be a big company. What do you think?"

Ella sat up and turned to face her. "I don't know. I hadn't dreamed of running a cleaning empire on a Caribbean island. My dream was to work in a dive shop. But that's not happening anytime soon, I fear, not with the rules about work permits." Ella frowned. "What about work permits? I don't have one, I get paid in cash under the table. Would I be allowed to buy a business?"

Mariette nodded. "Sure. They cannot control who buys or starts a business, they only control who gets work permits and who can take jobs that natives can do."

"How come you got a work permit?" Ella asked.

"I am Dutch, second best to a native so I got one. You're American, you will never get one."

"That's not fair. Well, I guess it is if there are Bonaireans without jobs, but will we be able to find cleaners? It's not a very glamorous job cleaning up after people."

"Well, it is better than a resort job."

"How do you figure that?"

"In a resort there are people moving out all the time and people make terrible messes in resorts. We do most of our work on the weekends and early in the week so the cleaners would have fulltime work and extra time off too. You're good with money, and I could use help with financial matters. I am not so good with balance sheets and stuff like that."

Ella leaned forward. "I can help with that no matter if I invest or not."

"I will not be able to buy the business if you do not invest."

"Oh. I guess I had better talk to Dan. Maybe Dan hung over will be more rational than the Dan I dealt with last night when he was talking about buying a boat and all new SCUBA gear."

"Whoa. That would eat away at your savings."

They heard the dryer stop running so they went inside to fold all the towels and put some of them in the bathroom and the beach towels in the rack inside the patio doors. The house they cleaned in the afternoon was average, not as tidy as the Crowns house and not as messy as the Shores house. They cleaned together so that they could talk about Mariette's idea of buying the business. Ella promised to crunch some numbers that night and bring a spreadsheet the next day for them to go over. Mariette said her husband Nathan was all for the idea. Ella said she hoped that Dan wouldn't blow up at the mention of it.

Ella drove past the Dive Inn on her way home but didn't see Dan's bicycle chained up alongside the fence, so she assumed that he had not gone to work that day. She was right. He was lying on the couch sleepily watching a telenovela with subtitles on the television mounted on the wall. When she walked in, he said, "Have you ever watched these things? They're crazy complicated. Much worse than the soap operas in the United States."

She put the car keys on the hook by the door. "Yes, I've watched a few times. They are kind of addictive. It's easy to get sucked into the story and start to care about the characters and their situations." She sat in the chair next to the couch. "How are you feeling?"

Dan muted the television. "Better. Foolish. I'm sorry, Ella, I don't know what got into me last night. I don't really need a boat and while new gear would be nice, I can do without it for a while."

"Don't give up on the boat idea."

"Why?"

"I talked to Mariette, and she said that Jack Slater is probably just stringing you along. He likes when you come into his shop and talk to him about selling but told anyone who would listen that he would let his heirs decide who to sell the business to."

"Why that old pirate. Did you tell Mariette how awful I was to you last night?"

"No. She proposed a business idea and I want us to look at it with an open mind. No temper tantrums, solid cold logical thought, okay?"

"Uh, okay. What did she say?"

Ella stood up. "Do you want a beer?"

"God, no."

"How about a soda or some iced tea?"

"I'll take a ginger ale if we have any."

Ella went into the kitchen and came back with their drinks. She set hers down on a coaster on the glass topped coffee table and looked at Dan. "Gina says Playa Palms is planning to sell the cleaning part of the business and Mariette wants us to buy it with her." She stopped, waiting for the explosion, but none came.

"Buy the cleaning business?"

"Yes, I know it was never a part of our dream to own a cleaning business but the buy in is only five thousand dollars and Mariette has plans to expand almost immediately. I'm going to crunch some numbers tonight and talk about it with her more tomorrow."

Dan took a swig of his ginger ale and set the glass back down. "What does that mean for our dive business dream?"

"If Mariette is right about Jack not intending to sell you the business, our dive shop dream is on life support. We could invest about a quarter of our savings in the cleaning business and start making a profit almost immediately if what I am thinking pans out."

"Where does a boat come in?"

"I was thinking that maybe you could contract with Babs to be her extra boat during the high season. You know she needs an extra boat especially when cruise ships are in port. You could still work part time for her and part time for us. Let's sleep on it and talk more tomorrow."

"Okay. Do we have anything like soup for supper? My stomach is kind of touchy."

Ella laughed. "I'm not surprised. You almost did yourself in last night."

He gave a weak chuckle. "I did."

They had supper, chicken soup for Dan and a mystery meat cutlet with a salad for Ella and spent the evening talking about the possibility of buying the cleaning business with Mariette and Nathan. They debated whether they were willing to let go of Dan's long held dream of dive shop ownership and chase owning a business that neither of them ever dreamed of.

"The thing that keeps popping into my head," said Ella, "is that there are always going to be vacation rentals that need cleaning."

"Playa Palms is not the only rental agency that needs cleaners," Dan said.

"Exactly. I don't know if the other agencies have their own cleaners or if they contract with an individual. What if we could organize the independent cleaners to standardize their wages and even pay them more for each job?"

"You mean like a union?"

Ella nodded. "Well, kind of. A company might have a better chance of making sure people are well paid for their labor and there is always safety in numbers. We could have pairs of cleaners, cleaning teams, which would make the work go faster and protect the cleaners from people like Bert Champeau. I can't imagine that he would assault a woman if there were two of them there. He backed off as soon as Gina arrived."

"I think you should talk to Gina about why Playa Palms is selling the business before you commit," said Dan. "It could be too much trouble to be worth investing in."

They sat at the table long into the night debating and discussing the pros and cons until Dan couldn't stop yawning.

"I'm dead tired," he said. "Last night really took it out of me. I'm sorry, babe, I need to crash."

"Okay," Ella said, "I'll clean up here. You go shower and hit the hay. I'll be along in a few minutes."

She ran a sink of dish water and got busy doing the dishes while Dan got into the shower. She was careful not to run the water too much so that she didn't freeze or scald him. The water in their apartment wasn't adequate to stay hot for both so she rinsed them in tepid water leaving the hot for the shower.

"Yow!" Dan said at one point.

She had forgotten and turned on the hot water. "Sorry," she said, and switched to lukewarm.

Doing the dishes while he was in the shower was a bad idea, so she let the dishes soak while she folded a basket of laundry that Dan had taken off the wash line before she came home from work. After she heard the shower stop, she went back to the dishes and was just finishing up when Dan came out of the bathroom, a towel wrapped around his hips.

"That little shower woke me up. How about you come to bed soon?"

He nuzzled her neck, kissing her shoulder and then up behind her ear. It made her shiver.

She turned in his embrace. "Let me take a quick shower and I'll be right there." She dried her hands. "I thought you were ready to crash."

He stopped in the doorway and leered at her over his shoulder. "I'm never too tired to make love."

She shook her head and went into the bathroom. As she washed herself, she thought about Bert Champeau and the way he had loomed over her at the beach. It made her feel cold and afraid, but she pushed the thought away. Dan wasn't like that. Dan would never hurt her. He had stood by her and been understanding and gentle with her bad dreams and her fears. She was sure he would continue to be gentle and understanding. She wrapped a towel around herself and went to double check that the doors were locked before turning out all the lights and going into the bedroom. Ella dropped her towel and slid between the sheets. She thought that Dan had fallen asleep, but he reached across to pull her close.

"I'm feeling a little nervous," she said. "I keep remembering Champeau looming over me."

"We can take care of that," said Dan, and he rolled them over so that she was lying on top of him. "There. Now you're the one in control."

She leaned down, kissed him, and felt his immediate response. "I like being in control," she said against his lips and felt her own desire begin to rise.

They slept all night with Ella snuggled up to Dan's back and her arm across his body. He held her hand as they fell asleep.

"I love you," she said, her lips softly brushing his shoulder.

"I love you too," he said gently squeezing her fingers.

CHAPTER 12

The next morning at breakfast Dan said, "I have an idea. Let's invite Mariette and Nathan over for supper on Monday so we can hash out all the questions about this possible investment. Do you think you can find time to talk to Gina before then?"

"That's a good idea. I'll call Mariette before I leave for work and see if we can't stop in at Gina's office on our lunch break to get more information."

"Good. I'll talk to Babs about your idea of working part time and chartering part time. See what she thinks about it."

Ella cautioned him not to start looking for a boat just yet. "This is only an idea, not a reality, so curb your excitement, and don't order new gear just yet."

Dan put on a sad face. "Oh, okay, if you insist."

She laughed at him. "Funny. As much as I complain about cleaning and not working in a dive shop, I am kind of excited about this possibility."

"As long as I can keep diving and teaching diving, I'm happy."

"That will be our priority."

Dan pedaled away toward the Dive Inn in the relative cool of early morning and Ella got her cleaning supplies organized and refilled before motoring off to meet Mariette. They had a noon appointment with Gina all set up so Ella made sure to have a notebook and pen in her car so that she could make notes about the information they received from Gina.

"What did Gina say when you called and asked for an appointment?" she asked Mariette when she arrived at the first cleaning job.

"She was a little surprised that I had asked you to go in with me, but she's willing to answer all our questions. I think she's tired of running two businesses, so she's eager for us to take this job off her hands. What did Dan say?"

Ella carried her bucket of supplies into the house, her mop and broom in the other hand. "He didn't say no immediately. He wants more information just like we do, and he's willing to consider the idea. We want to have you and Nathan over for supper on Monday so the four of us can talk about it."

"Good idea. I will text Nathan to keep Monday night open." She pulled her phone out of her hip pocket and her fingers got busy tapping out the message.

Almost immediately a text reply came back. She looked at the screen and said, "There. He's all for supper and talking about buying the business. Now what can I bring?"

"I don't know what I am making yet, but I'll let you know."

They got to work. Ella took the downstairs and Mariette took the upstairs. She tossed the sheets and towels down for Ella to get the washing started and Ella got to work on the kitchen which showed signs of an extraordinary amount of cooking. She had to run the dishwasher twice to get all the dishes clean and it took two sinks of dishwater for her to clean all the pots and pans. I wonder if they went out to eat at all or if they just shopped and cooked all week, she thought.

There was very little food left in the refrigerator and freezer, just a jar of mayo and a couple nearly empty jars of jelly--guava and passionfruit. Nothing worth saving there. In between sinks of dishes and sweeping up sand from every corner of the downstairs, Ella kept the laundry moving. She thought about hanging the sheets outside so they would smell like sunshine for the next guests, but the lines were broken so the sheets went into the dryer.

Dan had a busy morning with a boat full of novice divers. He and Samuel divided up the passengers and Dan directed Captain Bill to take them to Jerry's Reef which bottoms out at one hundred thirty feet but has lots of interesting sea life in the shallows to keep newbie divers entranced for a long time. He and Samuel took the divers down the wall to near one hundred feet and then angled back up to thirty-five feet for most of the dive.

The sunlight glittered on the wavelets above and sent rays of light down onto the reef, what some people call "God light" and made for good photographs if anyone had a camera. One diver had a camera, but he spent most of the dive trying to adjust his buoyancy and got back onto the boat after the dive complaining that he had missed more shots than he got. Dan consoled him by saying that he should stay close to Dan on the second dive, and he would help him with his buoyancy.

On the second dive at Sharon's Serenity Dan stayed close to the guy with the camera and helped him take some decent pictures of passing parrotfish and a lot of the small creatures and fish that inhabit that staghorn and elkhorn corals at the drop off. There was a lot of fish action in the shallows that kept the divers entertained on their three-minute safety stops. It was a complement of much more confident divers that got off the boat at the dock after the morning's dives. Most of them thanked Dan and Samuel for their help in making the dives a success. The diver with the camera sat at the table in the courtyard scrolling through his pictures and looking like he had won a prize.

'These are great," he said to Dan. "I can't thank you enough. I can't wait to show them to my wife. Especially the one of the orange seahorse."

Dan smiled at him. "We were lucky to find that seahorse. They're not very common on that site."

Ella and Mariette worked hard to get done cleaning the house in time for their noon appointment with Gina. They stopped at Subway for lunch to take to their meeting. They knew that Gina would have her lunch so they figured all three could eat and talk.

"I was disappointed that there wasn't any bread or cheese or fruit left in this morning's house," Ella said. "That way we could have cobbled together a sandwich for lunch instead of having to buy one."

Mariette grinned. "That is why I asked you to invest in the business with me, you are careful with money and do not waste food."

Ella laughed. "Dan says I'm a Scrooge McDuck when it comes to money; I would rather save it than spend it."

"That is not a bad thing."

Their lunch with Gina was very informative. Dan was right, Gina's cleaners worked for more than just Playa Palms Rentals. She was forthcoming with financial information too. Ella was impressed at the cash flow in the business even with them buying the cleaning supplies for the employees.

"It is much more economical to have bulk supplies for the cleaners," Gina said. "That way I can control the quality of them and focus on environmentally safe solutions. That is a good selling point these days."

Mariette and Ella didn't reveal all their ideas to Gina, they didn't want her to implement them and keep the business for herself. Ella filled pages of her notebook with the answers to their questions so that she would have all the information to share with Dan and Nathan when they met for supper in a couple days.

"We can make the transition smooth," Gina said, "if you can pay cash for the business."

Ella looked at Mariette who nodded. "If we decide to go ahead, that will be no problem."

They were excited driving back to get Mariette's car and move to their second cleaning job of the day. Ella was getting to be less concerned about people still being in the houses, but she and Mariette had gotten used to cleaning together and agreed that they got more done quicker that way.

Dan didn't get a chance to talk to Babs until the end of the day. Both the morning and the afternoon dive boats were packed, and they all hung around for at least an hour after the dives, so the courtyard was packed with people wanting their logbooks signed or to rent gear which kept Dan hopping. He was glad that Babs had hired another dive instructor named Cyril. He was from Switzerland and wasn't as outgoing as Dan would have liked but he was an experienced and competent diver, so it was good. By the time all the afternoon's boat divers had rinsed and hung their equipment and gotten their logbooks signed and had a chance to ask questions about what they had seen and what the next day's dives would bring Dan was exhausted.

Babs was tidying up her desk and had closed her computer when he leaned on her office door.

"Do you have five minutes to talk?" Dan said.

Babs looked at her watch. "Five minutes. Harry and I have dinner reservations. What's up?"

Dan crossed his arms over his chest. "Well, Ella and her friend Mariette are talking about buying the cleaning business from Playa Palms and that would mean we wouldn't have enough money for a down payment on a dive operation. You know that we were hoping to buy Jack Slater's shop when he retires but now we hear that he plans to hang on until he dies and let his heirs figure it out."

"That is what I hear too. He enjoys your visits though; he thinks you would make a good operator, but he's not ready to sell out. What does this have to do with me?"

Dan shifted from foot to foot. "Ella and I were talking about maybe buying a boat and doing some dive chartering. She wondered if maybe I could work for you part time and be your backup boat part time, especially when cruise ships are in port."

Babs looked down at her hands. "That's not the worst idea I have ever heard. When would all of this happen?"

"None of it's a done deal. Ella and Mariette are talking to Gina today and on Monday Mariette and Nathan are coming to supper so that we can go over the possibilities. Only after that decision is made would any of the boat stuff come into play."

"You know boats are like a hole in the water that you pour money into, don't you? There is mooring and gas and maintenance and you would need a captain's license to run the boat, or you would have to pay a captain to run the boat for you. Boats are not cheap."

Dan ran his hand over his face. "I know, I know, but I came down here dreaming of running a dive operation…"

Babs interrupted, "You essentially run this one, isn't that enough?"

"No, not really. I dream of owning the place and that's hard to give up."

Babs picked up her purse and her keys. "I have to run but I will think about what you said." She stopped next to him in the doorway. "Give some thought as to what you would do different around here and talk to me in the next week or so. Maybe we can work something out."

Dan's eyes followed the little middle-aged woman as she walked down the short hall and out into the sunshine. What did that mean? Was Babs thinking of selling off part of the business?

It seemed to Dan that the bike ride home got longer that day. He nearly ran into one of the wild donkeys that hung out at the big curve near the airport. He liked the wild donkeys even though they were a hazard on the roads. They were really the only wild things on the island, aside from the birds and iguanas. He wished that Ella had driven by the dive shop and picked him up for a ride home. He was getting tired of not having a car at his disposal. Ella was right that it would sit idle while he was at the dive shop, but it was impossible for him to go anywhere like the grocery or liquor store on his bike. He had to depend on Ella to pick up his beer. It made him feel like a kid or a kept man. That part of his rant the other night was true. He wanted his own wheels and not two wheels but four wheels. Dan knew it wasn't really in their budget to support two vehicles, but it was hard not to resent this daily bicycle trek. Maybe the cleaning business would be lucrative enough that he could buy a used truck, maybe one of those rental pickups that were everywhere on the island. There must be one with his name on it.

Dan got home first. He locked his bike inside the fenced

yard and went into the apartment. He pulled out a beer and quenched his thirst. Man, it was hot and that ride had seemed longer than ever. And where were the trade winds today? It was still, not a palm frond clattered, even the waves seemed to have laid down when he rode past Windsock Beach. It wasn't September, which was when the winds usually slowed and stopped. September was when you could dive the windward side of the island from shore and not get torn up on the rough iron shore rocks. This was March when the winds blew unceasingly from the east and kept the heat and humidity bearable, but not today. He looked off to the west to see if storm clouds were piling up, but the sky was clear, same in the east. Now he was out of reasons that the wind should die down. Dan heard tires on the gravel out front. Ella must be home. Was he supposed to have started supper? Was tonight his night to cook? He opened another beer and didn't even check to see if there was food in the fridge. He didn't care whose turn it was, he was hot, he was tired, and he was drinking his beer.

"Hi, I'm home," Ella said as she came in the front door. "Sorry I'm late but More For Less was jammed."

"Oh, you were at the market. Did you bring beer?"

She smiled at him. "I did. It is still in the car; I couldn't carry it all. Will you get it?"

He put down his green beer bottle. "Sure." He knew he sounded grudging, but he couldn't help it.

When he got back into the kitchen Ella was chopping onions, garlic, and bell peppers. There were a half dozen limes on the counter.

"What are you making?" he said as he loaded the six pack into the refrigerator.

"Ceviche," she said, "it's too hot to cook."

Dan pulled his head out of the cool and slammed the door. "What if I am not in the mood for ceviche? What if I want something cooked? Did you think to ask me before you went ahead with all your fancy fish salad making?"

Ella's mouth dropped open, and her hands stilled. "I'm

141

sorry. I didn't think that you wouldn't like this for supper. You usually like it when I make ceviche."

"I don't say anything when you make it, that doesn't mean that I like it. You're big on making decisions these days, aren't you? No discussion, whatever Ella wants, Ella goes ahead and gets."

A little voice in the back of Dan's head asked what he was doing, making a big fuss about what she was making for supper, but he couldn't help himself.

Ella put down the sharp knife she was holding and turned to look at Dan. "Exactly what is your problem today?" she said.

Dan looked back at her. "I'm hot, I'm tired, and it seems like my dream is getting swept away in favor of your new idea to buy the cleaning business."

"No," said Ella, "we're discussing the possibility of buying the cleaning business with our friends and working to figure out a way to get you as much of your dream as possible if we do. "If" being the operative word here, if things work out, if we buy the business, if you agree."

Dan drained his second beer and opened a third. He took a drink. "This is warm."

"I just brought it home and you just put it into the refrigerator."

"I know that."

"So, it would be warm."

"You couldn't buy cold beer at More For Less?"

"Not for three dollars extra, I couldn't. How was I to know that you would want more than the two beers we had in the fridge?"

He slammed the bottle down on the counter. "So now I am an alcoholic?"

"No, of course not, I just didn't think it would be a problem."

"Well, it is. Today it's a problem."

"I'm sorry," said Ella.

He slumped down at the table. "I don't know what I want

today. Can we have something different for supper?"

She looked at the vegetables, fruit, and fish all cut up on the counter and ready to assemble the salad. "I kind of have to keep going but I brought home some beef shawarma that I could make. We can have the ceviche another day."

Dan put his head down on his arms on the table. His voice was muffled when he said, "Good. I don't think I can face raw fish today."

She turned back to making the salad. "Okie dokie."

He raised his head and shouted. "Don't say that. You sound like a little kid when you say that."

Ella jumped and nicked her finger with the knife. "Ouch, dang it, I cut myself and this lime juice stings."

Dan put his head back down on his arms. "Great. Something else that's my fault."

Her voice was small when she said, "Can you get me a bandage please?"

Dan stood up so fast that his chair tipped over. "Yeah. I'll get one. Hold on." He came back with a bandage, tore the package open, and wrapped it roughly around her finger. "There," he said and sat back down at the table scraping at the label on his warm beer.

"Thank you," said Ella afraid to set him off again.

Once the ceviche was mixed, covered, and put away Ella got to work on fixing the beef shawarma. She put the pasta water on to boil and sauteed the beef and vegetables in a little oil. Ella didn't know what had gotten into Dan. He usually didn't drink more than a beer or two of an evening and he never lost his temper. Soon the food was ready, and she prepared two bowls of pasta and beef shawarma.

"Do you want a salad?" she asked.

Dan's head came up and he glared at her. "No, I do not want a sissy lettuce salad. Just like I do not want that disgusting raw fish salad you're so fond of. I want man's food." He got up from the table and grabbed the car keys off the hook. "I'm going out."

"But I made the supper that you said you wanted." All she

saw was his back as he left the kitchen.

"I changed my mind just like you changed your mind about the dive shop."

CHAPTER 13

The light from the setting sun hit Dan right in the eyes as he sat down in the driver's seat. Tears sprang to his eyes, and he dropped his hands to his lap. What was he doing? He was going to get a burger or a steak, that was what he was doing. He was going to get something that didn't have noodles or rice or too much lettuce and tomato. Man food. The tires sprayed gravel into the lawn as he sped away from the apartment.

Ella sat down at the table, two bowls of pasta and meat and vegetables cooling in front of her. What was going on with Dan? He had never been like this, not even when they had to repair his truck at home and spent almost all their savings to do it putting them back at square one to get to Bonaire. They had just doubled down on savings, cut back on eating out and started shopping at cheaper grocery stores then. Ella could stop going to the therapist, she didn't feel like she was getting much out of it anymore. There wasn't much she could do to lower the grocery bills, or the utility bills, and she wasn't really a clothes shopper. Their big expense every month was their cell phones, and they were on the lowest plan available on the island. She wondered if she could get a stateside plan that was cheaper and would still work on the island. She would have to look into it.

Ella took two bites of her supper before she started to cry. Great heaving sobs wracked her shoulders and she put her head down in her hands and cried.

That didn't last long, Ella wasn't much of a crier, then she got angry. Angry at Dan for putting her in this position. Angry at herself for thinking she could make all their dreams come true by investing in the cleaning business. A service business like that could never take the place of owning a dive shop, she should have seen that. It did look like a fast way to start making more money, but she would have to look at the balance sheets that Gina had given them. The way Gina told it the business nearly ran itself and made money hand over fist. If that was the case, then why was she looking to sell? Was this a case of something that looks too good to be true? Why had Dan blown his top when asking questions could solve problems easier?

Dan left the neighborhood and didn't know where to go. He could head to Karel's Beach Bar and probably run into some of the divers from the boat this week. They would be happy to buy him drinks but he wasn't in the mood to be "Dan the Dive Guy" tonight. He wanted to be "Dan the Angry Guy." There had to be a little neighborhood bar where he could go and just drink. Maybe down the Nikiboko Road he would find one.

He drove out into the darker neighborhoods at the edge of the town and found a little open-air bar where it looked like a man could get a drink. He parked at the side of the building and walked up to the bar and ordered a beer. All talk had stopped when he walked up, and he looked around to see a half dozen pairs of eyes watching him.

"What? Can't a guy get a beer here?"

"Yah, mon," said a voice out of the dark and the talk started again.

Soon Dan was in the middle of the group of men, all holding beer cans, all complaining about something, usually a woman.

"All I want is to buy a dive shop, but it looks like that's not going to happen," he said after a few beers.

The men laughed.

"Oh, you are the latest fish to bite on Jack Slater's line, eh?" said the man next to him.

Dan blinked at him. "You know about that?"

"Everyone knows that. Mister Slater has been stringing investors along for years. He likes to have someone sniffing around after his business, it makes him feel like a big man, but he means to keep his business until the undertaker comes to cart him away."

Dan peered at him through a beery haze. "How do you know that?"

The man slapped Dan on the shoulder. "I am Leo, I been working for Mister Slater for about ten years now and he always got someone on that line. He uses his age as bait, makes you think that he's feeble and just about ready to sell up, but he's fit and strong and means to hang on until the bitter end. Look at another business to spend your money on. Diving is big business on Bonaire, it costs a fortune to run one. Get a boat and charter dives."

"I been thinking about that," Dan said.

Leo looked at him and poked his finger in Dan's chest. "Think real hard about it. Miss Babs is looking to buy another boat and you can maybe slip into that slot with your own boat."

"How do you know that?"

Leo puffed up his chest. "My cousin Raul is a boat dealer and she been talking to him about another boat. Make a plan and see if you cannot work something out with her. Raul would just as soon sell you a boat as her. A sale is a sale to him."

"I should talk to Raul and then Babs," said Dan.

"You should do," Leo said, "and talk to your missus too. You got a missus?"

Dan waved his ringless left hand. "No missus but as good as."

"She got a job?"

"Yeah."

Leo laughed and elbowed Dan. "You gotta let her support you while you get your boat floated and get busy with dive charters. That is going to take some work, but you can do it, Dan."

Dan had a dreamy look on his face. "Let her support me. That's not a bad idea."

"Yah, mon, you play, and she works. That is the best of

both worlds."

Dan drained his beer, crushed the can, and set it on the bar. "I'll do it. I'll go home and tell Ella right now that I have a plan. She can support us while I go diving. I like that plan." He staggered around to his car and opened the door. "Now if I can only remember how to get home."

The group of men clustered around the bar laughed.

"You will figure it out," Leo said.

When Ella was upset, she cleaned. Not the superficial cleaning she did every day, this was deep down cleaning that had her attacking the tile grout with a toothbrush dipped in bleach cleaner. She swept away all the cobwebs that accumulated on the edges of the window blinds, she dusted all the books on the shelves, she took the pots and pans out of the cupboards and scrubbed the grease off the shelf paper. Ella knew that she would have a hard time getting up for work in the morning provided, that is, that Dan brought home the car with her cleaning supplies in it. As the night wore on, she kept one ear cocked for the sound of tires on gravel, but midnight came and went, and Dan didn't come home. She had finished refolding almost all the clothes in her dresser when she finally heard a car approach and park in front of the apartment. She heard keys jingle, the creak of the gate in the fence, and footsteps up the walk to the front door. Dan fumbled to get the key in the lock, mumbling and muttering but she refused to go and open the door for him. Let him struggle out there. The porch light turned on automatically, so he had that light to help him find the keyhole.

"Stupid door," Dan said but he finally got the key in the lock and shoved the door open. It banged against the wall and bounced back. "Ow, dammit," he said.

She heard him close the door and turn the lock, then he noticed the light in the bedroom and came to stand in the door.

"Are you mad at me?" Dan said.

"A little. Are you mad at me?"

He sat down on the edge of the bed. "Yeah, a little, but I

was talking to the guys, and I have a plan."

She finished folding the last tee shirt and closed the dresser drawer. "What guys? And what's your plan?"

He lay back on the bed on top of the covers and flung his arms out. "The guys at Julio's Bar out the Nikiboko Road."

She stood looking at him, her hands on her hips. "I've never heard of that bar. How did you end up there?"

"I drove around and lucked into it. It's a nice place if you don't need a chair or a glass. Julio has cans of beer and canned cocktails, but I think those are only for the ladies." He waved his hand around. "Anyway, the guys told me that Jack Slater is never going to sell me his dive shop, that he likes to have a fish on the line all the time and I have been this year's fish. Tomorrow I am going to cut bait and get off the hook. Jack can find himself another patsy to lure along with empty promises."

"What guy told you that?"

Dan sat up on one elbow. "Leo who has worked for Jack Slater for years and has seen other prospective buyers come and go. Leo says that Slater laughs about having a sucker on the line all the time, that he plans to keep working until he keels over."

"Yes, we were kind of getting that idea. What's your plan?"

"My plan is to let you buy the cleaning business while I buy a boat so you can support us while I dive. Brilliant, don't you think?" He flopped back onto his pillow, his hands behind his head.

"Oh yes, that's a brilliant plan," said Ella. "How are you going to work that one out?"

There was no answer. She looked over to see that Dan had fallen asleep. He was fully dressed, even had on his shoes, and was on top of the covers.

"Great," she said.

Ella went out to make sure that he had remembered to bring the keys to the car inside, then she got ready for bed, brushed her teeth, and slid into her side of the bed. It was a little awkward with Dan holding down the covers, but she managed to get comfortable, and it only took her a little while to fall asleep. It was getting light when the alarm went off the next morning. Both of them moaned and Ella groped to hit the snooze button. That gave them ten more minutes but after that she knew that they had to get up and get moving.

"Hey, Dan," she said, "I'll let you have the first shower while I make coffee."

He rolled onto his side and pushed himself upright to sit on the edge of the bed. "Oh, god, I need coffee."

"So go take a shower."

She pulled on shorts and padded out into the kitchen, the tiles feeling cool on her bare feet. "Don't go back to sleep," she said when she didn't hear him get up.

"Okay, okay, I'm moving."

She heard his shoes hit the floor and then she saw him shuffle into the bathroom. She got the coffee pot filled just before he turned on the shower. She hoped he didn't drown himself sleeping in the shower. It didn't take long for the aroma of brewing coffee to permeate the air. Ella put two slices of brown bread into the toaster and got out the gouda cheese and guava jelly.

She went to the bathroom door and called to Dan. "Do you want cheese or jelly on your toast?"

The answer was a little while coming. "Neither. I'll just have plain toast. My stomach is queasy this morning."

"Plain toast it is. Butter?"

"Just a little smear."

By the time she got back into the kitchen the toast had popped up and she put in two more slices. She sliced some cheese very thin to put on her toast and she spooned out a bit of fruit salad into a bowl for her breakfast. As the last of the coffee dripped into the pot Dan turned off the shower.

"Perfect timing," she said. She poured him a mug of coffee and carried it to the bathroom. "Do you want this here or are you coming to the table?"

He reached out for the mug. "Here please. I need coffee." He took it so quickly that a little of it sloshed out over his hand.

"Yow, that's hot."

"Fresh brewed," she said. "Your toast is ready when you are."

He put the mug down on the edge of the sink. "Let me brush my teeth and I'll be right there."

She went back into the kitchen to eat her own breakfast. She wondered if Dan would remember his grand plan now that he was awake and not full of beer.

Dan showed up in a few minutes combed and dressed and carrying an empty mug. "Is there more coffee?" he said.

"I made a full pot. We were both up too late last night so I figured we would need it. How is your head?"

"Groggy," he said around a bite of toast. "My stomach feels a little sloshy. I'm hoping the toast soaks up the acid."

"And any leftover beer."

He winced. "And that."

She finished her breakfast and went to take her own shower. Dan showed up in the doorway as she stepped into the shower stall.

"Did I tell you about meeting Leo who works for Jack Slater last night?"

"You told me a little, but you fell asleep pretty fast."

He proceeded to retell her about Slater not really intending to sell his business and how Leo had said that Babs was looking to buy another boat.

"How does he know that?"

"His cousin is the boat dealer."

"Ah."

She turned off the water and grabbed a towel to dry herself off.

"Leo says I should buy a boat and offer to rent it and my services to Babs."

"We did talk about that, remember?" She combed her wet hair and patted it into place. "Excuse me." She walked past him into the bedroom.

"I guess we did but I was so angry about buying the

cleaning business that I wasn't paying attention."

"I know. Spend some time today thinking of ways you would change things at Dive Inn like Babs asked you to. On Monday we'll sit with Mariette and Nathan to talk about investing in the cleaning business and then we can talk about looking at boats. Maybe you can work something out with Babs."

They talked around and around the subject as they both got ready for work. Dan shoved his bike in the back of the car and drove them to the dive shop.

"Maybe there will be enough left so I can buy a used pickup truck," he said, "maybe an old rental one."

Ella said, "That's not a bad idea if you can find one that isn't too beat up."

Ella left him there with his bike and drove up the island to the Santa Barbara neighborhood where it seemed like most of their clients were. Mariette was waiting for her, and she looked downcast.

"What's up?" Ella said.

"Oh, Nathan is worrying now about spending five thousand dollars on the business," Mariette said. "I told him that we had the balance sheets and would be getting together with you and Dan on Monday but now he's getting cold feet."

"Well, that's just great. Now that I think Dan might be on board, Nathan hesitates. Do you think he'll make you back out of the deal?"

Mariette shook her head. "I do not know. He just asked if I still thought it was a good idea to spend that much. I told him that we agreed to pay cash for the business, and he turned a little pale."

Ella looked at her. "I hate to ask this, but you have the money, right?"

"Right, we have the money. It is most of our savings but if Gina is right, we will start making it back almost immediately."

"If Gina is right," said Ella, "I'm nervous about that. If the business is so great, why is she looking to sell it? Why now? What's her hurry?"

Monday couldn't come soon enough for Ella. She was anxious to sit down with Dan and Mariette and Nathan to see if they could come to an agreement about buying the cleaning business. They had been kicking the idea around for weeks and now they were finally going to get together and hash out the numbers. Ella had every intention of sitting down with the balance sheets that they had gotten from Gina and putting them on a spreadsheet, but she had not had the time. Maybe if Dan had to work on Sunday, she would have the time. He had been less angry about the idea since talking to Leo in the bar that night he stormed out. Knowing that Jack Slater was never going to sell his dive shop to Dan or to anybody had made him think of how else he could get into the business. He had sat for two nights making lists of things that he would do different if he was the owner of the Dive Inn. They went over the lists together and pared it down to a manageable number of items to talk to Babs about. He had not gotten up the nerve to sit down with Babs yet, but Ella encouraged him to find the time and do it.

Ella decided to make stew for Monday supper. That way she could put it into the slow cooker and not have to run around like crazy when she got home from work. She was lucky to find small red potatoes, carrots, and onions at La Portuguesa market and there were some nice-looking beef cubes at More For Less that week.

Dan did have to work on Sunday so she sat at the computer and compiled the balance sheets into a spreadsheet document so that they could easily compare expenses and profits.

On Monday morning before work, she dredged the beef cubes in flour seasoned with salt and pepper and browned them in the fry pan before putting them into the slow cooker. She wished she had found some celery but there was none in the produce department or at La Portuguesa, so she sprinkled in a little celery seed and put in the last bay leaf from the plant she had to leave behind when they moved to the island. She made sure to remind Dan that the slow cooker needed to stay plugged in so that their supper would cook all day. Dan tended to unplug any small appliance before he left the house. He said that once when he was a kid his neighbor's house had caught on fire because a faulty toaster was left plugged in. He wasn't taking any chances.

"Are you sure that this is safe?" he said, his hand hovering over the plug.

"Yes, leave it alone. I used one all the time at home. If you unplug it, we won't have any supper to serve to Mariette and Nathan. All we will have is the salad they are bringing, the rolls I bought at the bakery, and the homemade chocolate pudding I fixed for dessert."

Dan turned to look at her, his eyes shining. "You made homemade chocolate pudding? Did you make extra?"

She chuckled at his eagerness. "Yes, greedy gut, I made the recipe that serves six so there should be some left for you to have tomorrow night."

He rubbed his hands together. "Or for a midnight snack after they leave tonight."

"Tomorrow night. And you had better save some so that I get another serving too."

He put on a sad face. "Oh, all right. I promise to share the leftovers with you."

She kissed his cheek. "Thank you."

Dan made sure that Cyril the Swiss dive instructor was assigned to lead the afternoon boat dive so he would have a chance to talk to Babs about his ideas. He had thoughts about how to rearrange gear storage to make it easier to fit divers when they rented gear, about where to put the tank racks to make it easier for shore divers to pick up tanks without having to weave their way through the whole courtyard around the table and all the loitering divers. His big idea was to offer certain specialty courses at reduced cost to people who had booked a week's worth of boat dives.

"Charge them for the certification card and maybe an extra fifty bucks and Cyril or I can do the certification dives on the regular boat dives like I did with the last Underwater Naturalist class," he said. "We don't get enough people doing specialties. There are easy ones that don't have a lot of book work that goes along with them, like Boat Diver or Night Diver, that would be easy to tack on to our regular weekly dives."

Babs started to say something, but Dan interrupted her. "I know that we only offer night dives twice a week if there is demand, but the first dive of the Night Diver certification is a site familiarization dive and that is done in daylight. A quick beach dive at Playa Chachacha across the street takes care of that requirement."

"That would mean that one of you would have to lead that dive."

Dan nodded. "Yes, that's true, but it doesn't have to be a long dive. It can be sort of in and out because you don't go deeper than thirty-five feet on a night dive so we would just go to the drop off and then turn around. Easy."

Babs looked at him. "That is good thinking. Boat Diver would be even easier because people are on the boat already, they would just have to do the little bit of reading and take the quiz and that would take care of the class work."

"A little lecture, a little question and answer on the dive boat and that one is in the bag."

Babs looked at the list that he had handed to her. "I think we can get Reg to fix up a tank rack in that niche opposite the rinse tank and you and he can talk over hanging pipes in the gear storage area so we can organize it a little better." She smiled at him. "These are good ideas, Dan. Have you thought any more about buying a boat?"

Dan leaned back and folded his arms. "We're meeting with Mariette and Nathan tonight to go over the numbers of investing in the cleaning business. If we invest in that we said that we'll consider spending some of our savings on a dive boat."

He remembered what Leo had said about everyone on the island knowing pretty much everyone else's business.

"Have you heard why Gina and Playa Palms Rental is

selling that cleaning division off? It almost sounds too good to be true if the numbers Gina gave Ella are right."

Babs started to shuffle papers on her desk. "I heard that Gina is expecting and thinks that will be too much for her to do with another child to manage. A lot of the resorts use her services for their cottages and condos because they do not have to pay employee taxes like insurance for the cleaners. That is not a small concern, it is big business for the island. It sounds like a good opportunity for you to get into."

"I hope we're not biting off more than we can chew," Dan said.

By now Ella and Mariette were like a well-oiled machine. They took turns doing the bedrooms and the laundry and got through the houses more efficiently than when they worked separately.

"I cannot wait until we're working for ourselves," Mariette said.

"Oh," said Ella, "is Nathan coming over to the idea that this might be a good plan?"

"He is not as against it as he was the other day. I am hoping that the numbers convince him that this is a safe investment."

"Nothing is a safe investment," Ella said, "but it looks like a stable business, so I'm hoping the purchase works out."

She swept all the sand from the kitchen and living room into a pile that she picked up with a dustpan and dumped back on the beach.

"Why people don't wipe the sand off their feet before they come into the house I don't know. Do they do the same thing at home?"

Mariette said, "It is a rental. People do not take care of a rental like they do their own things."

"I'll bet that they are all slobs at home too. Especially the young people, they're the worst. Remember that house with every dish and glass, sheet, and towel dirty, and spread out all over the place? I thought we would never get it clean."

"That was one for the books."

Ella opened the freezer and called Mariette into the kitchen. "There is ice cream in here and enough for two. Grab a spoon."

The two friends stood side by side dipping their spoons into the carton of Lover's Ice cream.

"Mm, honey almond frozen yogurt," said Mariette, "I have never tried this one before. It is good."

"Mm-hmm, it's one of my favorites," Ella said, "next to mango sorbet. And coconut. And chocolate. I guess you could say that every flavor of ice cream and frozen yogurt is my favorite, except mint. I don't like mint."

"Oh, I like mint. I will have your share. You can have my share of coconut. I cannot abide coconut; all those little pieces get stuck in my teeth."

Ella's spoon dipped into the carton. "Deal."

They cleaned the afternoon house as quickly as possible so that they would both have time to go home and shower before meeting again at Dan and Ella's house for supper.

"What are you making for supper?" Mariette said.

"Just some beef stew in the slow cooker. I got some rolls at the bakery and made chocolate pudding for dessert. Dan is in charge of the drinks. I think he got a bottle of red wine and a six pack of beer. I hope that's all right."

"That sounds perfect. I like a good stew."

"Me too, even though it really is not stew weather. I always think of stew as a winter dish."

"I am sure it will be delicious."

They finished cleaning the afternoon house and went their separate ways, agreeing to meet again at Dan and Ella's place around six-thirty. Ella drove by the Dive Inn to pick up Dan and save him the bike ride home. He left his bike locked to the inside of the perimeter fence in the courtyard and slumped in the passenger seat.

"What a day," he said.

"Yeah? What happened to make it a day?"

Dan pulled his seat belt around and buckled it. "The morning boat dives were full of a group from a shop in Indiana or Illinois, I forget which one. They had just finished their Open Water certification dives and are on their first dive trip. I'm not impressed with their Instructor. They all had difficulty setting up their gear and were all over the place in the water. Up, down, flying to the surface then crashing into the sand. I was glad that we went to Mi Dushi on Klein Bonaire where the mooring is shallow and in the sand flats, otherwise they would have broken half of the reef before getting themselves under control."

Ella navigated around a car waiting to turn into the airport. "That sounds like a real adventure. Did you have a Divemaster?"

Dan nodded. "Yes, Samuel was there, and we were both trying to watch everyone and keep everyone together. I was glad when the first dive was over. We went to Bari's Reef for the second dive because there is a lot of sand around the reef patches to minimize the damage. Plus, there are all those big orange barrel sponges that fish hover in to catch people's eyes. It was tiring to the max. How was your day?"

She turned off the shore road onto their street. "Good. Neither house was trashed so we could make good time getting things cleaned. Both times it was the laundry that slowed us down but we managed to get out early so we can get home and get cleaned up before they come over for supper." She pulled up in front of their apartment and made sure to pull completely off the street once Dan got out of the passenger door. "That way Nathan can park alongside and won't block the street."

"Good thinking."

Dan got first dibs on the shower since Ella wanted to check on the stew and set the table. She had bought some crackers and sliced up some gouda and set out olives and pickles for appetizers. She covered the plate with the cheese and the bowls with plastic wrap and stuck them into the fridge. She made sure that they had enough beer in the fridge too.

Dan was quick out of the shower and Ella ducked in right after him.

"Hey, you're steaming up the mirror," he said, "how can a man shave like this?" Then he grabbed a towel and wiped the mirror.

"Shaving at night?" she said, "You must want to impress them."

He peeked around the shower curtain and waggled his eyebrows. "They are not who I want to impress."

"I see," she said and went back to shaving her legs. Soon enough they were both dried off and dressed.

Dan said, "Did you get a chance to put all of Gina's info on a spreadsheet?"

She nodded. "I did."

"And how does it look?"

"Not bad. I have copies for us all to go over after we eat. There's a lot to talk about."

Mariette and Nathan arrived right on time. Mariette carried a bowl of salad and bottle of dressing. She and Ella went into the kitchen while Dan took drink orders. Nathan had a beer while the women wanted wine. Dan lit a mosquito coil so they could sit out on the patio and not be eaten alive by the little no-see-ums that were most active right after sundown. They asked Nathan how things were at the airport and Dan talked about his boat of novice divers and how scattered and awkward they all were.

"All except one couple who had their buoyancy well settled. They held hands and swam along like they had been diving for a long time. I complimented them on their skills, and they said that they had done a Discover Scuba at a resort in the Bahamas, so they had done a few dives there with an Instructor who helped them with their buoyancy. It really shows when people have a conscientious Instructor."

Nathan talked about a similar group of passengers who were on a trip together and he was sure that this was their first time in a foreign country.

"They all had too much baggage and kept looking for skycaps to haul it around to the rental car kiosks for them. I was glad to be at the check in desk rather than at baggage security that day."

"I wonder if they are the same people," Ella said.

Dan laughed. "I wouldn't be surprised."

Nathan asked Mariette how their day had been.

"Not bad," she said, "Ella found a half carton of Lover's honey almond frozen yogurt that we had to share, or it would have gone to waste."

They all laughed. Everyone had been nibbling at the appetizers for a while when Ella suggested that they adjourn to the kitchen table for supper. She ladled the stew into soup plates that she found at the Eastern Store, she passed around Mariette's salad for which there were little salad bowls at each place, and set a basket of rolls in the middle of the table. Dan refilled the wine glasses and brought Nathan another beer. Everyone exclaimed over the stew. It was meaty and full of vegetables. They all sopped up the gravy with the rolls.

"Save room for pudding," Ella said, and everyone protested that they were full. "Then how about we save dessert for after we talk about buying the cleaning business."

The suggestion was met with agreement all around. Nathan stood up and insisted that he and Dan would clear the table and put the food away while the ladies finished their wine. Ella could see that Dan would never have thought of doing that and was surprised at the idea, but he got out a container for the leftover stew and bagged the rolls.

Once everything was put away, the tablecloth removed, and the table was wiped off Ella brought out the spreadsheets and Gina's balance sheets. She gave everyone a pencil or pen and a couple sheets of computer paper for note taking. She passed out the spreadsheets.

"I spent some time on Sunday organizing Gina's information on a single sheet. I thought one month's numbers would be a good place to start our discussion." She paused. "I'll give you a couple minutes to skim the sheets so that you have some idea where we are before we start."

She waited while everyone shuffled through the pages and mumbled as they read down the columns.

"At first," she said, "Gina only showed us her profit sheets, how much income there is each month, but we made sure to get her expense sheets too." She pointed to the first column. "This is her office rent expense. I figure we won't need that, at least not at first. We can run the business out of our houses or one of our houses until we get an idea of how things are going."

Mariette nodded. "That is a good idea, but I wonder where we will keep the cleaning supplies. Gina has that closet of supplies that everyone uses. Have you thought about where we would keep those things?"

Ella looked at her. "I did wonder if there was a closet in your house that could be used for the supplies. We don't have an extra closet in the apartment."

Nathan nodded. "We could maybe clean out that closet by the back door, the one with all of the junk in it, and use that."

"Good idea," Mariette said.

Dan looked at the pages in front of him. "How many people are employed by her?"

"Seventeen," Ella said. "We need to find out if they are all paid the same wage or if Gina had some sliding scale. I can't imagine that she has nineteen people, including us, working full time."

Mariette said, "I think some of them work exclusively at certain resorts."

"Oh, that makes sense," said Ella, "That's a question we need to ask."

The discussion went on for another hour or so as each of them worked through the information in front of them. Ella was the one with the most business experience and she emerged as the one everyone turned to for answers.

"I think that ten thousand dollars cash is a fair price for the business. I worked out that during the season she takes in about that amount in a month. Of course, expenses and wages have to come out of that, but it's a good indicator of the health of the business."

They all agreed to study the spreadsheets and meet again in a few days to discuss the possibility of making the investment.

As they all gathered the papers Dan said, "Anyone like coffee?" Everyone voiced their assent, and he got up to make a pot.

"Use the Mt. Meru coffee," Ella said.

"I meant to," he said with a smile.

She got up and got out some Pyrex glass bowls to serve the chocolate pudding in. "I have whipped cream if anyone is interested." She brandished a can of Redi Whip.

"Oh, I will have some," Nathan said.

"Me too," said Mariette and Dan in unison.

"Whipped cream for everyone," Ella said, and she squirted a rosette of the creamy white stuff onto each serving.

By then the coffee was done brewing and Dan handed around mugs of coffee. "Sorry we don't have cups and saucers," he said, "but we do have a cream pitcher for milk if you take it. Anyone need sugar?"

No one used milk or sugar in their coffee so Dan sat back down. Ella passed around spoons and handed everyone a little bowl of pudding. She watched Mariette and Nathan take their first bite.

"Mm, this is amazing," said Mariette. "What brand is it?"

Ella smiled. "Thank you. It is not a brand it is homemade."

"You mean you made pudding from scratch? How do you know how to do that?"

"My mom used to make it for special occasions. It is a simple recipe, the hard part is stirring the whole time, so it doesn't scorch in the pan."

"It is delicious and rich. No wonder you serve a small bowl. I do not think that I could eat more than this."

Ella looked across the table at Dan. "Oh, I know someone

who can eat a lot more of it." Soon the pudding was just a memory, and the coffee mugs were empty.

"Time to go," Nathan said. "We all have to be at work in the morning."

They agreed to meet again in a week to give them time to go over the information and would make the decision then.

CHAPTER 14

Dan picked up the clipboard in the dive shop the next morning and ran his hand over his face. That same group of new divers was on the boat for the two morning dives. He heard their excited voices out in the courtyard and knew it would be an interesting day. He stepped out of the shop and voices hailed him.

"Dan!"

"Good morning, Dan."

"it's Dan the Man!"

He ducked his head and smiled at their enthusiasm. "Good morning," he said. "Everyone have their gear organized and ready to haul onto the dive boat?"

That question started people scurrying around to get their gear set up. Dan kept an eagle eye on them to make sure that they were setting things up right. He stopped one diver who was installing his regulator before his buoyancy control device.

"Your BCD goes on first," he reminded him.

"Oh, yeah, thanks. I'm a little excited to get diving again."

"Just take your time. The boat isn't leaving yet."

Samuel had already hauled his gear down to the boat and came back for Dan's gear.

"Oh, thanks, Samuel, but I can carry my own."

"That is okay, Dan. I have to take the extra weights down; I might as well take your SCUBA unit at the same time but do not forget your fins and mask."

"Right."

Dan was kept busy checking everyone's gear setup and lifting them onto the divers' backs for the short walk down the dock and onto the dive boat. One of the women stood with her hands on her hips. She didn't look happy. Dan walked over to her.

"Is there a problem?"

"Yes. I don't see why I have to carry that heavy equipment down the dock to the boat when there is that nice native man carrying your gear. Can't he carry mine too?"

Dan took a deep breath.

"Samuel did me a favor today so that I have time to make sure all the inexperienced divers on the boat have their gear set up correctly. He's not a porter or a bellhop, he's the Divemaster responsible for the safety of all the divers on the boat. Here, let's take the weight pockets out of your buoyancy control device. That will make it easier to carry. You can come back for your weights, fins, mask, and snorkel."

She didn't move to slip her arms into the vest's armholes. "Bob didn't make me set up my gear or carry it to the pool on my back. He set it into the water for me to get into." Dan set her SCUBA unit back on the ground.

"Here at Dive Inn, we expect our able-bodied divers to be self-sufficient. Do you have a disability that would prevent you from carrying your gear? I don't remember seeing it on your paperwork."

She shifted from foot to foot. "Well, no, but I don't think that I am strong enough to carry that all the way to the boat."

"I am confident that you're strong enough. I can tell that you work out at the gym, don't you?"

"I like to keep toned."

Dan lifted her SCUBA unit again and held it for her. "Slip this on and buckle it up. Walk a little hunched forward like you see the others doing and you'll make it. I have confidence in you."

She grumbled but turned around and slid her arms into the vest. Dan held the weight of the tank while she fumbled with the cummerbund and belt to secure it on her back.

"Now tighten the shoulder straps and you'll be able to walk down there easily. Samuel will help you get on board and guide you to your seat. You'll have to come back for your second tank too."

She straightened up and nearly overbalanced. "What?"

"You're planning to do two dives, right? You'll need that second tank then. Everyone carries their own tanks to the boat and away from the boat. Didn't you carry your tanks yesterday?"

She shook her head. "No, one of the guys carried them for me but he's not feeling well this morning, so he's going on the afternoon boat."

One of the other men came back for his second tank and said, "I'll carry your second tank, Sue. You're using these smaller ones, right?" He pulled two blue tanks from the rack, one tall and one shorter, and started carrying them across the street and down the dock to the boat. "Come on," he said over his shoulder, "let's get going. I want to dive."

She sighed and started after him. "I'll be back for my weights and fins and stuff."

Dan said, "I won't let you forget."

He grabbed his own dive bag with his fins, mask, snorkel, and chamois quick dry towel to take onto the boat. He tucked the clipboard under his arm and left the courtyard. Before he got to the boat Sue came hurrying past on her way to get the rest of her gear. When Dan was sure that everyone had all their dive equipment, he told Captain Bill and Samuel that they could shove off. Captain Bill said that he was hoping to stop at Forest for the first dive, but they were too late to get to the mooring. Someone was already there. They ended up two sites over at Munk's Haven. Dan was just as happy. The mooring was in twenty feet of water in the sand flats so again the divers had some room to get control of their buoyancy. He called for everyone's attention for the briefing.

"The site we're on is called Munk's Haven. You have to watch for currents and keep track of your depth. The site bottoms out at one hundred ten feet but I ask that you stay above one hundred feet for the dive. It's possible to see turtles at this site so keep your eyes peeled for one. Samuel will get in first and meet you at the mooring line for your descent. Use the mooring line to keep from crashing into the sand if you can avoid it. Remember to put little spurts of air into your buoyancy control vests as you descend. Be back on the boat with no less than five hundred psi in your tank. Pay attention to your depth and your air consumption. When everyone is in the water, I will lead a little circuit of the reef and then let you have time to explore at the top of the drop off. And don't neglect your three-minute safety stop at fifteen feet. Okay?"

There were nods all around.

"Then let's go diving."

There was a lot of activity on the boat. People struggled into their wetsuits and then slipped into their SCUBA units. Captain Bill helped Samuel into the water and then posted himself at one of the side entries on the boat to help the rest of the divers. Dan was at the other entry to do the same. They held tank valves to steady the divers as they put on their fins, checked to make sure that the air was turned on, and made sure that one diver cleared the area before the next one stepped off the boat and into the water. Sue, the reluctant gear carrier, was the last to come to Dan for help into the water.

"Which one is your buddy?" he said.

"I don't have one, I just tag along with another team."

"You can be my buddy if you'd like. I promise to swim slowly so that you can see the fish."

She gave him a small smile. "I'd like that. Thanks."

She put on her mask and got ready to get into the water.

Dan said, "I'll meet you at the mooring in just a minute."

She nodded, put her regulator in her mouth, and stepped off the boat. Dan slipped into his gear, put his mask around his neck, and went to the side of the boat where Captain Bill steadied him while he put on his fins and settled his mask on his face.

When he got to Sue, he said, "Ready?"

Her eyes were as big as saucers as she looked at him through her mask.

"Take a deep breath and let it out. Let's go."

He raised his inflate hose and purged the air from his

buoyancy control device and watched Sue do the same. As they descended under the surface he tipped over onto his stomach and started putting little spurts of air into his vest to slow his descent. Sue copied him and kept pace with him. They stopped about six feet from the sand bottom. He gave her a big okay sign and looked around to see the rest of the group hovering as best they could, waiting for him to lead the dive. He motioned for Sue to come stay by his side and turned into the slight current to begin the dive. They swam slowly down the slope away from the mooring, a pair of good size Tiger Groupers swimming away before them. Dan pointed out a big Green Moray Eel as they passed its hiding place in a niche in the reef. He turned around to make sure that the group was following, that he wasn't swimming too fast, and was surprised to see that Sue had turned around and was swimming backwards too. It made him laugh which sent a cloud of bubbles from his regulator.

All along the reef there were purple sea fans waving in the current and golden fuzzy sea rods waving like wheat in the moving water. He heard Sue grunt and looked up to see her pointing away from the reef. There was a big Hawksbill Turtle swimming up from the depths. He stopped swimming so that everyone had a chance to see the turtle. He checked Sue's air gauge and saw that she was well under fifteen hundred psi, so it was time to turn back toward the mooring. He led the group in a wide sweeping turn that took them up to the edge of the drop off and started swimming them back toward the boat. They got to the mooring, and he motioned that they could spread out and explore keeping an eye on their depth and air. He looked around to see that Sue had stuck to his side, so he swam slowly over to the shallows and started looking around to see the small critters that live there.

He pointed out a Banded Coral Shrimp, red and white striped like a barber pole, and a baby Spotted Moray Eel. She was fascinated by a Christmas Tree Worm that sucked itself back into its hollow tubular home and then slowly emerged when they held still to watch.

As Dan and Sue swam up into shallower water Dan couldn't believe his eyes. There were two divers standing on top of the coral with their heads above water talking to each other. He swam over to them and put air into his buoyancy control device so that his head was above water, but he refrained from standing on the coral.

"What are you doing?" he said.

"Talking," one of the divers said.

"You're standing on the coral, you're killing it," Dan told them, "Get off."

"We're not hurting anything. It is just rocks," the other one said.

"It is not just rocks; it is living organisms that take decades to grow. Get your masks on and get off the coral."

It took all of Dan's self-control not to reach over, grasp them, and pull them into the deeper water. The divers took their time getting their masks settled and putting their regulators in their mouths. They put air in their buoyancy control devices and floated away from Dan into the deeper water. Dan looked at the top of the coral where they had been standing and saw the outline of a fin where there should have been coral polyps. In every briefing before every dive Dan made sure to emphasize the fragility of the coral ecosystem and that divers should keep their hands to themselves. Any touch could damage a part of the reef and the damage was cumulative. He was tempted to turn the divers in to the Marine Park authorities. Maybe they would get fined, for sure they would get a stern lecture about preserving the reef for future generations.

He settled his gear back on his shoulders and turned around to swim back to Sue, but she had swum up to him. She showed him her air gauge and it was down to five hundred psi. Time to head back to the boat. He gave her the okay sign and they swam over to the mooring for the three-minute safety stop. Dan motioned for her to barely pinch the mooring line with thumb and forefinger to avoid the stinging crinoids that grow on the line, and they stayed there for three minutes by his dive computer. He motioned up with his thumb when the time was over and she swam up, her head breaking the surface just as his did.

"That was amazing," she said. "Did you see that turtle? It was as big as one of the tires on my car."

"Bigger, I think," said Dan. "It was a good dive."

Samuel was guiding the returning divers to the stern of the boat where Captain Bill had set out the trailing line so that divers could take off their fins and get onto the boat easily.

Dan stayed by the mooring line to make sure that all the boat's divers were headed back to the surface. The last pair were the ones he had caught standing on the coral. They swam around the base of the mooring and then slowly ascended until they stopped at fifteen feet for their safety stop. Dan watched them until they had been there for three minutes then he followed them to the surface and around to the stern of the boat. He floated behind them while they removed their fins and handed them up to Captain Bill along with their weight pockets, then they climbed the boarding ladder one by one.

Dan did a final check to make sure that there were no bubble streams from divers he had missed before removing his own fins and getting onto the boat. He settled his tank into the rack at his spot on the stern and picked up his chamois towel to dry off his face and arms. Dan saw Sue sitting in her wetsuit shivering and he went over to her.

"If you peel off your wetsuit and dry off you will be warmer," he said.

"I'm too cold to take off anything," she said with a shudder.

"Trust me, getting that wet neoprene off and getting some sun on your skin will warm you up. Give it a try. Just take off the upper body part of your suit, that will help."

She didn't look convinced, but she stood up and turned around to unzip her suit and take it off. She grabbed her towel and dried off her shoulders and arms.

"Hey, I feel warmer already," she said.

"Told you."

Dan turned away and went around to make sure that they had all enjoyed their dives. He called the roll from the clipboard just to double check that they were not leaving someone on the site before giving Samuel and Captain Bill the signal to unhook from the mooring and head back to the dock. The two men who Dan had chased from the coral head were sullen and silent. Dan left them alone but resolved to speak to them when they got to the dive shop. He didn't want to embarrass them in front of the others, but he also wanted to impress upon them the importance of staying off the coral and not touching the delicate flora and fauna underwater.

When they got to the dock and the boat was tied up, he made sure that everyone knew that they were responsible for carrying their tanks up to the fill station and reminded them to put the dust cap on their regulator before dunking it in the rinse tank. There were a few grumbles about having to carry the tanks back up to the shop but most of the people did so without fussing about it. Even Sue picked up her tanks and started the trek back to the shop. Dan was pleased to see that she had gotten over her need to be waited on. He was walking back down to the boat to check that all the gear was removed and to get his own duffel bag when he heard his name called.

"Dan!" He turned around to see Sue coming toward him.

"Thanks for diving with me," Sue said, "I don't think I would have seen half as much if I had not been with you. Everyone swims too fast for me to have time to look at things. You swam slowly enough for me to see stuff. Thanks."

"I am glad you enjoyed the dives. My first instructor taught us to swim slowly and look in every hole and cranny. It stuck with me."

They got onto the boat, and each retrieved their dive bag.

"Can I buy you a drink later?" Sue said.

Dan shook his head. "Thanks for the offer but no. We're having dinner guests and I need to get home to help."

They had the dinner guests the night before, but he

figured that was a good easy excuse to get out of going out for a drink with another single lady. Maybe he and Ella would go down to Karel's Beach Bar some other night to meet his divers but tonight he just wanted to go home and be quiet. It had been a stressful week already and it was only Tuesday.

CHAPTER 15

He had been thinking hard about whether they should invest in the cleaning business, whether they should buy a dive boat, or hold out to invest in a dive operation of their own. Right now, it looked as if owning a dive shop and operation was turning into a pipe dream. There were just too many dive operations on Bonaire for someone starting out to get a foot in the door. Damn that Jack Slater for building his hopes up for a year but he was glad to have met Leo who set him straight on the matter.

He had not been brave enough to approach Babs about investing in the Dive Inn. She asked him if he was still thinking of buying a boat so maybe that was her hint that she was open to him buying his way into the business. He knew that her daughter was getting to be high school age and she would need to go back to the Netherlands for secondary school. The schools on the island were not up to the standards of Holland or the States so a lot of expats sent their children back home for high school.

All of this was running through Dan's mind as he signed logbooks and pointed out the pictures of the hawksbill turtle in the Reef Creatures ID book.

He took time to talk to the two men who had been standing on the coral.

"Look," he said, "I am sorry that I yelled at you, but I thought I had made it clear in my briefing that Bonaire has a no-touch policy regarding reefs and marine life."

The men had the grace to look abashed.

"Yeah, you might have said something about not touching

things," one of them said.

The other one spread out his hands. "But that just looked like an old black rock. We didn't know that we could hurt something that looked dead by standing on it."

"I know that things look dead," Dan said, "but all sorts of creatures live in and on those dead looking rocks. All of Bonaire underwater from two hundred feet deep to the high tide line is a marine park and protected from being handled."

"What about those native guys who come in with fish to sell?"

Dan scratched his head. "They have permits to catch fish in certain areas, but they are taught the best practices to preserve the fishery and the reefs. People come to Bonaire for the healthy reefs and the abundant fish life. It's why you came, isn't it?"

They both looked at their feet. "Yeah, it's why we came."

Dan took pity on them and stopped lecturing. "Just be more careful. You can go to the surface to talk, just don't stand on anything while you do it, okay?"

They looked at him. "Okay."

Babs called him into the office. "I am going to Windsock Deli. Can I bring you something?"

He dug his wallet out of the dry bag in the corner. "I would love a crab salad sub." He handed her some money.

She waved it away. "My treat today. Let's eat together and talk about some of the other suggestions that were on your list."

Babs was gone for about half an hour in which time the dive shop courtyard cleared out. Divers rinsed and hung their rental or personal gear and took off to find lunch and maybe have a snooze before their afternoon dives. Many of the morning divers were already signed up for the afternoon dives. Dan had talked to the novice divers about the possibility of taking Advanced Open Water Diver course to expand their skills. A couple of them were especially intrigued by the idea of doing a night dive but so far no one had signed up. This week it was Cyril's turn to lead the Thursday evening night dive. Dan was relieved that he had the night off. Maybe he and Ella would go out with friends or meet the divers at Karel's Beach Bar for a few drinks. It had been quite a long time since they had gone out for fun. Now that the prospect of buying into Jack Slater's dive shop was lost, he felt like they could go out and spend some money. They should maybe go to Mona Lisa Restaurant for that steak he had been hankering for. If there wasn't a cruise ship in port on Thursday night, he would invite Ella to go out to dinner.

All the while he was thinking about that steak dinner, he was filling tanks and getting rental gear hung and organized by size. It was a new system he had instituted since his last talk with Babs, and it seemed to be working well. Having things in size order made it a lot easier to find gear when someone needed a particular size. He couldn't figure out why no one had organized it before.

Babs came back with a big bag of goodies from the Windsock Deli. She handed out salads and sandwiches to Reg, Samuel, Cyril, and Cecile and then invited Dan into her office to eat with her.

"Business," she said when eyebrows were raised.

Dan chuckled. "I bet they think I'm being called on the carpet for some offense."

"Probably," Babs said, "but it is more than that, isn't it?"

Dan nearly choked on a bite of sandwich. "Is it?"

"You know it is. You were the one who came to me with the idea of buying a boat and chartering it to me as a second boat on busy days. Have you changed your mind?"

Dan took a drink of his soda. "No, I haven't changed my mind. We met with our friends last night and went over the numbers and buying the cleaning business looks possible. I think it will be more work than Ella thinks it will be, but I also think it will make money faster than being employed by the business did."

"Have you thought about buying into a dive shop instead of owning your own outright?"

Dan nodded. "I did. Ella and I talked about it, and we think that isn't a bad idea. Are you interested? I know your daughter is about ready to go back to Holland to secondary school and wondered if maybe you're thinking of scaling back a bit."

Babs finished her salad and took a drink. "I am. That is very perceptive of you."

"Ella thought of it, I didn't."

"At any rate, I am considering the idea of taking on a partner, an investor to take some of the day-to-day load off so that I am free to go back to Europe if Amy needs me or just to visit family and friends. I have been running this business alone for a long time now. I could use a break and I wonder if you're the person to give me that break."

"What kind of money are you talking about? Buying a dive boat and the cleaning business would pretty much deplete our savings unless you want to buy the boat and have me invest in the business directly."

She smiled. "Oh, you heard that I have been looking at boats, have you?"

"It's a small island. Not much happens that doesn't get spread around."

"I heard you spent some time with Leo at Julio's Bar last week. Leo's cousin is the boat dealer so I assume that is where you got your information."

"Exactly right. Was it supposed to be a secret?"

She shook her head. "Not really. As you say, it is a small island, it is hard to keep secrets. So, what do you think?"

Dan finished his sandwich and cleared his mouth with a swig of soda. "I think that first we need to settle on whether we're buying the cleaning business."

"It sounds like a good investment to me. Gina is a good businesswoman, not given to overstating her prospects."

"That's good to know. I think we'll go ahead. Ella and Mariette have a good handle on things and work well together."

"Mariette used to work here, you know."

"No, I didn't know that."

"Yes, she worked in the shop when she first came to the

island, before she met Nathan and got married."

"It's a small world. A small island."

"It is indeed. Once you have that ironed out why don't you and Ella come to meet with me, and we can discuss the possibilities. Raul has a good-looking boat in his yard that would make a good second dive boat. You should go look at it and then we can talk."

He wadded up the paper his sandwich was wrapped in and put it into the paper bag it came in. He put the trash in the garbage can beside the door and stood up, taking his soda can with him.

"Time to get ready for the afternoon dives," he said.

"Back to work." Babs picked up her glasses and turned to the files on her desk. "Oh, Dan, any nibbles on the specialty courses yet this week?"

"No but I have high hopes that a couple of the morning divers will decide to do Advanced Open Water Diver so that they can do the night dive on Thursday."

His hopes proved prophetic when the pair of divers he had chastised for standing on the coral came to him before the afternoon dives expressing interest in doing Advanced Open Water. "What do we have to do so we can go on a night dive?"

Dan ushered them into the office and showed them the textbook for the course. It was thicker than the divers expected.

"You don't need to read it all," he assured them. "Only the sections pertaining to the dives you will do this week." He flipped to the contents page. "You've already done a Boat dive, so you just need to read that one and do the quiz at the end. Then read Night Diver, Underwater Navigation, Buoyancy Control, and one more."

"How about Underwater Photographer?" said the taller of the two. "I have an underwater camera that I am afraid to take into the water. You could show me how to use it."

"Great idea. So read that chapter. I'll give you some paper to write the quiz answers on so I can put it into your student folder. Do you have your camera with you?"

"Yes, it's in my bag."

Dan closed the textbook.

"Get it out and let's look at it and then we can do a little compass practice before the dives and get two of the dives done this afternoon."

The men looked a lot happier than they had after the morning dives. They paid Cecile for their courses, took their textbooks, and went out into the courtyard for their camera.

"We only have one camera between us. Is it okay if we share?"

"Perfectly fine," said Dan. "Now let's see how this thing works."

In just a few minutes he had shown the divers how to make sure that the O-ring around the door of the housing was free of sand.

"Sand grains are going to be the biggest cause of leaks," Dan said, using a clean paper towel to wipe the O-ring clean of excess silicone lubricant. "Too much silicone attracts sand."

He went over the features of the camera with the men and left them for a few minutes to get the rest of the divers started getting their gear organized for the dives.

"We'll board the boat in about half an hour," he announced, "so you can start carrying your tanks down and getting them settled in the racks. Captain Bill will direct you."

He went back to the men to teach them the rudiments of compass navigation. "The hardest thing I had to learn in Advanced Open Water was to trust my compass underwater. We will do a couple exercises here on land before you have to do it underwater. Each of you grab a towel."

He had them stand in a clear area, sight on a course, drape a towel over their heads, and have them walk a straight line following only the compass. The first time the tall one walked straight into the table and the shorter one angled off into the fence.

"I told you that it wasn't as easy as it seems. Make sure that you're holding your compass flat so that it is floating and take your time."

He set them up to try again. This time two or three of the other divers played along trying to learn how to use a compass. Dan knew that teaching the two men while others watched was an effective way to lure other divers into taking Advanced Open Water too.

"How do we get to take part in this?" one of the others asked.

"Sign up in the office," Dan said, "I'll be glad to teach anyone who wants to learn."

He was amazed to see four or five of the others hurry into the shop to sign up. Dan went to talk to Samuel about splitting the group into Advanced Open Water students and just divers. It promised to be a productive day.

Dan got the Advanced Open Water students started learning to use their compass and reading about navigation in the textbook while he went down to the dock to confer with Captain Bill.

"I would like to go to a site with a bit of current for the first dive this afternoon," Dan said. "I have Advanced Open Water students so a drift dive would be perfect."

Captain Bill nodded. He picked up the binoculars and sighted out to Klein Bonaire.

"So far there is not a boat at Southwest Corner. There is usually a little current there even on the calmest days. I will try for that one."

"Great. Thanks, Bill."

When he got back to the courtyard, he was pleased to see at least half of the divers walking a compass course with towels over their heads. The other divers were giggling at how silly they looked but they were also fiddling with their compasses and Dan knew that they would all pay more attention to their gauges on today's dives than they usually did.

"Okay, divers, get your gear organized and on the boat. Captain Bill has a nice site picked out for us and we should be on the move, so no one gets there before we do."

That announcement started everyone moving. The Advanced Open Water students put their towels into their bags and started down to the boat. Everyone else followed them. Dan paused to enjoy the sudden silence as the last of the chattering horde crossed the road to the dock. He hadn't realized how much noise six people pacing back and forth on the gravel courtyard made.

Babs caught his eye and said, "Good job getting people signed up for specialty dives."

"If I'm lucky some of them will decide to do more than just Advanced Open Water. Thanks. See you later."

He grabbed his duffel and followed the divers to the boat. Because this was a boat full of new divers, he went around to double check that all of them had their gear set up correctly. One person had their regulator on upside down and was trying to stretch the hoses to fit. Dan unscrewed it from the tank, turned it over, and put it back on.

"This will work better," he said.

"I'm used to standing behind my tank when I set up my gear, not in front of it like we are on the boat," said the diver.

"I suspected as much," Dan said. "Everyone got their weights?" he asked.

"Oh, no," said one of the divers. "I will be right back."

Dan held up a weight belt. "No need to run, I saw this and brought it along."

"Thanks."

"You're welcome."

By that time Samuel had untied the boat from the moorings and shoved them away from the dock. Since they had such a short ride to the dive site, Dan started the briefing right away.

"This afternoon we're going to Southwest Corner on Klein Bonaire. It is next to where we dove this morning, but has more reliable currents and I thought that you Advanced Open Water students might enjoy a drift dive. Instead of beginning to dive into the current we're going to let it carry us along, let the water do the work. The biggest tip I can give you is if you feel like you're going too fast, you can turn perpendicular to the current, letting the current push against the side of your body, so that you are less hydrodynamic and will move more slowly. Doing that will make it easier to see what is happening on the reef instead of just zipping by. If the current is strong enough don't kick, just let the water move you along. I'll lead the dive and Samuel will be at the rear of the group. Try to stay together to save him from having to chase you all over the reef."

Everyone laughed.

By now they were at the site and Samuel had snagged the mooring buoy and gotten the boat attached. He looked over the side to gauge the current and gave Dan the thumbs up that there was current at the site.

"Okay, divers, get geared up and get ready to quickly get into the water. We'll gather at the mooring buoy, and all descend together. That way we have a fighting chance of staying together."

Since this wasn't the first day of their dive trip the divers were more efficient at getting themselves ready to go. Dan got into the water first this time and swam over to the mooring buoy. He could feel the water wanting to push him away from the buoy and had to swim a little harder. He watched as pairs of divers stepped off the boat in a giant stride entry into the water and started toward him. It took a little time, but they all got into the water and gathered.

"Everyone, get ready to descend," he said once they were all there.

Hands lifted inflator hoses and he could hear the whoosh of escaping air as they sank under the surface of the ocean. Dan felt the push of the current as he got lower under the water and watched people's eyes widen as they realized the power of the sea. He watched divers check their gauges to make sure that they had not sunk too deep. Dan rolled over on his stomach and steered the group along the reef in a downward angle, the current getting stronger at about sixty feet. He kept them at that depth to let them feel the push and figure out how to let the water be in charge of their speed and movement. A couple of the divers turned across the current to slow down and see the fish moving around on the reef. The diver with the camera tried to stop to take a picture but ended up head down and twirling like a ballet dancer trying to stay in place. He finally gave up and settled down to enjoy the ride. As Dan started to angle the group to a shallower depth, he rolled over onto his back facing the group and held up his gauges telling them to check their air consumption. One of them signaled that they were down to twelve hundred psi so he moved the group up to thirty feet at the edge of the drop off where they would use air more slowly. The current was less up there so he could let them explore a little bit. When the first diver indicated that they were at one thousand psi Dan unfurled and inflated his safety sausage. That told Captain Bill that it was time to release the mooring and come pick up the divers as they floated in the current at the surface.

Captain Bill maneuvered the boat ahead of the group then he tossed out the trailing line so that the ascending divers could hold on, remove their fins, and pull themselves to the stern of the boat. One by one grinning divers clambered up the boarding ladders and staggered across the deck to their spots at the racks.

"That was amazing," said one of the divers.

"Yeah, it was like being part of the ocean."

"That must be what fish feel like," said another.

Dan and Samuel were last to climb onboard. Captain Bill pulled in the trailing line, so it didn't get tangled in the propellor. Dan took off his mask and slipped his SCUBA unit into the rack.

He turned to the group and said, "So, what did you think of drift diving?"

"Loved it."

"I never could have swum against that current, I would have stayed in one place the whole dive."

"Can we do that again tomorrow?"

Dan laughed. "I guess you liked it," he said.

"Can we still sign up for Advanced when we get back to

shore?" asked one of the non-students.

"Sure," Dan said, "just stop in the shop and tell Cecile that you started doing the class and she'll get you all signed up and give you the textbook so you can do the readings and quizzes. I need you to write the quiz answers on a separate sheet of paper so I can keep them in your student folders. Ask her for a couple sheets of computer paper if you don't have any paper with you."

Dan sat down and wiped himself off with his chamois towel.

"Where did you get that little towel thing?' Sue asked. "That looks a whole lot more convenient than hauling around a big beach towel."

"It is. I think there are some in the dive shop. I bought mine at home before coming here and you can get them in stateside dive and sports stores, probably online too."

One of the divers called out. "Where are we doing the second dive? It looks like we're headed back to the dock."

"We are," Dan said. "There is a broad expanse of sandy bottom there which makes doing compass work easier than trying to avoid coral heads and sea fans. There is a nice reef just past the drop off for those of you not doing Advanced. I know there is a resident octopus along there. Maybe one of you will be lucky enough to spot it."

Dan gathered his students around him once they were all in the water and set up a compass course for them to follow. He had them swim the legs of a triangle from the dock to a concrete mooring block over to the edge of the commercial pier and back.

"Remember to keep your head down and hold your compass flat so that it floats otherwise you will be way off course. Take your time and have fun."

He put his mask on and swept his regulator up and into his mouth. He lay on the bottom watching his students try their best to stay on course. Naturally, a few of them went off one way or another but they all eventually made it from the dock to the block to the pier and back.

When they were all finished, he gathered them together

again and said, "Good job, everyone. I saw that some of you had a bit of trouble keeping steady on course, but you all got it in the end. Go on up to the shop to take off your gear and don't forget that you have an empty tank and your dive bag on board the dive boat. Thanks for a fun afternoon."

There was a lot more chat and work after the afternoon dives than usual. All but one pair of the divers on the boat signed up for Advanced Open Water so Dan had a lot of people to guide through the course. He signed logbooks and answered questions about drift diving and underwater navigation. People were flush with enthusiasm for the new experiences they had and said they couldn't wait for the night dive the next night.

"We'll be diving at the same site we dove this afternoon, Playa Chachacha. The Night Dive will be a shore dive. Make sure you have a light. You can rent one if you don't own one. Speak to Cecile in the shop and she will put one on your rental gear list."

A few of the divers were crazy about the drift dive and asked if there were other sites on Bonaire where they could drift from one site to another.

"On the south shore of the island is Red Slave dive site. The water is always moving at that site, and it can be a shore dive if you're careful. The best way to do it is to take two vehicles. Park one at either Vista Blue or Atlantis so that you have a way to get back to the other truck. No one wants that long walk back in the blazing sun. Be warned it can be an advanced dive if the surf is high and the current is racing."

"Can we do it from the boat like we did today?" someone asked.

"We can but it would be the only dive of the morning because of the distance we have to travel to get there. If enough of you are interested, I'll talk with the owner and the captain and see what they say."

All of the divers in the Advanced Open Water class were eager to pursue another drift dive.

"If we do two more drift dives you will qualify for Drift Diver Specialty Certification," Dan told them.

That brought them up short and started a give and take between those eager to pursue more drift dives and those who wanted a bit more vacation on their vacation. Dan thought, this is when we could use another boat. He went to talk to Babs about diving Red Slave. Captain Bill would most likely agree to go wherever they wanted but Dan would talk to him when he got the matter discussed with Babs. When he came back out to the courtyard the divers were still debating whether they all wanted to do a drift dive again and sacrifice the second morning dive. Babs had given the go-ahead. She was pleased that Dan's idea to offer specialty courses and especially Advanced Open Water was working out so well so quickly.

"Tell you what," he said to the group, "let's do another dive on Klein Bonaire tomorrow morning and then come back to Playa Chachacha to do a Peak Performance Buoyancy dive. There's a buoyancy course laid out just south of the dock and learning how to control your buoyancy better would make it a lot safer when we dive Red Slave. What do you say?"

"That sounds like a good idea," Sue said. "I would feel better doing a more intermediate dive if I had some more experience under my belt."

There were murmurs of agreement so that was the plan.

"Spend some time this afternoon and evening getting your book work done and then you can just dive dive dive the rest of the week," Dan said.

The newly converted hardcore divers of the group cheered at that thought.

"If you do two boat dives tomorrow morning and one shore dive tomorrow afternoon, then do the night dive you will end up doing four dives in one day. That should be enough to satisfy even the most dive crazy of you. I'll talk to Cyril; he'll be diving with you in the morning because it's my night to lead the dive, so I need some surface time."

"Aw," a couple of them groaned.

"Hey, you wouldn't want your dive instructor getting bent now, would you?"

They all laughed and agreed that would be a bad thing.

"Besides, I have all this paperwork to do since nearly all of you are signed up for Advanced. I can't let the paperwork slide."

By then all of the divers had rinsed and hung their gear and started leaving to go back to their hotel which was right down the road in walking distance to Dive Inn.

"I'm doing my homework on the beach," Sue said. "I'm not going to waste this glorious sun and sand sitting indoors to study."

"Good idea," said another one of the women. "Can we join you?"

Their voices trailed off as they got farther away from the shop. Once they were all gone Dan sat down with a big sigh.

"Well, that was more than I bargained for," he said to Babs who had come out of the office to help get everyone signed up for Advanced and get their student folders filled in.

"But it is working out well," she said. "You will have almost a dozen new certifications and maybe some specialties too."

He nodded. "I should talk to Cyril about tomorrow's dives. He can put them through the Peak Performance Buoyancy course on the second dive, which will be their third Advanced dive. The Night Dive will be the fourth and then all we will have to do is maybe Underwater Naturalist for the fifth. Or if he lets them bounce down to a hundred feet on the first dive that could count as a Deep Dive. I am sure that the men will all want to do Deep. That's the macho choice. The ladies will want Naturalist, I think, that's the prettiest choice."

Babs laughed at him. "That sounds sexist to me. Some of those ladies looked pretty gung ho."

"Are you being sexist again?" came a voice from behind Dan.

"Hey, Ella," he said. "How was your day?"

She sat down on the bench next to him and pecked him on the cheek. "Oh good, you know, cleaning, sweeping, laundry. Same old, same old. How was your day?"

Dan grinned at her. "My plan to sell certifications came up

trumps today. Almost all of the novice divers in that group from Indiana, or is it Illinois, I get them confused, anyway almost all of them signed up for Advanced so I am leading specialty dives. We did a drift dive off Southwest Corner on Klein Bonaire and then came back to Playa Chachacha to do some underwater navigation."

"When is the night dive?" she said. "I might come along."

"It is tomorrow night here at Chachacha. I would appreciate another pair of eyes."

"You always put me to work."

He put his arm around her waist. "That's because you do such an excellent job. You should really get your Divemaster Certification so you can officially be my backup."

She shook her head. "I told you when I worked in the shop at home, that's my job and I don't want to do my job for free as Divemaster."

He nuzzled her ear. "It's not your job anymore. Now you're the queen of clean. Soon you'll be the boss of clean, I suspect."

"Yes, I think so. Mariette and I have been talking about nothing else. We took our lunches to eat with Gina today to learn more about the day-to-day operation of the business. I hate to say it, but it is sounding better and better, almost too good to be true. Makes me nervous."

"I know what you mean. There's a lot at stake if you decide to go ahead."

She bumped his shoulder with her head. "If *we* decide to go ahead. You have a say in this too."

"I know but you're the one in the trenches and you're the one with the head for figures."

She chuckled. "It's crazy. I always said that I was no good at math but now I can look at spreadsheets, balance sheets, and figure out a budget. You've been a good influence on me, Dan."

"You're welcome. Always glad to help a little lady."

She poked him in the ribs. "Who are you calling little lady? I am a woman."

"Hear me roar," he said.

She tickled him and said, "You go, Helen Reddy."

He pushed her hands away. "Cut it out. Let's get going. I am starved. Lunch was a long time ago. What's for supper?"

"We have that leftover beef stew and Italian bread. I could make a salad to go with it."

He gathered up all of the student folders and got up to carry them into the office. "Sounds good. I'll be ready to go in a minute."

While she waited Cecile turned out the shop lights and came out, locking the door behind her.

"Dan said you had a busy day today," Ella said to her.

"We sure did. That Dan is a good salesman."

Reg came out of the back of the repair and rental area. "You need a ride home, Cecile?"

"Today I could use a ride. I was run off my feet today with all the people in and out of the place. Thanks."

They walked off into the dusk their voices fading as they went. Dan and Babs came out of the office together.

Babs said, "Did Dan tell you about all the Advanced students he had today?"

Ella nodded. "Yes, he did. It sounds like the perfect idea for the time and the divers on the boat."

"A group of novices was just what we needed," said Dan. "And my winning personality, of course, that made it a sure thing."

All three of them laughed as Babs locked the gate across the courtyard entrance. Dan left his bike locked inside the fence and he took Ella's hand as they walked around the corner to their car.

CHAPTER 16

It wasn't there. They both stopped in their tracks and Ella looked around to make sure that she had not parked somewhere else on the street.

"Where did you park the car?" Dan said.

"Right here," said Ella, "right" she pointed at the empty parking spot, "here."

"It's gone."

"Yes, it's gone."

Ella pulled her cell phone out of her pocket and dialed 9-1-1. When it was answered she said, "I would like to report a stolen car. No, it's not a rental. No, I didn't leave the keys in it." She switched the phone to her other ear. "Can you just send someone?" She gave the dispatcher the address and hung up.

"They thought you left the keys in it?" Dan said. "You didn't, did you?"

She reached into her pocket and jingled them at him. "Nope, I never leave the keys in the car."

It wasn't long before a police car pulled up and parked where their car had been.

"You say your car was stolen?"

"Yes, it was stolen."

"Where did you leave it?"

Ella pointed. "It was right where you just parked."

He turned to look at his police car as if expecting to see their car instead.

"Did you leave the keys in the car?"

Ella jingled the keys at him. "No, I never leave the keys in the car. There are too many car thieves on the island for that."

The police officer took out his notebook and started writing. "Was the car locked?"

"No, and the windows were rolled down."

"What did you have in the car? Electronics? CDs?"

"All that is in the car are my cleaning supplies. My cleaning supplies! How am I supposed to work without my supplies? I listen to music on my phone. The radio in the car doesn't work," Ella said. Tears began to flow down her cheeks.

"What is the license number? I will call it in so that people can look out for it."

Dan remembered the number and gave it to the officer.

"You know we will find your car. Some kids probably took it for a joy ride and will abandon it out in the kunuku, out in the countryside."

Dan and Ella looked at each other. "Let's just hope that they don't wreck it. We can't afford to buy a new car right now. Not a new new car, but a different one."

The police officer closed his notebook and put it into his pocket. "I think we will find your car in a day or two, maybe without its wheels, maybe without its windows, but we will find it. Do not worry."

Ella said, "What do we do in the meantime? We need a car."

Dan looked at her. "I guess we rent one. There goes our savings, at least part of it."

The police officer was getting into his patrol car. He looked at Dan and said, "My cousin Jeremiah he has a car rental company. I can give you a ride to his place at the airport if you want."

Dan nodded. "I guess we might as well take the ride. We have no other way to get home."

So, Ella and Dan piled into the back of the police car and were driven the few miles to Flamingo Airport and its row of rental car kiosks.

"Island Rentals," the police officer said, "that is Jeremiah's company. Tell him Micah brought you, maybe he will give you a discount."

"Thanks for the ride and the recommendation," Dan said as he stepped from the car.

Ella slid over and got out behind him. "Thank you, Officer."

They turned and walked to the island Rentals window to see about getting a car for a few days. Jeremiah was happy to give them the "Micah rate" on a small four door Hyundai sedan in sun-faded blue that he kept for emergencies. It wasn't in good enough shape to be a regular rental, but it ran and would get them from home to work and back. Dan drove them home and they heated up the leftover stew for supper but neither of them were very hungry.

"Why would someone steal our old car? It is not pretty or fast, it's just an old beater that has seen better days," Dan said.

Ella looked at him. "Because they could. Because someone dared someone to do it. Because it was there when the mood struck. I picture a couple fourteen-year-olds riding around in it and laughing uproariously. I just hope they don't wreck it. We can replace the tires and the windows, but it wouldn't be worth it to do much body work, it is pretty rusty as it is."

Dan's phone rang. "It's Officer Micah," he said.

"Hello, Micah. Yes, we got a car from Jeremiah." He listened, his eyebrows raising. "You did? Already? And what kind of shape is it in?" Ella could hear talking but couldn't make out the words. "Okay, we'll meet you there." He hung up the phone.

"What did he say?"

Dan kept his eyes on his phone. "They found the car hung up on a rock on the road to Rincon."

"Is it drivable?"

"He didn't know. They're having it towed to the police station. I said we would meet them there."

Ella covered the bowl of stew and set it into the refrigerator. "Let's go."

Upon leaving they discovered that one of the headlights of the Hyundai was out. That made driving on the unlit roads of the island a challenge, but Dan was a careful driver and they made it safely to the police station. They went inside but the tow truck had not returned with their car yet, so they sat in the hot and stuffy waiting room until it arrived.

Officer Micah came out into the lobby to greet them and invited them to come back to his office.

"We think we found your car thieves," he said. "These two boys were hitchhiking on the Rincon road just toward town from where your car was wrecked. I picked them up to give them a ride and one of them broke down crying. I asked a few questions and they admitted to borrowing your car to go visit a girl."

"Borrowing? That's what they called it?" Dan was angry.

"It seems that your car looks a lot like the car of one of the boy's uncles. He thought it was a good joke to play on Uncle Stagger, but it turned out not to be Stagger's car after all."

"How did they figure that out?"

Office Micah chuckled. "The back seat full of cleaning supplies. Uncle Stagger's car would be full of beer cans and liquor bottles. By the time they figured it out they were too far out of town to turn back."

"Too far to turn back?" Ella said. "What does that mean?"

Officer Micah looked at his desk which was covered with files. "They are not experienced drivers. I think they were only good at driving straight, not turning around."

"So how did they figure to get home?"

"By thumbing," he said, "lots of people pick up hitchhikers on that road."

"They're lucky they didn't have a wreck making their way through town at the end of the day. There had to be lots of cars on the roads when they were driving," Ella said.

Officer Micah nodded. "Yes, they were lucky they did not hit anyone or get hit. Are you going to press charges?"

Dan sat up straight. "You mean we have a choice? Of course, we want to press charges. They hotwired our car and drove it across the island. I don't care that they thought it was Uncle Stagger's car, it was my car, our car and taking it is car theft." Dan's voice rose until he was nearly shouting.

"Be calm, Mr. Martinson," Officer Micah said, "there is no need to raise your voice. I merely asked the question."

Dan cleared his throat. "I'm sorry to shout. Yes, we want to press charges, don't we, Ella?"

Ella looked at him and then at Officer Micah. "How old are these boys?"

"One is fourteen and the other is fifteen. Their parents say that they are good boys overall, good students, they just did something dumb on the spur of the moment."

She looked down at her hands. "I hate the idea of this ruining their lives, but I also do not want them to get off without punishment. Is there another way to make sure that they are punished but don't have a felony police record?"

"Ella," Dan said, "are you nuts? They stole our car and drove it halfway across the island on a whim. They got it hung up on a rock and we don't know if it can be driven. What if we have a huge repair bill?"

"I was thinking about that," she said. "We're probably going to buy that cleaning business and I will need someone to take care of the outdoor work, someone to give Carlos a hand with the pools and gardens. Maybe the boys can work off the expense of car repairs for me that way."

Dan flung his arms into the air. "I can't believe that you're even thinking of hiring those boys when you know that they are dishonest thieves."

"I'm not sure that they are dishonest thieves, I think they're thoughtless boys who made a mistake." She looked at Officer Micah. "Can we talk to the boys' parents? Are they here?"

"They are here. They are in the next room with their sons, and I hazard a guess that those boys are not having an easy time of it."

"I say it again," Dan said, "are you nuts? These are proven car thieves, and you're talking about hiring them."

Ella touched his hand. "I haven't made up my mind yet. I would like us to talk to them and to their parents before we decide to press charges, that's all."

Officer Micah led them down the hall to the room where the two boys and their parents were.

Ella could tell that one of the fathers had been yelling at the boys. Their heads hung as low as they could get, and one boy had tears streaming down his cheeks. Both mothers were wiping tears from their eyes with balled up tissues. The room was stuffy, not well-cooled by the small window air conditioner. The air that it blew into the room smelled musty and made Ella think of her mom's basement at home.

"Have you come to take them away?" the father who was standing said.

Officer Micah said, "No, not just yet. These are the people whose car the boys stole. They would like to speak to you and to the boys before they decide whether to press charges or not." He introduced them. "This is Miss Ella Thomas and Mr. Dan Martinson. These are the Sandfords and the de Koops, the boys are Piko and Ned."

The police officer brought in another chair so that Ella could sit down. He leaned on the wall next to the door. Ella looked at the boys. They were so young, probably too young to shave, and they were both shaking, their knees bouncing.

"What were you thinking?" she said.

Neither boy responded.

The father on his feet nudged the nearest boy. "Speak up. The lady asked you a question."

The boy he had nudged shuffled his feet and leaned forward. "We wasn't thinking, we just did it."

The other boy chimed it. "We thought it would be funny to play a joke on Uncle Stagger."

"How did you get it started without a key?" she said.

The first boy said, "We learned from Dad, he has a garage and sometimes needs to start a car without a key. We learned from him."

The father on his feet buried his face in one hand. "Oh lord," he said, "you just made me an accessory to car theft."

"You did teach us, Dad," said the boy.

"But not so that you could go around and steal cars, knucklehead."

"What's your name?" Ella asked the boy who had been talking.

"I am Piko, Piko Sandford and he is Ned de Koop; we're cousins."

"Did you think about going to jail?"

Piko looked shocked. "No, we just wanted to play a joke on Uncle Stagger, but we got the wrong car."

"And our car looks just like your uncle's car?"

Ned nodded. "It looks some like his car. It is the same color, and he always leaves it open like you did."

Dan chimed in. "But we do not leave it open for people to steal it. That is supposed to deter thieves since there is nothing worth stealing in there, unless you want a broom and a mop."

The boys shrank from Dan's obvious anger and looked at Ella as if she would protect them.

She looked at the police officer. "How long do we have to decide about pressing charges?"

The police officer stood up straighter. "You should decide while you're here, Miss Thomas."

Ella looked at Dan and he shrugged.

"You know my thoughts," he said.

"I do not want to press charges," Ella said. "Instead, I want the boys to work for me after school and in the summer. I'm buying a cleaning business and I need some muscle. Our pool and yard man needs helpers and you boys just volunteered."

The boys looked shocked. The parents looked relieved.

"But, Dad," Piko said, "we were supposed to work for you this summer."

His father lifted his hands as if he couldn't do anything about it. "Looks like you have other plans. Unless you would rather go to jail and have a police record."

Both boys looked at him. "No," they said in unison.

Ned said, "We will work for her."

Mr. Sandford offered to take their car to his mechanic shop in Antriol and go over it to make sure the boys didn't damage it. "You have a flat tire on the right front but with any luck it is all right. No charge, of course."

Dan looked relieved that they wouldn't have to pay for car repairs even though he would rather have the boys in jail. No, that is not right, he would rather that the boys had to pay for their mistake, but he supposed that working for Ella all summer for no pay would be almost as satisfying.

"Of course," Office Micah said, "if Miss Thomas is not happy with your work she can always come in and press charges. This will not just go away like magic."

Piko and Ned looked shocked that they could still be charged even after they agreed to work for Ella. Ned looked like he wondered if this would be hanging over their heads for the rest of their lives.

Dan was quiet as they walked out of the police station and went to their rental car. They were halfway home before he said, "I can't believe that you did that."

Ella turned to look at him. "To be honest, I can't believe I did that either. I meant to go in there and see two tough guys and say, 'throw the book at them' but when I saw them, two scared boys, I just couldn't do it."

He glanced at her. "I guess now we have to buy the cleaning business, so you have some place to employ your convicts."

Ella laughed. "Yeah, look at me, I am starting my own chain gang."

Dan stopped at the Lover's Ice Cream store on their way out of town. "We need something for supper," he said.

Ella said, "We have that leftover stew."

"No, I'm buying a quart of something chocolate and when we get home, we're getting out two spoons and eating it all, right out of the carton."

Ella looked shocked.

"What," Dan said, "aren't you in the mood to eat chocolate

ice cream? I am."

"Sure," she said, "why not."

That is just what they did. Dan bought a carton of Triple Chocolate Crunch, they carried it home, and it didn't survive the night.

CHAPTER 17

Ella woke up before the alarm the next morning. How was she going to tell Mariette that she had essentially hired a pair of car thieves to work for them for the summer when they had not even bought the business yet? She slipped out from under Dan's arm and out of bed. The sunlight was barely a sliver in the east as she made her way silently through the house. In the kitchen she made a pot of coffee, using the Tanzanian coffee they saved for special occasions, and sat there sipping her brew and thinking. The events of last night had to mean that they both had made up their minds about buying the cleaning business. That meant that Dan would be shopping for a dive boat soon. Ella had gotten used to their savings account being nice and fat but with buying a business and a boat that nice fat bank balance would get skinny mighty fast. Their lives were changing, and she wasn't sure she was okay with it.

Change was hard for Ella, she liked things to stay the same, but she also knew that they couldn't pass up the opportunity to own their own business even if it wasn't the dive operation that they had been saving for.

The sun was just slanting in the kitchen window when she heard the alarm on Dan's phone ring in the bedroom. She waited until she heard him stirring and poured him a mug of coffee.

"Mm, coffee," he said as he shuffled into the room.

"Tanzanian coffee."

"What is the occasion?" he said, peering at her through half open eyes.

She refilled her mug. "Well, I was thinking that we both

seem to have made up our minds about the cleaning business so I thought we could celebrate with some special coffee."

"It's so good."

They talked over coffee, Ella hoping to convince herself that they had made the right decision. She ended up spreading out the balance sheets and her spreadsheet to double check the numbers, to see that she remembered them right.

"It still looks kind of too good to be true," she said as she pored over the papers. "There just don't seem to be any hitches in this. Can that be right?"

Dan looked at her over his mug. "Can you talk to Gina again and ask her if there is anything she's not telling you?"

"I guess so. I'll have to think of a way to ask that doesn't sound like I am calling her a liar."

Dan put down his coffee, got up, and got out the cereal and a bowl. "Raisin Bran?" he said waving the box her way.

"No, I think I'll have yogurt with some granola on top but thanks."

"Today's Thursday, isn't it?" he said.

"Yes, Thursday."

"Tonight's the night dive. Are you still interested in coming along?"

Ella turned from the counter, her bowl of yogurt and granola in her hands. "I think so. What time are you gathering at the Dive Inn?"

"Six o'clock," he said, "It's just getting dark then and that will give us a nice hour-long dive and still be early enough for people to have dinner at a reasonable hour."

"Sounds good. I will text you if I'm going to be late."

He finished his cereal, rinsed the bowl, and put it in the sink. "Then I had better make sure that our lights are working and in our dive bags," he said and left the room.

Dan dug out their dive lights and checked to make sure they worked. Ella's light was fine but his needed new batteries. He would stop at the mini mart on the way into town to pick some up. They were cheaper there than in the dive shop.

He was glad that Ella was planning to come diving. It seemed like life had gotten crazy busy lately and they had not had much time together. Dan was happy to be busy at the dive shop, but he missed time spent with Ella. The plan to buy the cleaning business sounded like a good one. He was still frustrated by Jack Slater's keeping him dangling on the hook with promises that he could buy Jack's dive business. Babs had not said anything again about him buying a part of the Dive Inn, but she had been glad to have his input into rearranging things to make it more efficient and his idea to push specialty courses and Advanced Open Water really worked out this week. He wondered how many people would be signed up for the night dive tonight. Maybe he would need a second divemaster to keep an eye on the novice divers. He would check with Samuel to see if he was busy tonight.

Ella came into the bedroom to get ready for work. "Do you want a ride to work this morning?"

He said, "Yes, I need to stop at the mini mart for batteries too, so I'll hurry and be ready in about fifteen minutes."

"Sounds good."

She went into the bathroom to clean her teeth and face and put on a little eye makeup.

"Why are you wearing makeup today?" Dan said.

"I'm not sure," said Ella, "maybe because I need a little extra confidence to tell Mariette about the car thieving boys that I hired to work for us this summer."

"That should be interesting. I wish I could be there for that."

She peeked around the door frame. "You could tell her for me."

He looked at her under lowered brows. "No, thank you. That's one conversation you're welcome to have all on your own."

The mini mart didn't look like a store. It looked like a plain old house stuck in a barren lot with a Salem cigarettes sign over the door. Ella wasn't sure that there was a door that closed on the place. She had never seen one, all they had were some strings of beads across the opening that didn't even keep bugs out. The store was dimly lit and most of the stock looked like it had been there for months if not years, but the prices were reasonable, so they stopped there when they needed to pick up one or two canned items. The store always had batteries so that's where Dan stopped when his dive lights were getting low.

When they got to the Dive Inn Ella pulled into the parking spot in front of the fence and went in with Dan to see how many people had signed up for the night dive. Eighteen. There were eighteen people signed up for the dive.

"You have to make time to come along," Dan said, "there is no way that I can keep my eye on that many divers at once."

Ella looked at the list. "How many of them are Advanced Open Water students?" she said.

"I don't know," said Dan.

"Ten," Cecile said, "I checked with the course list and all ten of the Advanced students are doing the night dive. They have all rented lights too."

Ella checked the time on her phone. "I had better get going. I need to meet Mariette at the first house in ten minutes and I am already late."

They kissed.

"See you later," Ella said.

Dan said, "Do you have your dive bag in the car?"

"Yes, it's in there. All I need is my light."

"I have that here, so you're set."

"See you before six o'clock," she said. "Now I really have to go."

She kissed him again and left. All up the island she rehearsed how she would tell Mariette what she had done.

"They are really good boys," she told the windshield, "I am sure that they will do a decent job."

Mariette was standing by her car as Ella pulled into the first house to be cleaned that day. "You're late."

"I'm sorry," Ella said, "only a few minutes."

"More like ten minutes." This was the first time that Mariette had been this sharp with her.

"What's up?" Ella asked.

"Oh, Nathan is not so sure that buying the business is a good idea. It would take nearly all of our savings and he's nervous about that. He keeps looking at the papers, adding up the numbers, and saying that it looks too good to be true."

Ella started to get her supplies out of the back seat of the car. "I know what he means. I keep looking at the numbers too and wondering what Gina isn't telling us."

They carried their cleaning equipment into the back door of the house. "Dan and I have made up our minds to buy the business. He's going to go look at a dive boat next week, but I feel nervous about spending so much of our savings so fast. I would like to have another meeting with Gina and ask more questions, but I don't know how to ask what I want to know without implying that she's been lying to us."

"Yes. I would like to meet with her again too. Let me call and see if she will meet us at lunch today."

"Good idea," Ella said. "I will strip the beds and get the laundry started while you call."

Gina was glad to meet with them again. She said, "I do not know what else I can tell you, but I am happy to meet with you if it will put your minds at ease."

So, they got down to work and got the house cleaned and prepared for the next guests in time to go down to Gina's office for lunch. They settled down in her cozy office, glad for the air conditioner humming away high on one wall.

"Now, what can I tell you that I haven't already told you?" Gina said.

"Well," said Mariette, "we were wondering if people paid their bills on time."

"And how do you deal with the resorts that use your service? Do they pay the cleaners or do you?" Ella said.

Gina set down her fork. "There are a few clients who are slow to pay their invoices but most of them come through in the end, after a reminder or two."

"Do you ever threaten not to clean until they pay?" said Mariette.

"I have done it once or twice," Gina said, "but usually they pay up in time. As far as the resort clients are concerned, they pay me, and I pay the cleaners. The resorts pay a negotiated rate, less than the rate that the vacation rentals people pay, and those cleaners get paid slightly less. I start out new hires in the resorts as the places are not people's private homes so if someone is careless, they are not breaking something expensive that I have to replace."

Ella sat forward. "Do you order your cleaning supplies direct?"

Gina shook her head. "No, I tack my order onto one from the Sand Dollar Resort, that way I get their volume discount. Our cleaning crews do not clean the hotel rooms, so we use the same supplies as the resort cleaners. People like that they are environmentally safe, and I get a price break."

"Do you have a contract with each resort or just an informal agreement?" Mariette said.

"Oh, I have contracts with each resort that we service. It would be too easy to abuse us if we just had an informal agreement. We used to have a handshake agreement but one of the resorts changed hands and the new owners were not as careful to abide by the agreement, so I had a contract drawn up, so we all know where we stand."

"I like that idea," Ella said. "Saves misunderstandings."

"And yet there are times when things go wrong, and you will have to deal with that."

They spent the rest of the hour going over the numbers one more time. Ella said that it looked good on paper and that they would give Gina their decision in a few days.

On the drive back to get Ella's car Mariette said, "I hope that Nathan agrees."

"I do too. We can't afford to buy the business on our own."

The second place that they cleaned that day was small and

easy. It seemed as if the guests had cleaned up after themselves. The beds were stripped, and the towels and sheets were in the laundry room. They did the laundry, emptied the dishwasher, and swept the sand out of the place.

They were watching Carlos vacuum the pool when Ella turned to Mariette. "I, um, I did something yesterday that I hope you won't be mad at."

Mariette looked scared. "What did you do?"

"Well, our car got stolen by two boys who thought it belonged to their uncle. They thought to play a prank on him but took our car by mistake."

"Oh my god," Mariette said.

"But the police found it right away. It only had a flat tire and I think that's all."

"I wondered why you had a rental car but thought yours was in the shop."

"It is."

"What did you do that I need to know about?"

"Instead of pressing charges I said that the boys could work for us this summer helping Carlos so that they didn't have to go to jail."

"Oh my god, who are these boys? Are they criminals?"

Ella shook her head. "I don't think so. Their names are Piko Sandford and Ned de Koop, they are fourteen and fifteen, and I think they were just stupid not criminal."

Mariette was silent for a while. "I know the Sandfords and the de Koops, those are good boys."

"I thought so too, that's why I suggested they could work for us. I didn't want them to have a police record over being foolish kids."

"What did Dan say?"

Ella picked at a hangnail. "He wanted them in jail, but I could see that they weren't criminals. Their parents were with them, their moms were crying, and the dads were angry. The boys were crying too. I just couldn't see them in a jail cell. I hope I did the right thing."

"I hope so too. I do not think I will tell Nathan that until after we have bought the business."

"Okay."

Just then the dryer stopped so they went to fold the last of the towels, got their supplies organized, and left for the day.

CHAPTER 18

Dan had parked his bicycle across one of the parking places in front of the Dive Inn so that Ella had a place to leave the car that wasn't around the corner.

"I thought parking here might make you feel a bit better than parking around on the side street would," he said.

Ella leaned over and kissed his cheek. "Thank you," she said, "all the way down here I was worrying about finding a place in the light to park."

She pulled her dive bag out of the back of the car and made sure that the windows were rolled down before she left the car to its fate. She was glad that it wasn't a shiny new rental car, that would just attract the attention of car thieves and vandals.

Samuel came to stand by her side. "Are you not happy to be diving tonight?"

Ella looked at him. 'No, I'm happy to be diving. What gave you the idea that I'm not happy?"

He motioned toward her forehead. "You have a big frown on your face and your mouth is turned down."

"Oh, I'm just worried about the car. Having our car stolen last night has made me nervous about leaving the car parked anywhere."

He patted her shoulder. "It will be okay there. Officer Micah is coming by every once in a while, to shoo away any bad people."

She let out a breath. "That is a relief." She looked around. "Did Dan go in the office?"

Samuel shook his head. "No, he's in the rental shed getting a lady fitted for a wetsuit."

"I think I'll go give him a hand."

As Ella walked into the rental shed, she heard laughter and then Dan's voice. "I think that one might be too small for you."

A woman's voice answered him. "Do you think so?"

Ella reached them and saw the woman squirming in the tight neoprene suit. "Can I help?" she said.

The woman looked at her. "Yes, can you help me get out of this suit? I think I am stuck for good."

She was indeed stuck in the suit. Her arms were pressed to her sides and the neck of the suit was wedged under her breasts.

Ella walked forward; her hands outstretched. "How did you manage to get it on this far?"

The woman turned like a penguin so that Ella could reach the suit and try to pull it off her perspiring skin. "I don't know. It was going on just fine and then it stopped. My arms are stuck in the sleeves, and he won't pull it away from my front."

Dan's mouth worked and his hands reached toward her but then fell back. "I can't grab anything that's not a private part."

"Just get it off me," the woman said. "I don't care if you touch me someplace personal. I'm stuck."

Ella tugged at the side of the suit, and it started to roll down her arm. "Turn so that I can do the same on the other side."

Working side to side Ella was able to peel the suit off the woman's arms so that she could help get the rest of the suit off. Within five minutes the offending wetsuit was off the sweaty woman and lying like a discarded chrysalis on the concrete floor.

Ella looked down at it and then up at the woman. "I don't think that is the right size for you."

"No fooling," the woman said. "I'm not sure I ever want to put on a wetsuit again."

Ella said, "You'll need one for the night dive. You'd get chilled after an hour in the water."

The woman looked at Dan and then at Ella. "I told him that I wear a size fourteen and that's what he gave me."

Ella smiled at her. "I used to work in a dive shop in the

States and I swear that whoever designs wetsuits for women has never met one. The sizes seem to be arbitrary. Here," she took a suit off the rack, "let's try this one."

The woman looked at her but took the suit and began to step into it.

"First fold the top down so that it looks like you're putting on pants," Ella told her, "that's easier than trying to put it on holding the shoulders. And have a seat on this bench so you don't lose your balance."

The woman got the suit on with a minimum of tugging and smiled up at Ella. "This is much better."

"Good. It's snug but not too tight," said Ella. "That will keep you comfy during the dive."

"I am glad because I get cold easily."

Ella motioned toward the door. "We should get out there and get our gear on the boat if we're going diving tonight."

"Are you coming too? Will you dive with me?"

Ella smiled at her. "First time jitters? What's your name?"

"I'm Arlene and I'm from Wisconsin."

"Hey," Ella said, "Dan and I are from Wisconsin too. Where in the state are you from?"

"I come from Appleton."

"Did you get certified at Divers' Realm?"

Arlene nodded. "I did. How did you know?"

Ella picked up her gear bag, slung it over her shoulder, and went to get a tank. "I used to work at Aqua Center, a dive shop in Green Bay and we traded regulator services with them. They're good people."

The two women kept chatting as they crossed the street to the dock and the dive boat. The boat was crowded, and they had trouble finding places for their gear.

Ella called to Dan, "Arlene and I want to dive together, is that okay?"

"Sure, I'm just figuring out buddy teams and who is diving with who."

Even though they were diving at Playa Chachacha across

from the dive shop Dan had decided that since the group was so big it would be easier to gather on the boat instead of on the sand, that way they could control entries and keep the groups together.

Soon Dan called for everyone's attention for the predive briefing. "Okay, everybody," he said, "since this is the first night dive for a lot of you, we have a few things to cover. Everyone have a light?"

There was a chorus of "yes" from around the boat.

"The biggest thing to remember is not to shine your light in your buddy's eyes." Everyone laughed.

"Thirty feet is the maximum depth tonight. I know a lot of you did an afternoon dive on this site, so you're familiar with it. There are plenty of eels and lobsters and shrimp hiding in the crevices for you to see if you take your time. If we're lucky, we may see tarpon which are silver and look like stainless steel or snook which are white and like to hunt at night. Sometimes there are octopuses out hunting too so keep your eyes peeled. Any questions?"

"What about sharks?" said Arlene.

"Sharks are rare on Bonaire so if you see one, you're very lucky. If you're frightened just vent the air out of your buoyancy control device and sink below the shark. They won't bother you. Now let's go diving."

Dan called Ella and Samuel over and asked them to get into the water with their groups and try to keep them together.

"I'll try," Ella told him.

Dan called out the names of the five divers that would be with Ella and had them follow her into the water. She gathered them together and they started off down the reef, Arlene tight to Ella's side.

Ella enjoyed the seep of the warm Caribbean Sea water under her tight-fitting wetsuit. She felt Arlene at her side fiddling with her light. The other two buddy teams in her group were spread out alongside them. She swam them down the reef, watching the light beams crisscrossing on the sand and off to the side where the coral reef began. There was the flicker of a silver fish and she looked to see a three-foot-long Tarpon hanging over the drop off. Ella reached out to Arlene to get her attention and pointed out the big fish. She heard Arlene inhale as she caught sight of it. Ella circled her light beam ahead of the other buddy teams to get their attention and pointed out the Tarpon to them too. She led her charges over to the edge of the drop off, checking that she didn't go below thirty feet, and started swimming slowly away from the entry. Soon the five divers relaxed and were discovering the delights of the nighttime reef. The red Soldierfish were out of their daytime hiding places and swimming in search of small fish to prey on. One of the buddy teams came over to her and tugged her to follow them. They had found a six-foot-long Green Moray Eel that was swimming along in a sandy spot on its own night hunt.

Ella kept an eye on her air gauge and looked for shrimp and lobsters that might be in the crannies of the reef. She spotted a splash of blue-white and saw a reef octopus blanch in the glow of their lights. The octopus immediately turned brown and bumpy to blend into the coral patch it was on. It always amazed her how quickly they could change the color and texture of their skin. It was the perfect camouflage. Ella heard a high-pitched crooning and turned to see that Arlene was swimming along, wide eyed, waving her light beam out into the dark. Ella took out her slate and wrote a question mark on it. Arlene took it and wrote "shark in the dark." Ella looked out where Arlene's light was, and she saw a pale flash of a fish. It was a Snook, a yellow white fish that also hunted for small fish at night. Snook grew to about eighteen inches to two feet long and were not dangerous. Ella wrote "Snook, not shark" on her slate. Arlene looked her in the eyes to make sure that she wasn't fooling her. Ella took her hand and swam along the reef. The Snook left the darkness and came over the coral and into their lights. Ella felt Arlene relax as she saw that it wasn't a shark after all and let go of her hand.

When her bottom time hit thirty minutes Ella turned the group around and started leading them back to the docked boat. They found a whole lot of shrimp in small nooks in the reef and the antennae of lobsters down on the sandy bottom. The shrimp claws' snapping sounded like popping corn. As they neared the boat Ella had them all turn off their lights and wave their hands through the water to excite the blue green glow of phosphorescence. She swept her hand through the water and blue-green fire trailed from her fingertips. The others were enthralled by the spectacle and mimicked her. One of the men waved his arms and legs in an underwater jumping jack and looked like he was juggling cold fire.

Ella showed them the dark red heart urchins that lived under the sand in the day and came up out of the sand to feed at night. She watched the slow progress of the urchins as they moved on tiny tube feet. By that time Arlene's air was down to six hundred psi so Ella escorted her to the trailing line by the boarding ladders. She went to the surface with her.

"I'm going to stay in the water to keep an eye on the other divers. I'll see you on the boat shortly."

"Okay. Thanks for diving with me," said Arlene.

Ella smiled at her. "Anytime."

The other two pairs of divers were investigating the small sponges and other sea life that was growing on the dock pilings. Small fish lurked around under there at night and tried to hide from the bigger predator fish. Tiny crabs skittered around on the surface of the pilings, in and out of the sponges, and waved their claws to warn the divers away. Soon there was a steady stream of divers swimming up to the boarding ladders. Dan and Samuel both jumped the line and got on board to help the arriving divers. They took fins and weight pockets as they were handed up and then steadied the divers as they climbed the ladders onto the boat. Ella stayed in the water to make sure that no one got left behind or had any trouble at the end of the dive. There was always one buddy team that lagged behind the others, trying to eke as much bottom time out of their tanks as possible. Ella swam down and gestured them to accompany her to the boat. They held out their air gauges to show that they still were not down to five hundred psi. They were so very close that she shook her head and motioned them ahead of her to the boat. Ella was tempted to just swim over to the beach and do a shore exit but then she would miss the debriefing and the excitement of the divers' first night dive. She was sure that they all would have seen wonderful things and wanted to be a part of that.

Ella checked her air gauge, fourteen hundred psi, and headed back toward the docked boat. She made one last visual sweep of the dive site to look for any columns of bubbles that she might have missed and then caught the trailing line in her right hand. She tucked the line under her arm and took off her fins, one after the other, then she pulled herself forward so she could hand the fins up to Samuel who was waiting for her at the stern of the boat.

"Good dive?" he said.

"Well, I brought back all that I took out so, yes, it was a good dive."

He laughed and extended a hand to help her up the last rung of the boarding ladder. She stepped to the side and sat on the bench in front of the tank rack. She felt the butt of her tank sit down into the rack and then shrugged out of her buoyancy control vest. Ella was a little chilled, so she hurried to peel off her wetsuit and dry herself off with her chamois towel.

Dan was walking around encouraging people to take their wetsuits off to avoid getting cold and having a hard time convincing some of the women. Ella trailed after him assuring them that they would indeed be warmer out of the wet neoprene suit than in it.

"I always take my suit off quickly and dry off, so I stay warm. The breeze will chill you if you're wet, so get dry," she said.

That produced a flurry of movement among all the divers, women and men. She knew that the men would be too macho to admit being cold, but they were quick enough to get out of their wetsuits. Once they were all dried off and settled down again Dan called for their attention to debrief.

"I hope everyone had a good dive."

Murmurs of assent went around the boat.

"Did everyone see that big Tarpon just as we got into the water?"

"Yeah," said one of the men, "that was a big sucker."

"Is that what that was?" said another. "I thought it was some metal in the water, like a boat hull."

"We saw an octopus," said Arlene. "It was amazing. It changed colors in a flash and went from smooth to bumpy in a second. Amazing."

"Did you touch it?" someone said.

"No, it was too fast, and I was afraid of hurting it."

"Good thinking," Dan said. "All of the fish and creatures in Bonaire waters are part of the Marine Park and are protected. What else did you see?"

"We saw parrotfish lying on their sides with a mucus bubble around them. I read about that in the Reef Fish book. It is a way that they protect themselves."

"Eels. We saw a big Green Moray out swimming and a bunch of little spotted ones in the reef."

"Phosphorescence is very cool, like blue-green fire from your fingertips."

Others chimed in. "We saw a lobster I would have liked to catch for supper. It looked big."

Dan laughed. "Good thing that you didn't catch it. They have spikes on their shells. They will tear up your hands."

One of the men said, "And how would you know that if this is a preserve?"

Dan said, "I went lobstering in Florida with my uncle when I was a kid. Florida has a lobster season when you can go catch a few. It's fun but it's hard on your hands."

One of the women said, "This is great, but I'm getting cold. What else do we have to talk about?"

"Nothing much," said Dan. "Let's get the gear and tanks back up to the shop. I have the list of light rentals so you can return those tonight and then you can get really dry and warm up. I can sign logbooks tonight or we can do it in the morning."

"Morning is good," said a man, "I'm ready for a drink."

Several people agreed and they all started to gather up their gear and move toward the dive shop. It took probably a half hour for people to rinse their gear and get it hung to dry overnight.

Ella said, "Be sure to hang your wetsuit inside out so that it has a chance to dry before your morning dives."

"Oh," one of the women said, "thanks for the tip. I have been putting on a damp suit all week."

"Eesh, that's cold," Ella said.

"It sure is," she agreed.

At last, all the divers were gone and only Ella and Dan were left. Ella had a plastic box with all the dive lights in it to return to the shop in the morning.

"I'll put that box by the compressor, so I remember to give them to Cecile tomorrow."

"Good thinking," said Ella.

They made sure that the rinse tank was drained and that no gear was left out in sight of the street. Dan locked the gate across the courtyard entrance and got into the passenger seat of the car.

"You drive, I am beat," he said.

Ella slung her dive bag into the back and slid behind the wheel. "Okay, you do look tired."

She realized when she turned on the headlights that she had meant to stop at Island Rentals to ask about getting the headlight fixed. Oh well, she would be careful and take it slow on the way home.

Dan said, "What did Mariette say when you told her about the boys you hired for the summer?"

"She knows the boys and their families and agrees that they are nice boys, but she's not going to say anything to Nathan until after we have bought the business. He's getting a little case of cold feet about the whole thing again."

"Oh great. Do you think they will back out?"

214

Ella shook her head. "I don't think so. I think Mariette is determined to buy the business and will talk him into it."

Dan leaned back against the head rest. "Good, because I'm on board too. I want to start looking at boats. We could use a second boat this week but don't have one."

"Did Babs say anything about buying into the business?"

"No, she didn't, but I haven't brought it up either. I am waiting until the cleaning business purchase is a sure thing."

By then they were pulling into the apartment and were both glad to be there. They hung up their wet bathing suits and chamois towels and then rummaged in the refrigerator for something quick to eat.

"All we have is bread and cheese, no ham or lunch meat," Ella said, "How about grilled cheese sandwiches?"

"Sounds good to me," said Dan.

CHAPTER 19

A week later the deed was done. Ella and Mariette bought Playa Palms Rentals cleaning arm of the business. They had hired a notary to go over the contract for purchase and he had assured them that there weren't any hidden pitfalls in there to trip them up. It had been hard for Ella to go to the Scotia Bank and get a cashier's check for five thousand dollars to bring to the meeting. Dan took the day off work as did Mariette's husband Nathan, but the women were the ones buying the business, so they did all the talking and all the signing. Mariette looked longingly at the cashier's check that she extended across the desk to Gina. Ella knew that her friend had worked long and hard to save that much money and it had been difficult for Nathan to agree to spend it.

They had crunched a lot of numbers over the last couple weeks of decision making doing their best to think of every argument for and against buying the business. Now they had done it. They were business owners. The four of them stood in the sunshine outside Gina's office and looked at each other.

"Should we go get a drink?" Dan said. "I feel like we need to toast the new venture and... and I'm thirsty."

Nathan laughed. "Yes, I am thirsty too. Nerves make my mouth dry, and I have been nervous all day. Let's get a drink."

Ella and Mariette looked at each other and shrugged. "Why not?" Ella said, "We can toast the new partnership. What's open?"

"Let us go to The Beefeater," said Mariette, "they have a nice bar, and it is sure to be quiet this time of day. I am not in the mood for a crowd."

They decided to leave their cars at the side of the road by Gina's office and walk into town. There was a cruise ship tied up at the Town Pier, so the streets were crowded with tourists. Sunburned people were rushing up and down the street and into and out of stores, not really paying attention to where they were going. It was a relief to get to The Beefeater and find that it wasn't full of people.

"What will everybody have?" said Dan, "I'll buy the first round."

He went up to the bar and ordered the Cuba Libres for the ladies and beers for the men. The bartender said he would bring the drinks to the table when they were ready. When the drinks were served, he held up his beer glass and said,

"Here's to many profitable years of Playa Palms Cleaning."

The four of them clinked glasses and drank.

"I think we need to change the name of the business," Mariette said, "since it is no longer affiliated with Playa Palms Rentals."

"I hadn't thought of that," said Ella, "What should we call it?"

"I was thinking something like Twice the Cleaning Service since there are two of us."

"Hey," said Nathan, "that is not bad. You're pretty clever for a cleaning lady."

Mariette elbowed him and almost made him spill his beer. "Have some respect, I am a business owner now, not just a cleaning lady."

"Yes," said Ella, "Have some respect. Oh my god, Mariette, we did it. We bought the business." Her face turned white, and she looked open mouthed at Dan. "We bought the business."

Dan put his arm around her and hugged her to his side. "We sure did. Now you two have to stop goofing around and get busy cleaning everything that holds still."

"We do not goof around, we clean," said Mariette, "but we also need to write letters to all the clients telling them that we have bought the business and that for now rates will remain the same. That will reassure them that we have their best interests in mind."

Ella nodded agreement. "We have to talk to the cleaners too. Do you know if Gina let people know that she was selling the business?"

"On an island this size I would be surprised if everyone didn't know it," said Mariette.

"I'm sure that their names and contact information is in the files that Gina gave to us," Ella said, "we should write a letter too, and then go around and meet them and introduce ourselves. I've met a few of them. What about you?"

Mariette said, "I know a few of them but none of the resort cleaners. We should probably split up and one of us clean and the other go meet them."

Ella frowned. "I don't know if splitting up is such a good idea. I think it might be better if we went to meet them together, present a united front, so that they don't get the idea that we're not equal partners."

"I had not thought of that."

The conversation went on with Dan and Nathan listening most of the time, letting the women get themselves organized. They agreed to take the next week to go around meeting the cleaning staff and getting acquainted with the resort managers. The walk back to their cars was much easier since all the cruise ship passengers were back on board the ship. In fact, they walked down the shore road past the pier to watch the tugboats pull the giant ship away from the dock.

"I don't think that I would like to go on one of those," Ella said.

"Me neither," said Dan, "too restrictive."

Mariette looked up at the glittering white ship with all its lights aglow. "I do not know. I think it would be a glamorous way to vacation."

Nathan tugged her arm to follow him down the street. "Well, now that we have spent nearly all of our savings it will be many years before a cruise is a vacation possibility."

They walked out of the bright lights of the town into the surrounding neighborhood and turned down the street past Bobbe Jan's barbecue joint to get to their cars.

"Oh," Ella said, "doesn't that smell good? I could go for some ribs and coleslaw right about now."

Dan smiled. "I'm game. What about you two?"

Nathan was already shaking his head.

Mariette said, "Thanks but I think we have already spent enough money for the day. You go on. Ella, I will see you in the morning."

Ella hugged her friend. "I'll get the employees' names from Gina's files and bring them along tomorrow. Good night."

"Good night."

Nathan and Mariette walked on into the darkness and Dan took Ella's arm and escorted her into the tiny restaurant.

Ella and Dan sat across from each other sipping ice water and waiting for their food to arrive. "I can't believe that we did that," Ella said.

Dan laughed. "But we did, we now own half of a cleaning business with employees and everything."

"We sure do."

They tried to talk about other things, but the conversation always came back to the business and their investment in it.

"I hope the employees are okay with us buying the business," Ella said.

Dan looked at her. "You won't know until you talk to them and maybe not even then. Some of them might resent you two expats overseeing them."

Ella sighed. "I know, I'm afraid of that too. We'll start meeting with them tomorrow and hope it goes well."

Their waiter, who also happened to be James the owner and bartender, delivered their food. When he set down the plates he said, "I hear that you spent a load of money to buy Playa Palms Cleaning today."

Ella's eyes flew up and she goggled at him. "Where did you hear that?"

James motioned over his shoulder with his thumb. "Their office is right around the corner, and we knew that Gina was looking to sell. She told us that you and Mariette were thinking of buying her out a few weeks ago. We figured that today was the day when you came in looking so excited and scared at the same time. Mariette and Nathan didn't want to celebrate?"

Ella shook her head. "We had a drink at The Beefeaters but then when we were walking back to the cars, I smelled your ribs and we decided to stop to eat. They went on home."

James smiled down at them. "Enjoy your meal." And he left to greet arriving diners.

Dan said, "Man, nothing is secret on the island, is it?"

"Nope, we should be used to it by now."

They finished their meals, walked around the block for their car, and drove home.

Ella and Mariette spent the next week going around to the resorts that contracted with Playa Palms Cleaning, introducing themselves, and meeting with the cleaners there. For the most part the women were friendly and relieved that nothing would change for the time being. One of them complained about the rate of pay and Ella told her that was something that they were looking at but first they had to get their feet on the ground.

Meeting with the house cleaning staff took a little more time as they had to visit each house and met each employee individually. They discovered that all the cleaners were not paid the same rate, and that they had been some of the lowest paid of them all.

"Well, how do you like that?" Mariette said, "I thought that all of the house cleaners were paid the same and that the resort cleaners were paid less, but you and I were just about the lowest paid employees."

"I don't like that, but I think I understand it," said Ella. "You and I were the last hired of the house cleaners and had not worked our way up the ladder very far. It is a good thing that it is the end of the month and time to bill the clients otherwise I don't know how we'll pay the employees next week."

Mariette looked up in surprise. "Oh yes, where will we get the money to pay them?"

Ella looked at the budget she had worked out. "I guess out of savings since we haven't had any income yet. Until those bills get paid all we will have is outlay."

"Why did we not think of that?" Mariette said.

"I did think of it and planned to use savings for it until we can replenish the funds. I'll get the invoices prepared and sent out. Let's get the cash rolling in the right direction."

Dan wasn't happy. "What do you mean you need to use more of the savings to pay your employees?" he said.

Ella handed him the balance sheet. "We don't have the cash to pay them. I only sent out invoices a few days ago and no one has paid yet. Tomorrow is payday and we need to use our savings to pay the staff. I am sure that the invoices will be paid quickly and soon we will be able to repay the savings account but for the time being that's our working capital."

"Does that mean no boat shopping?"

"Maybe. Have you looked at boat prices? What are you planning to spend on a decent boat?"

Dan stood up from the table and started to pace. "At least ten grand, maybe more, maybe a lot more."

Ella swiveled in her chair to watch him. "More than ten thousand dollars? I was thinking that would be the top."

Dan stopped pacing and stood looking at her. "I can't buy a cheap boat that isn't safe, and we have to think about fuel and mooring costs. Suddenly our big savings account is looking small."

Ella shuffled her papers and looked at the table. "I guess we didn't plan as well as we thought we had."

"Why are you having to pay the staff when they've been working for Gina the last two weeks?"

Ella looked up at him with a smile on her face. "We never thought of that. I need to call Mariette." She reached for the telephone. "Maybe Gina mailed out invoices too. We need to talk to her tomorrow and get this straightened out."

Ella was right. Gina paid the employees for the last two weeks and mailed out the invoices billing the same period. "You need to start your books on the day that you bought the business," Gina told them, "That way your income and outlay will balance."

Ella was relieved and Dan was ecstatic.

"It is a good thing that I asked that question, isn't it? I'm a handy guy to have around."

Mariette pressed Nathan and Dan into service hauling the cleaning supplies from Gina's office to Mariette's back hall closet. Ella set up the files in a corner of the living room and laid a plank across two file drawers to use as a desk.

CHAPTER 20

Dan came into the apartment humming and smiling.

Ella had a long day and wasn't in the best mood. "What are you so happy about?" she said.

He dangled a key in front of her. "I bought a boat today."

Ella's eyebrows shot up. "You did what?"

Dan turned and got a beer out of the refrigerator. "I found a good boat and I bought it."

"Without discussing it or going over finances, you just bought a boat," she said.

He took a long swallow of beer. "You knew I was looking at boats. I found one today in Rincon, took it out, liked it, and bought it."

She reached both hands up and grasped her head. "Did you buy it from Raul? Did you have a mechanic look at it? Do you know anything about its maintenance history? How much did you pay for it?"

Dan sat down at the table and made condensation rings on the surface with his beer bottle. "The guy wanted eighteen grand for it, but I got him down to fourteen."

Ella sat down across from him. "You paid fourteen thousand dollars for a boat without talking it over with me? Isn't Rincon on the windward side where the surf is too rough for boats?"

"Well, the owner lives in Rincon, but the boat is in the marina next to Sand Dollar."

She looked at him as if he had slipped a few cogs. "Does that fourteen thousand dollars include the slip rental fee?"

Dan shook his head. "No, it doesn't but the fees aren't that bad, only six hundred dollars a month."

"Six hundred dollars a month? That's a fortune. How can we afford to pay that when you aren't earning money with the boat?"

Dan slammed his empty beer bottle down on the table making Ella jump. "I knew you'd be like this. I knew that you'd tell me that it was too much money and how would we pay the slip fees. I've already talked to Babs, and she'll need another boat twice next week when the Viking Princess is in port. Those two days should pay for the first month's slip fees." He paced up and back in the small kitchen, then he reached into the fridge for another beer. "This is just like you. Now that you've got your little cleaning business and think you're a big deal you don't want me to have my boat."

Ella put her hand over her eyes and rubbed down her face. "I didn't say that you couldn't have a boat, but I would have liked to be part of the decision. Can I see the boat?"

Dan downed the rest of his second beer. "Sure. We can run up to the marina and you can look at it." He turned away and muttered, "As if you know what you're looking at."

"What was that?" she said.

"Nothing, nothing. Let's go before it gets too dark to see anything."

They were both quiet on the ride up the island to the marina. Dan parked the car in the gravel lot and escorted Ella to the end dock and down to the end slip where a pontoon boat swayed at the moorings. The boat looked a little battered and there was a slick of oil around the stern.

"Here she's, the Muddy Albatross." He waved his arm like a TV model showing off a new car.

"The Muddy Albatross? Can you change the boat's name? That's not a very appealing name for a boat."

"Yeah, we can change her name if you insist. I thought it was pretty funny."

She looked over the boat in the last rays of the setting sun. "Can I go aboard?"

"Why?"

She gave him a sharp look. "Is there a reason I shouldn't go aboard?"

"No, not really. Some of the deck planking is a little mushy but that's something that I can easily fix."

She pointed to the outboard motor. "And what about the leaking gas and oil? Can you fix the motor easily and cheaply too?"

He ran a hand over his face. "I don't know. I'll need a marine mechanic to look at it."

Ella folded her arms across her chest. "Do you think that maybe having a mechanic look at it before you paid money for it might have been a good idea?"

"There wasn't time. There was another guy ready to buy the boat if I didn't. I had to jump on it fast or I'd have lost it. The other guy was standing right on the dock waiting to see if I'd buy it. He had ready cash in his pocket Zeke said."

"Who is Zeke?"

"The guy I bought the boat from."

"Did it ever occur to you that Zeke might have had his cousin pose as a potential buyer so that you would jump into buying it just like you did before you had it inspected? I'm afraid you might have bought a pig in a poke."

Two men walked down the dock and turned to board the boat tied up next to the Muddy Albatross. "You don't want that boat, missus," one of them said.

"Why not?" Ella said. She shot a look at Dan. "Is there something wrong with the boat?"

"It's called Albatross. Did you never hear of the Ancient Mariner? The albatross is a burden to whoever owns it."

"Yeah," said the other man, "that is one unlucky boat. Zeke has been trying to sell it since the day after he bought it. Seems like every week something else goes wrong with it."

Dan let out a weak laugh. "It's an unlucky boat, huh?"

Ella jabbed him with her elbow. "And you just bought it. How much money have you given ol' Zeke so far?"

Dan rubbed his hands down his thighs. "I gave him a check for seven thousand dollars as down payment. I said I'd pay the rest monthly."

"With interest?"

"No, no, no interest."

"Well, that's something, I guess. Let's go home."

They walked up the dock and across the gravel parking lot to their car. They were halfway home before Dan said, "I guess I should have taken more time to decide before buying the boat."

"Yeah. I suppose we can stop payment on the check and get out of the sale, if you want."

"Maybe I can get someone to look at the boat, give me a repair estimate, and then renegotiate the price based on that."

"Maybe."

They were quiet on the remainder of the ride. When they got home Ella took a shower and went straight to bed. Dan sat at the kitchen table drinking another beer. It was quite a while before he took his shower and turned in.

Dan realized that he couldn't drive the Muddy Albatross and lead the dives. He needed a captain. Captain Bill's nephew, Jerome, had just gotten his captain's license and was looking for a job. Now that the Albatross' deck was repaired, and the motor had been serviced it was time to take her out for a shakedown cruise. Ella had taken the day off so that she could go along on the first dive from their new boat. Captain Jerome had the boat all gassed up and cleaned for their first sailing. They loaded their dive gear into the back of the car, stopped at the Dive Inn for tanks, and drove up to the marina. Jerome helped carry the equipment to the boat.

Ella couldn't believe the change in the old boat. There was new green AstroTurf on the deck and the boat sparkled in the sun.

"I never thought that it would turn out like this," she said.

Dan beamed. "I knew that it would be all right."

Once they got their gear set up on their tanks, Dan cast off and Captain Jerome motored out of the marina.

"Where are we going?" Ella said.

"I thought we'd just go up the coast to Bon Bini Na Kas, it's an easy dive that usually doesn't have much current," said Dan, "I feel the need for an easy dive and a short boat ride."

"Sounds good to me." Ella turned her face into the wind with its tangy salt aroma and let out a sigh. "I'm just glad not to be working today."

Dan was lucky to catch the mooring buoy on his first try and got the boat secured. The sun sparkled off the clear turquoise water and the little waves rocked the boat toward the shore. "This mooring is really shallow so be careful where you enter," Dan said, "We don't want to break any of the staghorn coral. Let's swim down the wall to around eighty feet and then work our way back up to the boat. I heard that people have been seeing turtles and big parrotfish here lately."

They finished putting on their wetsuits and shrugged into their SCUBA gear. Bubbles engulfed Ella as she sank under the warm saltwater. She adjusted her mask and looked around for Dan. He was right beside her. They gave each other the okay signal and let the air out of their buoyancy control vests to descend. On that sunny day it was like diving in an aquarium. Fish darted around the stands of coral, and Ella could hear the chiming of broken coral rolling in the small surf at the shore. The edge of the reef drop off was close to the mooring, so they swam over and down toward the bottom. Visibility was good and they could see all the way to the sand at one hundred twenty feet.

Dan touched her arm and pointed out into the blue and there was a pod of three dolphins swimming by. That was the first time Ella had seen dolphins underwater and she was tempted to try to swim with them, but they were gone before she kicked their way. She looked at Dan to see him grinning back at her. They exchanged enthusiastic okay signals and turned back to the wall.

Azure vase sponges and yellow tube sponges stood out

among the drab coral boulders and golden gorgonians waved in the mild surge like wheat in the wind. Nestled in the nooks of the reef purple-tipped anemones lived with their small clear cleaner shrimp companions that waved their antennae to attract fish to clean. Big turquoise and yellow Stoplight Parrotfish swam by munching on the coral. Ella could hear the crunch of their beaks as they nibbled away at the rocky structure.

The water felt like silk on her skin as Ella swam along. In the shallow area atop the reef Damselfish tended their algae gardens and chased away marauding Blue Tangs that swam by trying to steal a mouthful.

She looked at the base of a stand of gorgonians and saw a bright yellow seahorse with its tail curled around one of the stalks. Ella reached out to touch Dan to show him the seahorse only to find him hovering over an octopus that was leaving its burrow. When the octopus noticed them, it blanched as white as the sand, then scuttled to the protection of the nearest patch of coral where it changed to the mottled brown of its surroundings.

Dan motioned toward the boat, so they slowly swam that way. Captain Jerome had lowered the boarding ladder and thrown out a trailing line to make it easy for them to take off their fins before climbing back on board.

Ella climbed first and carefully walked to her place along the side where she could slip her tank into the rack and take off her buoyancy control vest. "What a great dive," she said. "That was the first time I've ever seen dolphins underwater and we saw a seahorse and an octopus too."

Dan sat across from her and grinned. "I'm glad you liked it. I think this might turn out to be one of my favorite dive sites. It's a little far from the Dive Inn's dock but it would be a good second dive, don't you think?"

The ride back to the marina was swift and uneventful. The Muddy Albatross ran like a dream and Ella had to admit that Dan had been right to buy her.

CHAPTER 21

Ella raised her eyes from the spreadsheet she was working on. "What did you say?"

Dan snorted. "I said, when was the last time you went diving with me? When was the last time you spent the day with me at all?"

She looked around at the files and invoices spread out across the board that passed for her desk and blinked. "I guess it's been a while," she said. "Why?"

Dan threw up his hands. "Because we were going to dive together a lot. That was our dream, to move to Bonaire and go diving together." His hands landed on his hips. "What happened to that dream?"

Ella stood up. "Well, we couldn't find a dive operation to buy, I couldn't get a job in a dive shop. I ended up cleaning vacation homes and bought the cleaning business with Mariette. You bought a dive boat and are investing in Dive Inn." She looked at Dan's frowning face. "Is any of this making sense?"

"Yeah, but you're not diving."

"No, I'm not. I've been too busy to break away for a day to go diving. I miss it. I'm jealous that you get to go diving nearly every day and my dive gear sits in the back of the closet dry and unused."

"You should come diving with me tomorrow. We're going to Red Slave early in the morning and you should come."

She looked at all the paperwork piled up around her computer. "I don't know if I can or if I should. I need to get these second notices sent out." She picked up a sheaf of papers with a Twice the Cleaning Service logo on it. "I suppose I could get them done today," she said, longing in her voice.

"I could really use an extra set of eyes," Dan said.

She put the papers down with a slam. "Oh, the only reason you want me along is so that you don't have to hire an extra divemaster? That's flattering."

"No, that's not what I meant. You're such a good diver that you're an example to the bozos that are usually on the boat. I want you along because I like being with you." He folded his arms across his chest. "Besides, I miss you. You've been so busy with the cleaning business that you've barely spoken to me all week."

Ella ran a hand over her forehead. "I'm sorry, Dan. It's the end of the month and time to send out bills and time to pay the staff. I have a zillion things on my mind and I've been neglecting you. I'm sorry." She crossed to him and put her arms around his waist.

He lowered his arms and wrapped them around her. "I miss you, babe. I feel like we're leading two separate lives, not what we dreamed of at all." He pulled her close and rested his chin on the top of her head. "Some days I'm sorry we bought the business."

She squeezed him closer. "Me too. This is not the life that we imagined when we were freezing up in Wisconsin. We're not carefree, we don't own a dive operation, and we aren't diving every day. Well, you are but I'm not."

"Yeah. This isn't what we planned, is it?"

"Not really but in some ways it's better," Ella said.

He pulled back and looked down into her eyes. "What do you mean, better?"

She looked into his eyes. "I think it's better that we aren't in the same business, in the same building day after day. This way we have different days, different things happen to us that we can share in the evening."

"That's true."

"And our savings account is growing faster than it would be if we were both in the dive business."

"How do you figure that?" Dan said.

"Well, if we had a dive shop, we'd have to have inventory. That would mean a big cash outlay and trying to guess what the fickle diving public would like to buy. Our only inventory is the cleaning supplies that we piggyback onto the Sand Dollar's supplies order. We don't have tanks and weights and wetsuits and rental regulators and BCDs that we must pay for, maintain, and replace when needed so anything over and above our operating costs gets split between us and Mariette and Nathan and banked."

"Yeah, I guess that's right."

She nodded. "Plus, you're able to pay for fuel and slip fees out of the money you make taking out divers."

Dan looked up, thinking. "And don't forget Captain Jerome, I pay him too."

"Yes, plus we get a percentage of his sightseeing charters. It all adds up."

She pulled Dan's head down and kissed him. "It's been a while since we sat down and went over the books. Maybe we should spend an hour later so you can see how things are going." Ella stepped out of his embrace. "Let me get back to work on these invoices and I promise to go diving tomorrow. Now scat." She sat back down at her desk and Dan planted one last kiss on top of her head before heading to the kitchen to rustle up a sandwich for lunch.

Dan felt like that conversation had gone well. He missed having Ella along on dives and was tired of hearing about the cleaning business. Her stories weren't as interesting since she had stopped cleaning and started running things. Ledgers, spreadsheets, and invoices were not Dan's preferred topics of conversation. He liked to talk about the antics of his dive students and the customers on the boat. He wanted to wow Ella with tales of giant hawksbill turtles and barracuda that hovered over the edge of the reef and scared the unwary. He finished his ham and Gouda sandwich, chugged the last of his soda, and fished his keys out of his pocket.

"I'm off for the afternoon dives," he said as he walked toward the door.

Ella waved over her head. "Enjoy. See you later."

She bent back over her computer as Dan went out to the car to head back to the dive shop.

The sun was barely above the horizon when the divers began to gather at Dive Inn for the early morning trip to Red Slave. It was a long boat ride almost all the way down the leeward coast of Bonaire, so they needed an early start. Dan was using his own boat, the Muddy Albatross, so that Cyril and Captain Bill could take another group of divers out to the less challenging dive sites on Klein Bonaire. He and Captain Jerome had conferred on the way he wanted the drift dive to go so that there would be no confusion, no slipups. This was the first time that they had taken a group to Red Slave, and he wanted everything to go smoothly. Dan was glad that Ella had agreed to come along. She could swim at the back of the group to help him make sure that none of the divers strayed. There were six divers signed up for the dive and they straggled in looking bleary eyed and a little hung over.

"Did everyone have an early night last night?" Dan said when they were all gathered at the table in the center of the courtyard.

Random mumbles and a few "yeah, sure"s was the response.

"I don't want anyone impaired on this dive. The current can be strong, and I need you to be aware of yourself and your gauges on this dive. It's an advanced dive so be sure you're up to it."

He looked around at the six divers, not encouraged by their slack faces and slumped shoulders. Ella looked at him over the heads of the divers and shrugged.

Captain Jerome brought the boat in to the dock and Dan went over to help him tie it up.

"I think it's going to be an interesting dive," he said.

Jerome just nodded and settled his sunglasses more firmly on his nose.

Dan went back and got the group started moving toward the boat. "Remember that you'll only need a single tank. Because the site is so far away it's a one-tank dive trip."

A couple of the divers groaned.

Dan shrugged. "You're welcome to snag a tank and do a shore dive across the street when we get back."

One by one the divers got up, picked up a tank, and set up their BCD and regulator before carrying it over and settling it onto the boat. Weights were carried separately, and masks, fins, and cameras were all stowed on board.

When Ella climbed aboard with her SCUBA unit and dive bag, she wasn't surprised to see that she was the only woman on the trip. Great. Six macho men and one woman to keep track of them. Wasn't that the way it always went? Men did dangerous things and women cleaned up the mess. She grinned to herself.

Overhearing the talk among the divers she had to smile at the boasts they were making—how deep they had been, giant man-eating sharks they had fended off, currents that nearly swept them out to sea. She would wager that she had been deeper, seen more sharks, and battled more currents than all of them put together.

She said, "Any of you wreck divers?" A couple of them nodded. "We did a lot of deep wreck dives in Lake Michigan," she said. "Cold and dark down there."

"Holy crap," one of them said, "did you dive in a wetsuit or a drysuit?"

Ella kept fussing with her gear. "I did Ice Diver specialty in a wetsuit but did the deep wrecks in a drysuit. It was just too cold in the lake to hang there for decompression stops in a wetsuit."

Silence greeted her statement. Suddenly she was a more macho diver than any of them. There, she thought, that ought to keep them in line and she smiled.

While they had been talking Dan got all his gear settled and untied the boat from the dock. Captain Jerome turned the bow of the boat to the south and soon they were speeding along, Flying Fish sailing away at their approach. All the moorings along the way were empty except for one of the three moorings at the *Hilma Hooker*, the only wreck dive on Bonaire.

Captain Jerome took the boat past the Red Slave mooring and turned it around.

"Get suited up," Dan said, "while I give a little briefing. Red Slave is past the south end of the double reef system that is a feature of this part of the island. Current sweeps this area all the time so you'll notice that the sponges like the Azure Vase Sponge are fan-shaped rather than round. If the current is pushing you too fast for comfort turn your body across the current so that it pushes against the greater part of your body. That should slow you down. Remember the next stop from here is Venezuela so pay attention. That's it, let's go diving."

The six divers shrugged into their buoyancy control devices, buckled the straps, and snugged them onto their shoulders.

Ella watched them, making sure that each of them had their air turned on and their gear assembled correctly. She also paid attention to the demeanor of the men to see if any of them was having second thoughts. A couple of them looked nervous but excited. She looked to see the color of their fins so she could keep an eye on them.

Dan got everyone gathered at the side exits of the boat and said, "I want us all to be in the water at about the same time so we can descend as a group and stay together. Be sure not to be in front of me in case someone has a problem. Let me know when you get to one thousand psi so that we can begin our ascent. Please put your fins on now so you're ready to go."

By then Ella had her gear on and was standing at the back of a trio of divers ready to giant stride into the water at Dan's command.

"Let's go!" Dan said and the divers surged forward, splashing into the sea almost as one. Dan felt the current tug at him as soon as he was underwater. He looked back and saw that his six divers and Ella were grouping themselves together, settling their gear as they descended following his lead.

The golden gorgonians which looked like tall stalks of vegetation bent to the north in the direction the current was flowing. The purple sea fans were bent nearly double. To their right the rising sun started to shoot long rays of light into the water illuminating the coral and sponges. They shot past a big orange sponge that at any other site would be the shape of a barrel but at Red Slave it was a narrow fan shape that looked like a giant clam.

Dan felt the water rushing past him, happy to be in the water leading a dive off his new boat. He was even happier that Ella was along to enjoy the dive with him. True she wasn't by his side like he wished she was, but he knew he could trust her to keep a close eye on the divers and step in if anyone had a problem.

They flowed along with the current, at the mercy of the rushing water, amazed at the ease with which fish swam against it. One of the divers came up alongside Dan and showed him his gauges, fifteen hundred psi. Dan nodded, gave him the okay signal, and started easing the group to a shallower depth. Leveling off at the edge of the drop-off in about thirty feet of water where they could see much more life. A big silver barracuda hung motionless over a coral head. Dan marveled at the fish's ability to maintain its position in the current. To their right stretched a wide sand flat dotted with patches of fire coral and staghorn coral. All the corals leaned away from the current, testament to the constancy of the water flow at that location. Another of the divers came up to his side brandishing his gauges —nine hundred psi—time to surface.

Dan took the bright orange safety sausage from his BCD pocket, unfurled it, and inflated it with his octopus safe second regulator. He held onto the tether and motioned the divers to approach and hang on with him. They stopped at fifteen feet to perform the required safety stop and to be deep enough underwater that the arriving Muddy Albatross wouldn't injure anyone. Once the boat was in position Dan sent the divers to the surface in pairs, giving each team time to pull themselves to the stern of the boat, hand up their fins and weights, and climb aboard. Ella stayed with Dan until all the rest of the divers were safely onboard, then they ascended to the surface and got back on the boat.

"Well, what did you think?" Dan said after settling his gear into the rack and wiping his face with his chamois towel.

"That was some current," one of the divers said and there were murmurs of agreement all around. "I couldn't have stopped to look at something if I'd wanted to."

Dan smiled. "That current is why Red Slave is considered an advanced dive. You all did a good job staying together."

"I don't get how fish swim against that current so easily. They just flap their fins and move into it. It made me feel out of control most of the dive," said another of the divers. "I don't think I'd do that dive without a boat and divemaster."

"Aw, come on, Clay," said the man beside him, "we can dive here again as long as we park one truck down the shore."

Clay looked at him. "Did you see how far we drifted, Mac? We were three or four sites up the coast. I wouldn't have parked a truck that far away. It never occurred to me that we'd float that far, that the current was that strong." He shook his head. "No, I'm not doing that as a shore dive."

Mac looked disgusted. "That's just great. Then you can sit in the truck, look out for our safety sausage, and drive down to get us. You can be shore support if you're too much of a chicken to dive."

Clay threw down his towel. "Who are you calling a chicken? Just because I'm not willing to risk my life on a dangerous dive I'm a chicken?" He stood up and leaned over the man next to him. "You're a fine one to talk, Mac. I'm not the one who stayed on the surface when we went in those caves in Aruba last year."

Mac stood up nose to nose with Clay. "I'm claustrophobic, okay? I wasn't the only one who didn't go down in those caves.

Plenty of people decided not to go because of the bats." Mac lifted his hand ready to push Clay who leaned toward him.

Dan stepped in between them. "Hey, guys, let's not get into a fight over this. One of the best things about diving is that everyone gets to set their own comfort level. What you can do today you may not feel safe to do tomorrow. Mac, you feel like you've got the experience and the skills to do this advanced dive from shore. Clay, you don't. There's no shame either way. Get your gear stowed so we can start back to the dock." He turned away to make sure his own equipment was put away, then he nodded to Captain Jerome and sat down to enjoy the ride. He kept his eye on Mac and Clay who sat beside each other and continued to talk.

By the time they reached the dock the two men were silent. Clay had his arms crossed over his chest and Mac had his fists clenched on his thighs. Both men shouldered their SCUBA units, picked up their dive bags, and started to get off the boat. They met at the side of the dock each one trying to shoulder their way ahead.

"Out of my way, chicken," Mac said.

Clay turned his shoulders and bumped Mac with his tank which jostled him away from the side of the boat.

"Hey, watch it," Dan said. "No shoving matches on the dive boat. Take care of your gear first, then you can settle this."

Clay stepped off onto the dock and strode up the steps, across the road, and started to disassemble his dive gear. Mac came up beside him and dropped his bag on Clay's bag.

"Move your shit out of my way," Clay said.

Mac ignored him and started taking his gear apart.

Clay picked up Mac's bag and slung it aside. "Fetch."

Dan walked up just as Mac hauled off and shoved Clay, knocking him and his tank over. Before Dan could react, Mac had leaped on top of Clay and was punching his face. Dan lay his SCUBA gear on the ground and grabbed the hose next to the rinse tank. He turned it on and sprayed the fighting men. "That's enough."

Other divers in the group helped Clay and Mac to their feet and held them apart. Everyone looked shocked.

Dan looked from one to the other. "I thought you guys were friends. Didn't you come down here in a group?" Heads nodded.

Clay pulled away from the restraining hands and rubbed his swelling lip on the back of his hand. He looked down to see blood. "You bloodied my lip."

"You deserved it," Mac said, shaking off the hands that held him. "You threw my bag."

"Well, you dropped it on my gear. Just stay away from me for the rest of the trip." Clay reached down to finish disassembling his gear.

Mac laughed. "That'll be easy, we're roommates."

Clay looked up at him. "I'll get another room."

Dan kept a close eye on the men as they rinsed and hung their dive gear. The rest of the group was subdued, quietly coming to Dan to have their logbooks signed and then leaving without the usual camaraderie. The group members that hadn't gone on the dive to Red Slave were puzzled at the atmosphere when their dive boat docked, and they came up from their two-tank dive. They all chattered like magpies about the fish and critters they saw and asked eager questions about the drift dive. The divers who had been on the Red Slave dive boat were quiet about the dive and cut their eyes to Clay and Mac who sat on opposite sides of the big table in the courtyard filling in their logbooks without speaking to anyone.

One of the women stood in the middle of the courtyard with her hands on her hips and said, "All right what happened?"

No one said anything but everyone from the drift dive looked at Mac and Clay. Dan looked up to see who would talk.

Clay said, "Mac called me a chicken because I said I didn't want to do a shore dive at Red Slave, so I pushed him."

She stared at the men. "And he pushed back, I assume."

"Yeah."

"You two disappoint me. You both struggled in class and

helped each other through and now you fight over Clay not wanting to do an advanced dive? I'll bet your behavior really impressed the Instructor. Mac, you apologize to Clay for calling him a chicken and Clay, you apologize to Mac for shoving him." She raised her hands. "I don't care who started it. You are not twelve years old and in middle school. You are grown men, I'm the leader of this dive trip, and I'm disappointed that a group from my shop behaved like this. Honestly." She shook her head and went back to rinsing and hanging her gear.

The rest of their group followed her lead and soon everyone except Clay and Mac had their gear taken care of, their logbooks signed, and had left for lunch.

Dan and Ella waited until everyone had finished at the rinse tank before taking care of their own equipment. They watched Clay and Mac sit at the table, heads down, hands still beside their logbooks. Neither man said anything for a while. When Ella took their wetsuits into the gear locker to hang them up, she heard one of them say, "Sorry." She looked out the door and saw them looking at each other. Dan came out of the office and walked over to stand by the table.

"I don't want to get into the middle of this fight, but I want to say that no diver is ever obligated to do a dive that feels wrong. There were times that I sat out a dive because it didn't feel right that day. That's one of the things that I love about diving; you're allowed to back out and not give an excuse. Now I hate to break up the party, but we need to go to lunch. You're both welcome to sign up for the afternoon dive if you'd like to head back out to Klein Bonaire with the rest of the group."

Mac stood up. "I'm sorry, Clay, I shouldn't have called you a chicken. Feel like going on the afternoon dive?"

Clay used both hands to push himself to stand. "And I shouldn't have pushed you. It was stupid and juvenile. Yeah, I could go on the afternoon dive."

"I'll sign us both up," Mac said, and he turned to go into the shop.

Dan and Ella watched the two men walk side by side down

to their hotel which was just a block away. "That could have been so much worse," Dan said.

"You bet it could have," said Ella. "I didn't realize that Julia was the leader of the group, she seems like just one of the crowd."

"It's called leading by example, I guess, but she sure defused that ticking time bomb in a hurry. Let's eat, I'm starved."

CHAPTER 22

Dan was proud to be able to tie his own dive boat up next to the dock across from the Dive Inn. He and Babs came to an agreement about him investing in the Dive Inn and the use of the Muddy Albatross for overflow diving when cruise ships were in port. Babs made use of Dan's boat more often than either of them imagined. Dan started to get a reputation as an Instructor and guide who could make your dive vacation one to remember.

Babs called Dan into the office. "I just had an email from a dive shop in Illinois. They heard about you and wanted to make sure that you'll be leading their dives when they come down next month."

Dan leaned on the door jamb. "What? Why? I don't do anything different than any other dive leader. I take them to a site, give a briefing, and send them off to dive."

"Well," Babs said, "evidently you do something special because this isn't the first email I've had making sure that you'll be the one leading dives when the group comes to Bonaire. They're also interested in doing Advanced Open Water while they're here, especially Drift Diver."

"Oh, I bet I know who they are," Dan said. "They must be another group from the same dive shop that crazy bunch last year came from. You remember, almost the entire group did Advanced, and I think they really had a great time with it. Hey, I don't care how we get recommendations, I'm just glad that people come to us to dive. More divers mean more profit."

Babs grinned. "Now that you're invested in the Dive Inn you're more interested in the bottom line."

"Yes, you bet I am. Ella's doing all the books for Twice the

Cleaning, and she keeps talking about income versus outlay and figuring out ways that they can make more of one and not the other. I guess I'm learning from her."

"I'm all for more income and less outlay," said Babs. "If Ella has any ideas about dive shop economics, please don't hesitate to share them."

Captain Jerome was interested in island history and grew a reputation for leading interesting and informative sightseeing tours around Bonaire. He had a sign painted that he hooked to the bow rails so that people passing the dock would see his offer for tours. He even got a new cellphone so that he wouldn't miss any calls. Captain Jerome's sister-in-law worked for the Tourism Office, and she was very helpful spreading the word about his new venture. Since the only other tours on the island were land-based he had an advantage. People seemed to enjoy riding on the Muddy Albatross learning about the island's history from a native islander and not have to endure a hot and dusty drive around the island. He even paid an annual fee to be able to dock in Washington-Slagbaai National Park at the northern end of the island where there were old plantation ruins to explore and the remains of docks for people to snorkel around. With the profits from tours and dive trips Dan was able to pay slip fees, maintenance, and Captain Jerome without dipping into savings, most months anyway. It was a pretty sweet arrangement for all concerned.

The cleaning business was going well. Ella and Mariette had gotten all of the cleaners' pay rates coordinated by setting up a merit and seniority scale so that the newest hires were paid less than the more experienced employees. The business ran smoothly for the most part and there were no big problems with staff discontent. A few of the long-time cleaners resented that two expats were now in charge, but Ella and Mariette were careful to be fair and transparent with their decisions, which seemed to mollify them. As time went on Ella and Mariette needed to spend more time on the running of the business and less time cleaning houses. That suited Ella. She wasn't bored by the day-to-day running of the business. There were enough challenges that every day was different.

Mariette and Ella met weekly for lunch to go over any problems or concerns. One day Mariette said, "I have an idea."

"What's that?"

"What if we expanded to include offices around Playa?"

Ella thought for a moment. "That's not a bad idea. How would we approach them?"

"Well, we could make up a flyer and one of us could go around to the banks and offices offering our services," Mariette said.

Since Mariette had been on the island for much longer than Ella, she was the one who went around to banks and offices in and around Playa offering them the cleaning service. Quite a few of them were happy with the cleaners that they had so Mariette talked to the cleaners about possibly joining forces with them at Twice the Cleaning Service. Many of the cleaners agreed to join Twice the Cleaning because of the cleaning teams that Ella and Mariette instituted which made them feel safer. They had all heard about Ella being assaulted by Bert Champeau and were afraid of it happening to them.

Ella discovered that she was good at dealing with clients, especially those who were slow to pay their invoices. Mariette was better at working with their employees to make sure that they were happy and productive. Over time Nathan grew happier with the fact that his wife was a business owner and was even more happy when their savings account began to grow again with profits from the cleaning business.

The teams made the cleaners feel like they were part of something, and Mariette had the idea to throw a monthly get together where the employees could compare notes and get to know each other better. She pressed Dan and Nathan into grilling fish and sausages for the picnic and she and Ella made salads and desserts. After a couple months the cleaners suggested that they would bring the dishes to pass if Twice the Cleaning provided the main course. It turned into quite a family affair and went far to dispel any lingering resentment. It also made Ella and Dan feel like they belonged on the island.

CHAPTER 23

One rainy Sunday when neither Dan nor Ella was working, he turned from watching a game on the TV and said, "You know, we should get married."

Ella looked up from her book and said, "What did you say?"

"We should get married. Mariette and Nathan are married. Babs and Harry are married. We should get married."

"I guess so."

"Don't you want to marry me?" Dan looked a little shy and nervous.

Ella put her book down and turned to face him. "Of course, I want to marry you. I've wanted to marry you for years; you just caught me off guard. Should we have a big shindig or just go to the registry office one day and get the job done?"

Dan shrugged. "I don't know. I just thought I'd like to be married. We could do it however makes you happy."

"Our families would want to be here, I think, so we'd have to have some sort of ceremony and reception. I'll ask Mariette where they held their wedding. We don't go to church, so I suppose we'd need a judge or a justice of the peace if they have those on the island."

Dan laughed. "We could get married underwater. I saw pictures of an underwater wedding in Skin Diver magazine once."

"I don't think so. Mom and Dad aren't divers, neither are your folks, and they'd all want to be there. Nice idea, though. Let's make a guest list and see what we're looking at." She went to the desk and got a legal pad out of a drawer, picked up a pencil, and sat back down on the couch. "Now, who do you want to invite?"

They spent an hour calling out all of their friends and family names. They were surprised to have two hundred people when they stopped.

"I didn't think we knew that many people," Dan said.

"Me neither," said Ella, "but most of them are family and we can't leave them out. I don't think a lot of them would fly down here, do you?"

Dan rubbed his hand down his face. "Maybe not. It's too far and too expensive to get here. Would it be a better idea for us to go home for a wedding so only the two of us have to fly overseas?"

"I don't know. Maybe we should have a small wedding here and fly home for a reception. That might be easier."

"Maybe we should elope," said Dan.

Ella looked at him. "I thought you didn't like it when people eloped. You had a lot to say when Ben and Felicia ran off to Vegas."

Dan looked chagrined. "Yeah, but that was because Ben threw such great parties when we were in college. We were all looking forward to a big, blowout bash when he got married and he ruined that when they skulked off to Vegas and got married by some Elvis impersonator in a chapel decorated like the jungle room at Graceland. Man, them eloping, that was a big disappointment, I'll tell you."

"Let's not elope. My mother, for one, would have a lot to say about that and for years. She's not one to let things go. I'm not sure that she's forgiven me for "running off to the Caribbean with a man you hardly know."

Dan looked hurt. "I thought your mom liked me."

"I think she does, in theory, but in actuality you lured her one and only daughter into selling off her possessions and moving to an island that's more than a day's travel away. I think that deep down she resents it."

As soon as the school year wrapped up Ella contacted Piko Sandford and Ned de Koop, the boys who had stolen their car and arranged for them to meet her at her house. They rode up on their bicycles and stood shoulder to shoulder at the door looking like they were in for a beating.

"Come in, boys," she said. "Let's talk about the work I expect from you this summer."

"Yes, ma'am," they said and stepped into the house.

Ella motioned them to the couch and sat at her desk across from them. "I told Carlos who does the pool and garden work for Twice the Cleaning Service that you two would be his helpers this summer and he's really glad to have the help. I'll give him your phone numbers so he can arrange to pick you up of a morning since I don't expect you to ride your bikes to the houses."

"Yes, ma'am," they said.

She looked at the boys who were talking to their sandal-clad feet. "People like it when you meet their eyes. It makes them think that you're listening and that you're honest. Now I know that you two will cooperate with Carlos and do your best for us. I hope that we won't have any trouble with dishonesty or laziness."

They looked up at her. "No, ma'am."

"Carlos is going to stop by in a few minutes to get to know you and to let you know the kind of things that he will need your help with. It won't be the most glamorous work and it will be in the sun, so I hope that you both have a hat to wear. I don't want you frying your brains."

Piko looked at her. "That would be bad. Ned doesn't have that much brains to spare."

Ned sat up straight and elbowed his cousin. "You should talk. I am not the one who nearly failed seventh grade."

"I did not nearly fail seventh grade. I was sick a lot and missed school, so I had to go to summer school, that's all."

Ella held up her hands. "Boys, that's neither here nor there.

I just don't want you getting sunstroke."

She heard a vehicle pull up and saw out the window that it was Carlos' old truck. He stepped out onto the street and came up the walk tugging his khaki shorts up to his waist. He knocked on the door and Ella went to greet him.

"Hello, Missus Ella," he said. "I come to see those car-stealing boys you tole me about."

Ella held the door open. "Come in, Carlos, the boys are here and they're eager to meet you and learn about how their summer is going to go." She saw out of the corner of her eye the two boys look at each other and shrug. "Ned, Piko, this is Carlos. He'll be directing your work this summer. He will report to me on a daily basis how you're doing, and I'll report to Officer Micah."

At that the boys' eyebrows went up almost to their hairlines. Evidently, they thought that once they started working for Ella and her company they were off the hook with the police.

Carlos looked down at the boys and shook his head. "I heard about you stealing Missus Ella's car and won't tolerate no stealing or shirking on my watch. I expect you to get your work done in good time and not grumble about it."

The boys said, "Yes, sir," in unison.

Carlos went on. "We will be cleaning pools and hot tubs, trimming the plants, and raking gravel. You tell me where you live and where I can pick you up of a morning and we'll get along fine. You will ride to the jobs with me, and I will take you home when we are done. Be sure to bring a lunch with you because there will be no going off to restaurants to eat. And water. Bring a water bottle that you can fill through the day. What we will be doing is hot and thirsty work. I don't want you getting sun sickness."

Piko and Ned looked as if they'd never heard of sun sickness and wouldn't get anything so wimpy sounding. After all they were children of a sunny place and had never been sick from it in their lives.

"And you will need gloves to keep from getting blisters. You will be doing a lot of raking and that raises blisters if you do not wear gloves."

Ella could see that the boys had begun to tune out Carlos' advice and worried that they wouldn't pay attention to him when it came to getting the work done. She began to wonder if pressing them into service had been a good idea after all.

Piko and Ned worked out better than Ella had hoped they would. At first the boys tried to dodge the hard work, but Carlos kept a close eye on them and molded them into decent workers. Ned showed a talent for gardening. He kept the bougainvillea hedges trimmed and seemed to know instinctively how to care for the cactus that dotted many of the properties. Uncle Stagger got into the act when one of the Air B&B owners expressed a desire for a traditional cactus fence around their property. Stagger knew the old way and taught Ned how to cut the cactus arms and lace them together with wire to make a formidable barrier around the lot.

Babs and Harry decided to move back to Holland permanently which gave Dan full control of the Dive Inn. Babs was still part owner, but she was an absentee owner and left the daily running of the operation to Dan. He hired another Instructor and Divemaster so that he could stay in the office and take care of business many days. That wasn't the way he wanted to work as a dive shop owner, but it was necessary. He still got out into the water a few times a week, usually with Ella along, which he liked. It wasn't as good as diving a couple times a day, every day, but it was better than being in the office all the time. Ella had more time to go along on dives with Dan since she'd stopped cleaning and just ran her part of the cleaning service operation. She did Divemaster training and got certified so that when Dan pressed her into service she was qualified and insured to do the job.

The Muddy Albatross stopped living up to its reputation

as a problem boat. Captain Jerome and Dan worked together to maintain it which made the boat run smoothly and without a lot of down time. There was enough demand and Dan's reputation spread among US divers and dive shops that they needed two boats almost year-round, high season and low.

The dive shop was more organized thanks to Dan's suggestions and Ella helped tidy up the recordkeeping in the Dive Inn. Dan kept using the "friends for supper" excuse whenever an unattached vacationing woman asked him out for a drink. It worked perfectly every time. He and Ella would go down to Karel's Beach Bar about once a week to have a drink or two with the divers and build a bit of brand loyalty among the traveling dive public.

CHAPTER 24

The day of the Bonairean wedding dawned bright, sunny, and hot. Dan had spent the night with Leo, who still worked for Jack Slater, so that he and Ella wouldn't see each other before the ceremony and jinx it.

Ella had a white wedding dress made by Mariette's sister-in-law who had a custom sewing and repair business. The dress was made of a polyester linen blend that wouldn't wrinkle as much as pure linen with white floral appliques on the bodice and down the front to the hem. The dress was sleeveless and A-line which just skimmed Ella's curves.

Dan wore a guayabera, pale blue that matched his eyes, over a pair of black slacks. They both wore sandals.

Their mothers surprised them by showing up at the registry office for the ceremony. The mothers had contacted Mariette and she helped them find lodging and got them to the office in time for the surprise. Ella couldn't believe her eyes when she walked into the registry office and saw her mom and Dan's mom there, both dressed in summer dresses with big hats.

"Mom, what are you doing here?" Ella said. "You too Mom Mortenson. How did you keep it a secret? You've never been very good at secrets."

Ella's mom had tears in her eyes when she said, "Do you think either of us would miss our children getting married?"

"But we're coming home in two weeks to get married again and have the reception. We've been planning it for months."

Dan's mom touched her shoulder. "But this is your real wedding, your first wedding, and we couldn't miss that, so here we are."

Ella looked around. "Are the dads here too?"

The moms shook their heads.

"No," said Mrs. Taylor, Ella's mom, "the dads stayed home. Dad is looking forward to walking you down the aisle at home."

Mrs. Mortenson leaned in. "I think the groom and the judge are ready. Time to get married."

Ella turned to see Dan standing at the front of the room, Nathan beside him. Mariette handed her a bouquet of white roses and red bougainvillea then Ella straightened her shoulders and walked to stand beside Dan.

He leaned down to whisper, "You look beautiful."

She gave him a quick smile, barely looking at him so she didn't start to cry.

The ceremony was short and straightforward.

"Do you Ella Marie take Daniel Charles to be your lawfully wedded husband?"

"I do."

"Do you Daniel Charles take Ella Marie to be your lawfully wedded wife?"

"I do."

"Do you have the rings?"

Nathan stepped forward, a pair of plain gold bands on his extended palm.

"With this ring I thee wed." They exchanged rings, their hands shaking as they slipped them onto the ring fingers of each other's left hand.

"I now pronounce you husband and wife. You may kiss the bride."

Dan touched his lips to Ella's every so sweetly and she heard a pair of sniffs from the mothers who were seated right behind them.

After the ceremony everyone drove to Windsock Beach where they had their monthly cleaning service parties and where their friends and employees were waiting to celebrate their marriage. The moms were a little nonplussed when they realized that they'd have to take off their shoes to be comfortable walking in the sand, but they were good sports and left their sandals in the shade with all the other shoes.

Ella was surprised that the husbands of a few of their cleaning employees had a steel band, so they were serenaded by "Here Comes the Bride" in a way they'd never heard it before. Wine and beer flowed, and children played in the sand. There was plenty food, and a grill kept the party supplied with burgers and hot dogs.

"How did you get all this arranged?" Mrs. Taylor asked Ella.

Ella laughed. "I didn't arrange it. This is our standard monthly Twice the Cleaning Service get-together with a few extra guests thrown in. We have a party like this all the time so the system was in place, all they had to do was figure out who would grill the meat since that's usually Dan and Nathan's job." She looked over at the grill, surprised to see Ned and Piko wielding the tongs and spatula, cooking the meats, and keeping them from burning.

Two weeks later Dan and Ella flew back to Green Bay to get married again and to have another reception, this time for their extended families and hometown friends. They wore the same things that they had for their Bonairean wedding but instead of red bougainvillea in with the white roses there were red roses in her bouquet. Ella's dad was so nervous walking her down the aisle of the Unitarian Church where Dan's family worshipped that her bouquet quivered.

The reception and dinner after the ceremony were much more traditional than their Bonairean party. The wedding party, Ella and Dan and their attendants, sat at the head table on a dais. The rest of the guests and their parents sat at round tables that filled the rest of the room. One of Dan's cousins had a DJ business, so he provided dance music throughout the evening.

As they danced their first dance Dan leaned to whisper in Ella's ear, "I think I liked our beach party better than this."

Ella smiled up at him. "Agreed. I guess we've turned into island people."

THE END

If you've enjoyed Island Dreams, please consider going to Amazon or Goodreads and leaving a review. They help people decide to read my book. Thank you.

ACKNOWLEDGEMENT

Island Dreams would never have been possible without my husband, Don, convincing me that we should learn to SCUBA dive in 1990. He promised me if I learned to dive, he'd take me to the ocean where the pretty fish lived. He kept that promise time and time again. Of all the places we dived, Bonaire was our favorite and we planned to move there after we retired. Poor health prevented the move, but I never lost my love of diving and Bonaire.

Special thanks goes to Aqua Center in Green Bay, WI and to Divers' Realm in Appleton, WI for allowing me to use their business names in this story. If you ever want to try SCUBA diving, these are the places to go.

BOOKS BY THIS AUTHOR

The Seaview

She knew it would be hard work, but what she didn't plan on was the electrically charged subcontractor and the way he made her feel.

Despite her son's vehement objections, Rose buys the ramshackle Caribbean beachfront bed and breakfast. She's confident that she can oversee the work in time for the start of tourist season. That is until the Health Inspector locks them out of the building.

Desperate to get the crew back to work she pleads with the plumber to get the key and finish at least one bathroom. The plumber has his own agenda. Rose's confidence is nearly destroyed by this major setback.

Can Rose and her crew finish the job before the first guest arrives?

The Seaview is the first book of The Seaview Series. If you like engaging islanders, breathtaking scenery above and below water, and a little romance this book is for you.

Open For Busiiness

It's opening day, and Rose eagerly awaits her first guest. Juggling excitement and nerves, she's determined to keep her new bed &

breakfast afloat despite bad weather and a lecherous plumber.

Now that Seaview is refurbished and reopened Rose's dream seems to be coming true, but the arrival of Hurricane Alphonso might end her dream before it can really begin. Her first guests are in residence and one of them acts like the hurricane with its wind, rain, and power outages is a personal affront.
Her attempts to fit into the island community are thwarted by nasty rumors spread by a local woman who resents Rose's romance with Ignatius "Iggy" Solomon. And a lecherous plumber just won't take "No!" for an answer.

In Open For Business, the second book of The Seaview Series escape to the Caribbean island of Anguilla. Enjoy Seaview with its changing cast of guests and the ever-faithful Iggy for delectable homemade breakfasts, beachside dancing, and rum punch as you dive into a tropical women's fiction story. Grab your copy today!

Spies Don't Retire

Some secrets refuse to stay buried... even in paradise.

Rose is settling into being a newlywed and hosting guests at Seaview Bed & Breakfast on the Caribbean island of Anguilla. Whispers of spies on the island begin to circulate. Someone threatens to unmask them. Rose's peaceful retreat risks becoming a battleground.

At a lavish party, the hostess introduces a British couple to a Russian one, and the tension seethes. Recognition. Sizzling hostility. Delicious gossip makes the grapevine hum. Were the men spies on opposite sides? Or do the wives share a more dangerous past?

As rumors fly, Rose finds herself caught between keeping

Seaview's reputation intact and navigating the conflict between feuding friends. In the meantime, she's fighting to clear her name from the lingering lies of her nemesis.

Can Rose mend fences with the local women who distrust her? Will the two warring couples declare a truce—or set the island ablaze with old rivalries?

Spies Don't Retire, the third book in The Seaview Series, takes you back to the tropical shores of Anguilla where intrigue, scandal, and delectable island fare await. Escape to paradise.

Horizon

Gail Logan, a widow in her mid-fifties, has lived her life by what other people think. That has to change.

Signing up for a watercolor class and thrifting a new wardrobe with a young classmate makes a good start. Replanting her regimented flower garden is another idea, but at the garden center, Abel Baker dismisses her plan and tells her what to buy. Gail doesn't appreciate his interference.

Widower Abel turns up in Gail's path again and again, but she buried one bossy man, and she's not interested in another. Should she give Abel a chance?

Her sons and her best friend feel threatened by all of Gail's changes. Should she go back to her dull existence or keep moving forward?

Immerse yourself in Gail's journey for a fresh perspective on life in Horizon. Enjoy her adventures learning to paint with watercolor, making new friends, and changing her life to please herself in this mature love after loss women's fiction story.

Better Than Mom's

Better Than Mom's is a neighborhood diner in a small city in Wisconsin where good food and interesting people come together.

Meet Brady, the warm-hearted owner who takes pride in making homemade food for his customers, Fay, the sassy morning waitress who cares for people more than she lets on, Naomi, the welfare mom who cooks like an angel and needs a job, Steve, who sits in the back booth and won't let anyone see what he's writing, and Officer Bates, who comes to investigate a crime but ends up sweeping Fay off her feet.

Stop in at Better Than Mom's for a bowl of homemade soup, a lighter-than-air biscuit, and a visit with people who could be your neighbors.

Anneke's Legacy

Lucia answers the buzzing phone on her desk, and her life changes forever

Tasked with settling her great-aunt's estate on the arid Caribbean island of Bonaire, cynical editor Lucia Vandersteeg clashes with Burke, a rugged fisherman living on the property. As she uncovers her family's past and confronts a dangerous treasure-hunting scam that puts her in peril, Lucia must decide whether to trust the man who infuriates her most, or return to her lonely life in the city, leaving behind a chance at unexpected love.

While navigating the island's slow pace and the complexities of the estate, Lucia develops a simmering attraction to the fisherman, all while being pursued by the more suitable attorney.

Can the tangled lives of the people on this small island be sorted out before someone gets hurt? Will Lucia and Burke acknowledge their attraction before it's too late?

Christmas At Seaview

Her daughter wants to get married. At Seaview. In four days.

Rose is excited about Christmas. Her children and their partners arrive on Christmas Eve at Rose's bed-and-breakfast on the island of Anguilla in the Caribbean. Two bombshell announcements on Christmas Day make her ecstatic. But her happiness turns into panic when her daughter makes a decision that turns the week upside down. Can Rose plan a wedding and take care of her paying guests during the most stressful week of the year?

The days tick away, and Rose is powerless to slow things down. Friday is coming fast. Will her guests feel ignored in all the wedding prep hubbub? Food, flowers, officiant. How will she get everything arranged before it's time to say, "I do?"

Pick up your copy of Christmas at Seaview, a novella that takes you along on Rose's wild ride through the week she never expected. Escape to the Caribbean this Christmas for a heartwarming story filled with joy, chaos, and family cheer.

ABOUT THE AUTHOR

Barbara Angermeier Malcolm

Barbara Angermeier Malcolm, a Green Bay native, is an avid traveler and former retail SCUBA sales professional.

She has journeyed to countless islands with her family on diving vacations, collecting inspiration and stories along the way. A passionate storyteller, Barbara has been crafting tales for years.

When she's not writing, you'll find her sketching, painting with watercolors, knitting, cooking, or doting on her grandchildren. She is an active member of the Green Bay writing community and a proud member of the Green Bay Area Writers Guild and Wisconsin Writers Association.

www.ingramcontent.com/pod-product-compliance
Lightning Source LLC
Chambersburg PA
CBHW060623260626
47161CB00008B/2784